DEATH
IN THE AFTERNOON
MEETING

A Film Noir Fairy Tale

by Eric Stromquist

Death in the Afternoon Meeting, A Film Noir Fairy Tale
by Eric Stromquist

Astoria Publishing, Astoria, Oregon
www.astoriapublishing.com, info@astoriapublishing.com

Published in the United States of America
ISBN 978-0-578-78588-2

To Lori, my Darlene

AUTHOR'S NOTE

After closing a restaurant in Portland, Oregon and opening
a new chapter of life in Astoria, I expected to have more time to
read, but had absolutely no intention of writing. So of course
I did. This fractured tale began almost 40 years ago when I
wrote a couple of episodes of Nick Clam: Chowder Head for
the short-lived Jake's Crawfish Snapper Review. At the time,
I was the director of Jake's Famous Products and my job was
to sell canned clam chowder to people who didn't want to buy
it. I'm not sure why, but I found it funny as I plied my futile
trade to imagine myself a hard-boiled, hard-drinking 1950s-style
private detective, and that became my "voice". Soon thereafter
the *Snapper Review* died, as you would expect, and that voice
inevitably got lost as my head became crowded with restaurants
and cooking schools and love and life.

Again I'm not sure why, but the voice popped back into my
now empty head while walking along the Columbia River one
sunny summer day and when I got home I sat down and started
writing. And didn't really stop. At first it was a free-wheeling
satire of corporate and popular culture. For those of you who
know me that will come as no surprise. What did surprise,
however, was how much and how quickly the story evolved.
The characters emerged from a murky bowl of soup filled with
my own life experiences, as well as people I've watched and read
about. I guess the main character, E.C. Poole, is somewhat a
reflection of me, but only in so far as he is handsome and hard
drinking. The rest is pure fiction. Basically, it is the story of a
guy living a painfully prosaic life who copes by creating a fantasy
world to make it somehow seem tolerable. Or even exciting.

A couple of chapters in, I realized to my horror that just riffing on the absurdity of modern life and corporate miasma did not a book make. I needed a plot. Gradually the idea formed to hang the satire on the bones of a corporate reorganization plan that represented an existential threat to the main character and those around him. Then the book became a tale of fear and paranoia and cowardice and courage. A mystery novel of sorts I suppose. And that's when Ernest Hemingway popped into my head and bullfighting was rather absurdly woven into the story and the title. Finally, after introducing the lovely Darlene Camper as a character early on, and then later flirting with the idea of a romance novel, I slowly realized that E.C. Poole was indeed smitten and I was actually writing a love story. From that point on, the arc became easy for me to follow and the words wrote themselves. And if you've ever met my Lori you know why.

So, there you have it. After diving into the deep end with no plot or purpose, and following no rhyme nor reason, this book amounts to a literary train wreck. Above all else, *Death in the Afternoon Meeting* is a silly story whose sole purpose is to make you laugh. Or at least chuckle. It is probably best thumbed through while basking in the sun by a swimming pool and nursing a tall drink. "Poole-side" if you will. But then that's the way I think all books should be enjoyed.

Eric

FOREWORD

I've had the privilege to enjoy a long friendship with Eric Stromquist. Originally as fellow waiters at Jake's Famous Crawfish Restaurant in Portland, Oregon, and then for the subsequent forty years sharing similar career paths, together and separately, but somehow always related to the food industry. For the last twenty years I have owned a nonfiction publishing company, Arnica Creative Services, known for creating beautiful coffee-table-style cookbooks and hardcover children's books.

Occasionally over time, Eric has mentioned to me that he might one day want to write a book. When he recently asked for advice regarding the publishing of a manuscript, I was only too happy to help. I received an electronic version of *Death in the Afternoon Meeting, A Film Noir Fairy Tale*, printed out a hard copy, and with my editor's visor in place and red pen in hand, began to review the work. I moved through the manuscript quickly and found it well written and an enjoyable read.

Eric is smart, clever, and witty, and his first published work is smart, clever, and witty as well. Choosing a film noir stage set and voice for the book was a challenge but is executed beautifully. The work has great structure and the dialogue is particularly well done. The words between the protagonist, E.C. Poole, and his counterparts are smooth and believable, and the strength of the conversations carried me into the unfolding story with movie images in my mind. I liked that.

The main character, E.C., is frenetic inside his own head. He is self-absorbed, non-trusting, calculating in every move while carefully studying others, and overthinks the aftermath of everything he says. Getting to know E.C.'s character was fun. The dialogue is peppered with "dame, toots, doll, etc.," and his tough-guy grammar usage had me in a film noir state-of-mind. I also found it hilarious that E.C. refers to himself in the third person as Chucky. There is a similarity to the characters in television's *Modern Family*, who all have separate and direct conversations (wink, wink) with the viewer audience. E.C. has the same link to his readership and I felt privileged to have secret access to his private thoughts.

Eric is humble. His enthusiasm for self-promotion is pretty much nonexistent, and he is shy and reticent about wanting to share his work with others. For Eric, the joy is in the writing and the journey is his reward, not the end. On his behalf, I encourage you to appreciate the quality of the writer's craft and enjoy the reading of a film noir fairy tale well told. And, if you are fortunate enough to be a member of the Jake's Crawfish family and friends community, you will be reminded of familiar people, places, and events wrapped in your own historical memories. Enjoy.

Ross Hawkins

DEATH
IN THE AFTERNOON
MEETING

The dream is always the same. I'm walking towards light at the end of a long tunnel. I'm terrified and want to run away but I can't. When I reach a small doorway with a huge wood frame I'm suddenly blinded and deafened by a roar. I slowly realize I'm standing in a huge arena filled with thousands of people. Horses are dragging a dead bull through the dust and his lifeless eyes are fixed on me. Accusing me.

But it is not me who is the killer. A small man in a glittering white and gold suit is walking away with a sword at his side. We're floating in a sea of waving white handkerchiefs and shouts of olé. Somehow the man is instantly at the other side of the arena. He accepts two giant human ears dripping with blood, bows deeply, then struts from the ring waving to the crowd.

It was a great day for him. He was an artist playing with death, and a brave bull died well at the hands of a master. I look up and see bright sun and faceless judges and know where I am. This is a bullfight, and my bull is next. I am next. Now it's dead quiet and I start to shake, first my arms holding a large cape, then my legs. Out of nowhere a bull bursts into the ring. I try to run but am stuck in the ground. I look down and see my feet wrapped in absurd little slippers.

Why am I here? I'm not a matador. My entire body goes limp. I stiffen and tell myself I'm not afraid.

1

I was a big baby. Ten pounds six ounces if you're keeping score and it couldn't have been easy for my poor mother, Mary. She was probably mad as a wet hen by the time the sawbones brought me into the world and maybe that's why she gave me the handle Ellis Charles Poole. I hate the name. It makes me sound like I'm the Duke of Earl or something. The kids in grade school made fun of me because of that. It was the kind of name that got you stuffed in a locker if you weren't careful who was tailing you in the halls.

Anyway, I'm not going around calling myself Ellis Charles so I go by E.C. My friends call me Chuck but I have more enemies than friends so I mostly go by E.C. Sometimes I call myself Chucky. Anyone else calling me that better be ready to plant her ruby reds on me. But that's not what I wanted to tell you.

A guy like me can't afford to let his roots get too deep but I was born and raised and lived my whole life in Portland, Oregon, so I guess you could say it's home. The Rose City they call it. I'm not sure we've got more roses than other cities but there seem to be plenty, and there's a festival every summer when old guys in white suits and hats get to coronate a teenage queen and name a new rose something or other. There are a couple of big parades too but I hate parades.

They also call us Stumptown because we used to have a lot of trees here and they cut them all down to make room for the city. You see that a lot nowadays, big housing developments and business parks named after what used to be there until they got rid of it to build big housing developments and business parks. They've all got fancy signs that say things like Pine Village, or

3

Goose Point, or Copper Ridge, but I guarantee you won't find any pine trees or geese or copper left. They should've called this burg Douglas Fir City. Anyway, it rains a lot here.

I'm not the type who turns heads on the street or needs a lot of attention but looks can be deceiving. Even though most people think I'm just your average guy I've got a nose for trouble. In fact trouble could've been my middle name. But it's Charles. Despite being a scrawny kid all the way through high school, I filled out pretty good and know how to take care of myself. I guess you could say it's my specialty. I'm not afraid of dark alleys and can be a tough customer if people are trying to sell me something I don't want to buy. I would've made a good cop or a private dick but I'm an associate sales director at United Food Distributors. It pays the bills. We distribute a lot of paper goods and chemicals and restaurant equipment, but like the name implies we mostly distribute food. It's big business, food distribution. Sometimes in meetings they tell us how big, and how much bigger it needs to get, but I'm usually asleep so I couldn't say how big that is. That's what I wanted to tell you though. There's a sales meeting today and I have to go.

The rain was beating on the window of my little office hovel and I was staring out at the parking lot dreaming about drinking and dames. Maybe I should've thought twice about that grande burrito for lunch because it was two in the afternoon and I needed a long chair nap. When I glanced at my laptop, staring me right in the face was an Excel spreadsheet of my quarterly sales figures. I hate Excel. Fact is I hate the whole Microsoft Office suite. The meeting's at three and my report is all screwed up. There's a corrupted cell somewhere causing trouble with my formula and when I find it I'm going to hit delete so hard that sniveling, little cell won't be able to find work in an old Texas Instruments calculator. But right now that spreadsheet was just sitting there threatening me with cold, black, columnar eyes.

I drifted for a minute when those eyes took me back to my salad days in the copier business and a loan shark I used to know named Peter Anders. A real shylock. A man who was known only as Little Peter. He was half Danish and half Russian, which is not generally a good mix, but he oozed charm and charisma. He was also whip smart and as vicious as they come. He worked in HR so he had access to all kinds of useful information about people and he wasn't afraid to squeeze them with it. If I'd stalled one more day paying off the entry fee in the March Madness pool I might've ended up sleeping with the goldfish in the office park water feature. Or with a bad performance review. I can't remember how I scared up the cash but it probably wasn't legal.

That memory sent chills down my spine. It felt like they might be going up my spine but everybody says they go down so I guess they were. Up or down, I opened my bottom desk drawer and reached for the bottle. A long pull of Smartwater calmed my jangling nerves and I started scrolling. Fifty-two minutes to meeting time.

I had turned that damn spreadsheet every which way but loose when I suddenly became aware of the little digital clock in the upper right-hand corner of my screen. It was ten to three and there was no way this crazy, mixed up thing was going to get fixed. I briefly entertained the idea of making a fast PowerPoint presentation to cover my butt, but the boss would see through that before I could make it to slide two.

I scanned the cells, checked the little clock again, and it was five 'til. I was out of time. I had to go face the music. I'm no

Fred Astaire or Paula Abdul or anything but I can dance around a problem if I have to. I've also got an air of confidence about me you just can't teach. It came factory direct and it's helped me out of plenty of tight jams. So I took a deep breath, packed up, and headed downstairs to the conference room armed with a pretty good excuse. My laptop crashed. The suits are never happy when I dust off that old saw but the guy above me on the org chart isn't exactly the sharpest knife in the drawer. Besides, he's got a meeting to run and there are lots of other sales figures to yell about.

As I reached the door of the conference room I got a funny feeling, a feeling I've learned the hard way not to ignore. I probably should've turned tail and ran but that's not my style. Walking in I remembered why I hate the room so much. It's stuffy and hot as hell, and that hit me in the face like a hard right. The thermostat is supposed to be locked on a program but the women who work in the office know how to get around that. They've got their ways. One of the things I'll never understand about dames is how cold they always think it is. Seventy degrees is sweater weather for them. They should be wearing bikinis. Anyway, they'll do whatever it takes to jack the heat.

The room doesn't get any better. There are no other doors, no windows, no fake plants, not even any asinine sayings on the walls. No nothing. No escape. There's just a tired old whiteboard wearing the writing of a thousand meetings gone by, a rectangular table made of fake wood that's the size of a tennis court, and a bunch of mismatched broken office chairs. Some of them don't swivel or go up and down anymore. I hate those. Swiveling can keep you awake and I usually need something to keep me awake. But the goody two-shoes who show up early take the good chairs.

Jack Girard is always last to arrive. Because he can. He's the regional sales director and top dog at this branch of United so it's a power move he thinks makes us all nervous. Some of us it does, but not me. I'm cool as a cucumber. I dropped into one of the crap chairs and felt a sense of foreboding, and my mind drifted to that dark place again. It finally dawned on me what it was. The room reminds me of doing time in the can. I didn't do a long stretch but it left a mark. It was the state pen in Salem on an 8th grade field trip and I can still smell the desperation and feel those four walls closing in on me. I shuddered thinking about it.

It was meeting time.

2

Except for Girard everyone else was there. Daniel Conner, Scott Sorenstam, and Victoria Mannheim are the other associate sales directors. Dan's got East County which is mostly fast food joints and big chain restaurants. Easy money. Scott has the Willamette Valley south to Eugene so he burns a lot of gas running up and down the I-5 corridor. I've got Portland Metro, which is like having a Catholic family with too many screaming kids. Vicky has everything else and she kicks ass. I don't have the numbers to back me up but she probably hasn't missed a sales quota since Clinton got caught with his cigar out in the Oval Office.

Michael Willard is the regional logistics manager and the steadiest guy in the world. He also happens to be the guy who makes sure a couple hundred million dollars' worth of stuff goes where it's supposed to go. Mark Westerling's the controller and he's a tool. Sue Ann Pennington is the marketing director who comes up with all the sales initiatives and stupid slogans we're supposed to pitch. Mostly though she just plans office parties and enforces the Casual Friday dress code. Chucky doesn't do casual. I wear business casual of course, but I'm not going out on any calls wearing dad jeans and a Tommy Bahama shirt. I always wear slacks and the company-issued United Food polo shirt, even on Fridays. I don't think Sue Ann likes me.

Then there's Darlene. Darlene Camper is Girard's secretary, although they call them administrative assistants now. Just like people pulling minimum wage are "associates" or "team members" or something. And janitors are "custodial engineers". Anyway, I always snap to when Darlene's in the room. She's a real looker with more curves than Skyline Boulevard and obviously comfortable in her own body. I would be too. She's got the kind of body that can take your mind off what you're working on and put it on other things. But it's those long brunette curls, luscious red lips, and big hazel eyes that get me. She's no sex kitten either, she's a full-grown cat. Even though we haven't gone out yet I think she has a thing for me. Dames usually do. My square-shouldered good looks aren't easy to resist. I should probably ask her before she gets bored with the chase but I've been pretty busy lately and when we hit the town I want to give her the attention she deserves.

I had conveniently situated myself across from Darlene's spot near the head of the table where Girard would park.

"Hey, E.C.," she purred in a throaty voice, "some of us are going to Manning's later for happy hour. Why don't you come?"

"Not my kinda place, honey," I said with an air of indifference she could see through like a lace teddy.

"Okay, suit yourself."

The little curl at the corner of her lips and twinkle in her eyes told me I should maybe give Manning's another shot. Darlene is some flashy bait on the end of that hook but I like my bars dark and divey. Manning's is bright and cheery with perky twenty-something waitresses pushing appetizer and drink specials like the Avon lady who knocks on your door and won't leave. Kids these days don't remember the Avon lady but I do. The one who came to our house up on Council Crest was pretty hot and I was always happy when mom let her in and she stayed awhile. Everybody buys their stuff online nowadays. I hate that. You can't have a decent sexual fantasy with Amazon Prime.

Anyway, I like dive bars and I drink scotch and soda, not

some fruity concoction or one of those complicated craft cocktails that take twenty minutes to make. I usually drink beer though because scotch and soda doesn't taste that good.

Just then Jack Girard walked in the room and blew my happy hour reverie like a bad fuse. We call him Jerk Girard behind his back and he doesn't just walk into a room, he struts. That's one of the reasons we call him Jerk. The biggest one though is that he's a jerk. He's not very tall with wavy black hair, a thick mustache, a hawk nose, and eyes like a lizard. He's ignorant, arrogant, aloof, greedy, hot-tempered, and demanding as all hell. And Girard's not too careful about hiding the fact that he's a little bit racist and a sexist pig. Other than that he's the perfect boss.

"We've got a lot to cover today so I want quick summaries of your third quarters relative to the stretch sales goals," he barked out while taking his seat in the only new chair. "Scott, let's start with what's happening down south."

Scott Sorenstam stood up and started passing around papers. He's skinny as a rail and tall, six-three or maybe six-four, but carries himself with stooped shoulders like he's embarrassed about it. He's not bad looking with high cheekbones, thick lips, thinning blond hair, and watery blue eyes. Scott's one of those born-twice Christians but doesn't talk about it much. I like that about him. He doesn't smoke or swear, and even though he'll have a beer now and again he doesn't drink them like he means it. He also doesn't hit his sales goals very often.

Scott handed me a colorful chart that was carefully doctored to cover his ass but I was busy thinking about stretch sales goals. What the hell is a stretch sales goal? We have sales goals at the beginning of every year but a while back some lowlife came up with the idea to "stretch" the goals mid-year and make them go from hard-to-reach to impossible. Probably just a way to screw us out of our bonuses and pad the bottom line. Not that they need to do that. Why can't they just say we have new sales goals?

When I snapped out of it, Sorenstam was droning on about results from the Willamette Valley region. His sales come mostly from Portland suburbs like Lake Oswego and Tualatin but to hit the numbers Scott has to make some hay in Salem, and Eugene which is 100 miles south.

"The legislature wasn't in session last quarter so Salem's off six percent, and enrollment is down at U of O so we're trying to pump up the organics and gluten-free stuff in Eugene. They just eat that up down there."

He smiled weakly delivering that line but it was obvious Scott missed his mark. Girard gave him a few seconds more before he sat up in his chair and shut down the report.

"Net, net, net, Scotty, where are we at?"

"Down three percent from Q2 and down five percent quarter-to-quarter from last year."

"Well that's a pretty picture, isn't it?" he said sweeping the room with hard, deliberate eyes, daring somebody to speak. "I want a plan to turn that around on my desk by Monday morning."

His look lingered on Sorenstam long enough to make all of us uncomfortable. Turning abruptly to his left he zeroed in on Dan Conner and snarled, "Am I going to hate East County as much as I hate the valley now?"

Girard thought he was being funny and you could see unnaturally white teeth gleaming from under his creepy mustache. But there wasn't anything funny about the way he smiled.

I suddenly flashed on Burt Reynolds and *Stroker Ace*. He was playing himself in that movie. A dick with a porn 'stache.

I guess those were happier days for him and Loni but he was still a dick. Fact is *Stroker Ace* just wasn't a good movie. And I never could figure out what Gomer Pyle was doing in it. Must've needed the money. Anyway, Girard reminds me a lot of Reynolds so I drifted off and found myself floating down that river in *Deliverance* wishing it was Lewis not Bobby who made friends with the hillbilly.

Conner didn't bother standing up or handing anything out. Dan's no gym rat and hasn't missed any meals in a while so he'll stay seated unless there's a damn good reason to get up. He didn't hit his numbers either but he wasn't going to make any excuses. Well, maybe one.

"We're down five from Q2 and off three from last year, Jack. It was a really hot summer so I guess people were eating salads instead of double bacon cheeseburgers."

Funny thing about Dan Conner. His voice somehow fits his body. Short and thick. He's got a bushy, disheveled mop of brown hair partially hiding a happy face with rosy cheeks, and he looks like the guy next to you at the bar who's had a few. He doesn't show any teeth when he smiles so it comes off as a crooked grin and gets lost in the folds of flesh. He was wearing that grin while he waited for the Jerk to swallow his cheeseburger excuse.

"They've got salads at Burgerville you know," Girard growled, glaring at Conner.

Dan ran through the details but nobody cared and he was just wrapping up when Darlene and I locked eyes. She gave me a coy smile that made me think of *Boogie Nights*.

Burt was much better in that one but I was thinking more about the subject matter when my gaze dropped to her cleavage.

She must've been reading my mind because Darlene was tugging on her surplice top and the cotton-polyester fabric was clinging to the peaks and valleys thanks to static electricity in the room. I love surplice tops. Not as much as tank tops mind you, especially the ones with spaghetti straps, but I love them just the same.

"Poole, sorry to wake you but I'd *really* love to hear how Portland Metro is blowing away the stretch goal and making me look good."

He meant it. The part about him looking good I mean.

"Sorry, Jack," I said without being the least bit sorry.

I leaned back in my chair but it didn't budge. Wouldn't swivel either. It looked like I was going to have to run this con game without any help from the furniture. My mind started to race and I briefly considered racing to the men's room. A lot of people in the office know I've got IBS and Girard would have to let it go, at least for now. But I don't think Darlene knows so I decided it was time to start dancing.

"My laptop crashed this afternoon so I don't have the exact numbers," I stated flatly without a hint of fear in my voice.

I can be pretty direct with people and sometimes it rattles their cages. I guess I could learn to stutter so it would be easier on them but I've got to live my life a certain way and stuttering isn't it. Anyway, I threw in the *exact* part as a smoke screen for exactly how bad my third quarter was. And it was.

"Oh, really?" Girard snarled. It obviously wasn't a question.

"Yeah. If IT will ever give us laptops from the 21st century this might not happen."

Girard looked surprised at that but I'm the kind of guy who punches first and asks question later. And I know from playing some rough games that the best defense is a good offense. Or is it the other way around? That's always bothered me. I guess it can work both ways. Anyway, I know the Jerk well enough to know that if I can get him on his heels he'll probably drop his gloves and that's when I can land a haymaker. I hadn't figured out what that punch would be but I've got a fast brain and was working on it when he countered with a hard left hook to the midsection.

"Well, if you'd ever hit a sales goal maybe we could afford it."

Working the body is smart. I've seen boxers throw in the towel plenty of times without ever taking one on the chin but that's not going to happen with Chucky in the ring. I'm a fighter and my body doesn't like being worked. I never made Golden Gloves champion, but I would've given it a go and probably could've been a contender if I wasn't such a bleeder.

"I've read the annual report, Jack, and it sure looks like United could afford a few new laptops," I responded, snapping his head back with a sharp jab.

Mark Westerling doesn't usually say boo unless the Jerk gives him permission but after hearing my smart remark he leaned into the table and stared at me. Corporate controllers can make your life a living hell but they don't often look like much in the flesh, and Westerling doesn't look like much. He's on the short side with a small head and no chest. Probably was the last kid picked for kickball. Even so, he's got sharp features and beady eyes behind thick glasses, and he can dish out some mean looks. His face screwed into an angry bird and he flashed a sneering grin in my direction.

"If the company doesn't meet sales expectations, to hit budget we have to offset that with expense reductions." He paused to let the weight of those words sink in. "I look at expenses as food, water and air. You can live for a month without food, maybe a week without water, and no more than a couple minutes without air. Fuel for our trucks? That's air. Software to keep our on-line ordering system current? That's water. New laptops for our sales team? That's food."

I'd heard this business school BS before and knew he had another load to dump so I gave him a mouthful of fist before he could open his trap again.

"Well I'm pretty hungry, Mark, and *your* brand new laptop looks good enough to eat."

At this point the tension in the room was thick. Like a venti extra-whip mocha frappuccino. It was that thick. I glanced to my left and saw Mikey Willard not at all trying to hide a grin that was asking me how I was going to get out of this one.

I could tell Westerling was really steamed and wanted a piece of me, and that Girard wanted to keep boxing too. I was ready to go fifteen rounds with either one of them, but the Jerk had other things on his mind today so he raised a hand to cut us off and said to Westerling, "Get him a new one."

Turning to me he snarled, "I want that report by EOB today."
Jawohl, mein Führer.

Yeah, I used my inside voice but I think he heard me just fine. I was spoiling for another round but I guess the referee stopped this one and gave me the TKO. My fists unclenched slowly under the table and I started to breathe easier.

Girard looked defeated and was none too happy about it. He motioned toward the indomitable Ms. Mannheim with a weary wave and pursed lips.

"Can you help me clean up this mess, Vicky?"

Vicky Mannheim is a big-boned gal from Southern Oregon. You just couldn't call her small. You could call her Vicky of course, but we usually call her Vic. I guess because Vicky takes too long to say. She's average in height, plain but not unattractive, energetic and earnest to a fault. Her piercing blue eyes and bobbed blond hair make her look like Steve McQueen. If Steve McQueen were a dame. Vic takes her job seriously and knows her stuff. She could sell ice to an Eskimo. As a matter of fact she does. There's a native Alaskan Aleut who made a ton of money selling blubber or something and bought a bar in Hillsboro. He does a lot of catering and buys dry ice from Vicky.

Vicky bats cleanup in these meetings for a couple of reasons. One is that she almost always blows away her sales goals, stretched or not, and makes up for the rest of us so Girard can claim all the credit for a successful quarter in his region. The other is so he can use Vic's bat to beat me and Dan and Scott over the head.

"We lost the Claim Jumper account last month, Jack, so I came up short of where I wanted to be," she said with sad puppy eyes that didn't hide the pit bull lurking within.

"Goal was six percent quarter-over-quarter and the stretch goal was eight," Vic mewled. "I was hoping for twelve but we came in at ten and a half."

Girard stalled for a minute looking at Vic like she was goddamn Mother Teresa, then turned and threw daggers in the general direction of me and the boys. We were all girding our loins because normally he'd pile it on thick right now, but there must be something big brewing because he just thanked Vicky and slammed his laptop shut. My mind was like a cart racing ahead of the horse when Girard abruptly stood up and jerked the reins.

"Sue Ann. Michael. Sorry to skip over you two today but we've got important business to discuss. Maybe some of you have heard scuttlebutt about this, and if you have I'm going to find the leaker and scuttle his or her butt," he said jabbing a finger at nobody in particular. He was obviously amused by his own stupid joke and the smug grin he was savoring was hard to swallow. "Today we're going to talk about the upcoming reorg. Darlene, get that PowerPoint up now."

Nobody gets a PowerPoint up like Darlene so my train of thought went off the rails just then. She was wearing a pair of dark gray slacks that could pass for yoga pants in most jurisdictions and they did a nice job showing off her gorgeous gams. Which was fine by me. I think I may have already mentioned the surplice top. It was the color of cream. Not half and half, the real deal. And completing the get-up was a pair of strappy sandals with stiletto heels. They were dark gray too. She made for a pretty picture that hung in my mind.

I was thinking to myself that no reorg was necessary for *that* finely stacked beauty when the first slide came up and Jack Girard's raspy voice snapped me back to reality.

"There's a memo waiting for each of you in your inbox with detailed instructions on how we're going to proceed so I'm just going to hit the highlights here. No questions until I'm finished. Are we clear?"

I was trying to prevent my right arm from shooting up in a Nazi salute when Girard launched his lecture.

"This is not just a reorg, this is a reinvention," he said pompously with his chin stuck out. "No, it's a *rebirth* of United Food Distributors."

Pointing vigorously toward the first slide on the whiteboard he continued, "We've had the same sales regions and sub-regions since United was founded. That's a long time folks and people have gotten a little too comfortable and a little too complacent."

I'm sure the first slide was fascinating but nobody could see it because the whiteboard was wearing a heavy coat of stale dry-erase marker residue. The poor thing had been beaten into submission through years of business meetings and humiliated by countless airhead executives who forced it to advertise their unoriginal crap. This was a whiteboard that had given up on life. Anyway, you couldn't read much.

"This reorg was Gloria's idea but I had a lot to say about it. She just wrote her MBA thesis," he said snapping his fingers at Darlene to get the second slide up. "It's called *Sales Stagnation and Competitive Dynamics*. It's attached to the memo I sent and I strongly suggest you read it before she visits next week."

Gloria Summerhill is an east-coast silver-spoon baby and the executive vice president of sales and marketing for United Food Distributors. She's the kind of broad who was born on third base and thinks she hit a triple. Or at least a solid double and stretched it into a triple on a fielder's choice. She's got her bread buttered on both sides that's for sure. Anyway, I've been on plenty of conference calls with Summerhill and she can be a tough cookie. Never met her in the flesh though and it made my flesh crawl just thinking about it.

"Gloria will be here Tuesday for the team-building exercise and I expect everybody to be up to speed on this reorg by then. If not sooner. Long story short, when you have a system in place long enough people learn to game the system. She calls it the petrified forest of sales. You have the same territories, the same quotas, and the same accounts. The same old same old."

Girard loves to use the same old sayings and he paused to relish the same old same old one before continuing.

"Again, I had more than a little input here but Gloria's theory is that only pure competition can sustain double-digit growth."

What is it with corporations and double-digit growth? Maybe it's because they're run by idiots with double-digit IQs, but all it means is they keep raising prices and cutting costs until customers can't or won't buy their crap anymore. How is that sustainable? I'm no communist but sometimes capitalism doesn't seem any better.

"So in a nutshell here's what we're going to do. Starting a week from Monday there won't be any more sales territories. We'll be consolidating all accounts in the region, shuffling the deck, and dealing them out again to the four of you."

I could swear he was looking at me when he nodded his pointy head and grinned.

"Corporate IT has come up with new software to track sales performance and any account that is underperforming will be given to a different sales rep. Bonuses will be based on customer acquisition and retention relative to the other associates and that's all explained in the memo. I'm not going to lie to you, the goals are challenging. But I think you'll find the rewards to be very generous."

Customer acquisition and retention? Oh, you mean sales?

The goals will of course be unattainable and the rewards out of reach, but what was left unsaid and hung in the room like cheap cigar smoke was if we start losing accounts we lose our jobs. There have been reorgs at United in the past, but usually they're something like consolidating warehouse operations or creating new business units that look like the old ones but have new names. They never amount to a hill of beans. But this one sounded like the apocalypse. Now. Or in a week at any rate.

Girard spent another ten minutes bumping his gums and patting himself on the back. I wasn't paying much attention but he told us how exciting this change would be and even shoveled some BS about how we'd all be richer and happier. He finally stopped at about ten after four, checked his Rolex with a flourish, and motioned for Darlene to put up the last slide.

Up on the not-so-white board were the big blurry words, *Winners never quit, and quitters never win.* It was a quote from Vince Lombardi, the legendary coach of the Green Bay Packers back in the '60s. It's one of those dime-a-dozen inspirational sayings that went up on locker-room bulletin boards back in the day to try and motivate a bunch of meatheads who probably couldn't read. Girard stared at it with his back to us for a long moment and then wheeled around beaming like he just pulled off a magic trick. He pointed to the words on the wall, then put his hands on the table and paused.

"Change is hard, people. I know it. You know it. Everybody knows it. This is going to upset some of you, but if you're not coming with me on this then get out of my way. We want winners at United Food, not quitters. So go home this weekend, read my memo, read Gloria's thesis, maybe have a couple of brewskis and watch a game or a movie, get some rest, and come back Monday ready to roll up your sleeves." He paused again, pointed his finger guns at us, and fired, "You're my team. Confidence is high."

Normally what the Jerk just did would make me sick. The guns. The stale business tripe. The "we're a team" crap. Hell, the only thing missing was that idiotic book *Who Moved My Cheese?* But today I was sick to my stomach for a bigger reason.

Girard motioned for Darlene to kill the PowerPoint.

We all rose from our chairs like the undead. Except for Sue

Ann of course, who always rises from her chair like she's in a hurry to go out and make it a great day. I took a quick look at Conner and rolled my eyes. His eyes were hollow and had that thousand-yard stare. It gave me a cold shiver, remembering guys in the war who had just lost a buddy or seen something they couldn't unsee. I've seen some pretty awful things myself. I think it was in the first part of *Saving Private Ryan*. Anyway, I brushed past Darlene a little closer than I needed to on my way out and Girard shot me one last nasty glare, whipping me with a snarling smirk.

"The report, Poole. EOB today."

3

I'd been back in my office exactly a New York minute when Westerling marched in and slapped a new laptop on my desk. Hard.

"Careful, Mark. Don't ruin perfectly good food."

"If you think you're being funny, Poole, I'm all out of laughs."

I smiled serenely at him while he took my old, perfectly good laptop and shoved a thumb drive in the USB port like he was using a shiv on a stoolie. It didn't take long to download the few paltry bytes of information I had and upload onto the new one. I wanted to tweak him with another joke about bytes of food but it wasn't going to take him long to figure out there was nothing wrong with my old laptop, and I didn't need to make him any sorer than he already was. Westerling stood up abruptly and tried to look intimidating, which isn't easy for a five-foot-nine bean counter. He gave me a thin smile.

"Sorry, but now you're going to have to actually file that report. By EOB today."

"Muchas gracias, amigo."

I'm not sure why I went south of the border just then but it seemed suitably snarky without being outright rude. Westerling said nothing and gave me a funny look before he turned on his heels and disappeared.

It was now ten 'til five. Almost happy hour. Well, most places start their happy hour at four, or even three, and they run until six or seven, so it's not really a happy *hour* at all. It's an hours-long bacchanalia when restaurants break even on food and make a killing on booze. Everybody does it. Makes me wish I was in the bootlegging business instead of peddling frozen chicken strips and slider buns. But I'm not. Anyway, I had drinks and Darlene on my mind and was in no mood to file a report for the Jerk.

Maybe it's because I was putting fresh eyes on the thing, or maybe I just got luckier than usual, but it took me all of two minutes to find that scumbag cell and send it to cyber hell. The formulas flowed now and all I had to do was plug some numbers into the report and hit send. Girard won't like what he sees when he opens the attachment but I'll be on my second scotch by the time he does.

I lost a little more time because I forgot the attachment on the first email, which seems like something I do a lot. Everybody does it, right? After re-sending *with* the attachment I shucked my jacket over my shoulder and headed for the parking lot. I hadn't made it ten feet down the hall when I froze in my tracks. There was Girard with Sue Ann standing outside her office door. They were obviously wrapping up a conversation, and as usual both of them were talking louder than they needed to.

"Jack, this is *brilliant!*"

Sue Ann says brilliant a lot and always does it with a little shake of her head. And a slight British accent. I hate that. Her whole body quivers when she gets excited, which is pretty often. With her curly permed hair and tiny frame she looks like one of those lap dogs people shave except for the little afro on top and balls on their ankles. She sounds like one too.

"Well, Sue Ann, we need to thank Gloria for this but really it was just an idea of hers and I did most of the heavy lifting."

"I *knew* it," she said practically shrieking the words.

Without warning, Girard pivoted toward me, and using skills I can't tell you where I learned, I made a catlike move into the break room and stuck my head in the mini-fridge to avoid detection. It was there things got sketchy in a hurry. I almost passed out from the stench of a days-old kale and quinoa salad, and an open container of vanilla yogurt sporting a five o'clock shadow. Luckily I'm able to hold my breath longer than most and I popped my head out just in time to see Girard's back and listen to his Manolo Blahniks clicking down the hall. I had to escape but couldn't risk the elevator, so while shaking the cobwebs out and trying not to lose the grande burrito, I made for the stairs.

It had stopped raining during the meeting and when I broke out into the warm October sun and crisp fall air it wasn't a second too soon. Sucking in big gulps of fresh air I took the beeline to my Subaru. I always have to make my car honk with that key fob thing because there are a hundred other crossover SUVs in the parking lot. Seems like almost everyone has a crossover SUV nowadays. And everyone else has a pickup truck. Which are all bigger than a house. Anyway, the crossover SUVs all look the same so it can get dicey trying to find mine. After I finally located my slightly worse-for-wear 2012 Outback, I settled into the driver's seat for the short hop to Tualatin and Manning's. And Darlene.

Manning's Lakeside Grill is like a lot of suburban restaurants. It's got a big dining room with tables by the windows and rows and rows of faux-leather booths. It's important to have lots of booths because Americans love booths. Europeans will sit elbow-to-elbow at tiny tables in bistros and trattorias, and they don't care. They just stare into each other's eyes and murmur suspicious things in their foreign languages. Americans won't do that. I guess a few Americans actually do speak foreign languages but I mean the elbow-to-elbow part. Americans need personal space so they love booths. It's like their own little world in there.

Problem is they talk so loud they might as well be sitting in each other's laps.

Anyway, Manning's has lots of booths. They also have this cavernous event space where the Rotary Club meets once a month, and they can make the room smaller so people who don't know any better can have meetings or reunions there. Or, God forbid, a wedding reception. The bar is plenty big too, with even more booths and lots of big-screen TVs. The real draw at Manning's though is the patio. And the lake. Which is fake. Some greedy developer just dug a hole so they could charge more rent in the business park, but customers love it. The patio overlooks the fake lake, and if the weather is anything short of life threatening that's where people want to be.

Not me. I don't get the obsession with eating and drinking outside. It's too hot in the summer, too chilly in the fall, and too windy in the spring. Hell, I've seen days when there are so many napkins and menus flying around it looks like a twister in a trailer park. And don't get me started on insects. I'm not easy to bug but let's just say I'd rather not spend my time swatting flies and yellow jackets away from the food. It's annoying. And I'm no Howard Hughes or anything but it's unsanitary.

Still, Darlene likes the patio so that's where I'm headed.

When I walked in the front door, the host, a very large Hawaiian or Samoan or something, was dancing to Wham's *Wake Me Up Before You Go-Go*. Literally.

Jitterbug. Jitterbug. You put the boom boom into my heart. You send my soul sky high when your lovin' starts.

The big guy was light on his feet so I couldn't help but watch. When he noticed me, a huge infectious smile crossed his face and he danced out from behind the desk to greet me at close range.

"Hi! Welcome to Manning's. You've been in before haven't you?"

You usually don't get this kind of greeting nowadays. Walking into most restaurants you're welcomed by blank faces staring at computer screens loaded with room management software. These cold fish cling to the security of the reception desk like a local news anchor not wearing pants. And when they finally do look up they may or may not actually say something.

You're in the hospitality business, asshole. We're supposed to have a conversation, and you're supposed to go first.

Anyway, this guy floored me.

"Yeah, I've been in a few times. Nice place. I'm meeting some friends from work and they're probably on the patio," I said with a smile I couldn't help.

"You work at United Food, right? I thought I recognized a couple of people but I haven't seen Scott yet." Manning's buys from United and this is Sorenstam's account.

The happy host introduced himself as Tui, which he explained is short for Tuituilomo, and pronounced "Tooey".

"Where you from, Tui?" I asked as he guided me outside.

"Tonga," he replied with eyes twinkling as if it's a magic kingdom. It probably is.

It was a sunny Friday afternoon so the patio was packed. Tui gracefully navigated the sea of junior executives, and the amateur beauties under their inspection, with his head on a swivel looking for some sign of my party.

"Hey, E.C."

I turned to my left and spotted Dan Conner huddled at a table by the lake with three familiar faces. Darlene wasn't one of them so my crest fell a little. Dan motioned me over and Tui led me through the crowd using better blocking technique than most NFL fullbacks. I followed the big guy in a wake of strong cologne.

"Thanks, brother," I said as I grabbed one of the chairs and sat down with my back to the fake lake.

Tui blew a quick kiss to the rest of the table, gave me a friendly squeeze on the arm, and then disappeared. I thought to myself Manning's is damn lucky to have that guy. Portland's a foodie town and there are plenty of places to get fancy food. A lot of those places are "chef-driven" concepts that critics get excited about and award a bunch of stars. Maybe half-stars too. I've had good eats at those joints but sometimes I feel like a guinea pig in a culinary experiment gone wrong. And unlike the guinea pig I have to pay the bill. Anyway, there's some good food around town but hospitality is definitely a lost art.

I reached over and patted my war buddy Dan on the back. Across from me was good old Mikey Willard and his warehouse manager Cesar Castillo. Mikey looks like a boxer. He's compactly built with a round face under a grizzled head of receding gray hair. He's a little past his prime but looks to be in good shape and like he could still take care of himself in a fight. And he has big hands with thick fingers that were custom made to be fists. Mikey gave me that timeworn, knowing grin again and a barely noticeable bob of the head by way of greeting. Cesar is a wiry Mexican with a nice face, a sweet smile, and a sweep of slicked, jet-black hair that makes him look like a supermodel. If it wasn't for the two missing teeth. He reached across the table and offered a fist to bump.

"Que pasa, E.C.?"

It comes out A-Say when he says it but sounds cool. Cesar's a good guy and we get along just fine, and it's not a bad thing to have him in your corner when the chips are down and you need a drop shipment for a customer at night or on the weekend.

"Livin' the dream, Cesar."

That's our standard exchange and it never fails to make him laugh. Right next to Cesar was Marta Blakely. She's the United Food event coordinator and the gal that Sue Ann treats like a summer intern. She's fresh-faced and all of twenty-five but has a mind of her own and doesn't buy the corporate crap. And thank God she hasn't yet contracted the degenerative perkiness disease that will eventually kill Sue Ann.

"Hey, Marta. Nice to see you but I thought you were doing that Taste of Gresham thing tonight."

Gresham is the biggest suburb east of Portland and it's Conner's bailiwick so he jumped in before Marta could respond.

"That's next weekend, E.C. Really looking forward to it," he said with more sarcasm than was necessary. "I'm pretty sure I'm going to be deathly ill next Friday so Marta will have to solo it."

Marta just giggled and said, "Hi, E.C.," then abruptly added "I heard about the sales meeting today and the reorg. What's *that* all about?"

Maybe the not-so-tiny dancer at the front door chased this afternoon's meeting out of my brain but now the reorg came charging back in like a bull. I shot a quick look at Dan and he just shook his head before taking a long pull on his pint.

"Not sure, Marta," I said, mostly because I wasn't sure. "They probably hatched this reorg just to reduce head count." I used air quotes for the head count. "The Ice Queen and the Jerk want us at each other's throats. If they go through with it at least one of us is getting the chop, that's for sure."

Head count. What the hell does that even mean? Do they not have time to count the rest of us? I guess body count is too obvious, even for corporate devils like Girard, and they probably think we're flattered they're aware we have heads. Anyway, they can go to hell as far as I'm concerned.

Conner wore a baleful expression but tried to keep it light.

"It'll probably be you, Poole."

"You're probably right," I mumbled nodding my head. I was starting to feel like I *would* be the one to come up with the dirty end of the stick. "Not trying to change the subject but where's Scott?" I added, trying to change the subject.

"He's a family man," said Mikey. Other people have families but we all knew what he meant. "I saw him walking to his car and he looked pretty shook up. Probably went home to tell the wife."

I was sure I hadn't ordered a drink yet, so when a cute waitress appeared with a scotch and soda I eyed the rest of the table suspiciously. Mikey knows what I drink so maybe it was him, but Tui the Tongan somehow zoomed to the top of my suspect list. Before I could figure out how the hell he would know what to send me, the hair on the back of my neck stood up. I suddenly became aware of the soundtrack for the first time since being whammed at the front door. Manning's plays one of those *Hits of the '60s, '70s and '80s* channels. The twenty-somethings on the deck mostly ignore it but it's right in Chucky's wheelhouse. And *Hit Me With Your Best Shot* hit me right where it counted.

You're a real tough cookie with a long his-to-reee of breaking little hearts like the one in me. Before I put another notch in my lipstick case you better make sure and put me in my place. Hit me with your best shot. Fire awaaaaay.

Pat Benatar was wailing that line when I caught a flash of creamy surplice top out of the corner of my eye and instantly I knew why the song had penetrated my gloom like a laser. Darlene

Camper was sashaying through the throng of revelers in perfect step with the music, and she had one of her curvy cohorts in tow. I reflexively stood up to greet her.

"Well, look who's here," she said playfully.

"Wouldn't miss it for the world, doll."

With a grandiose wave of her arm she presented her friend. "Guys, this is Suzanne. She lives downstairs from me and works at Bed, Bath & Beyond."

She came around to my side of the table, gave me a peck on the cheek and whispered, "Glad you came."

Glad I did too.

The fact that Darlene issued similar kisses to Mikey, Cesar and Dan didn't register. I was lost in a cloud of her perfume.

I sat back and took in the usual chit chat about friends, family, and of course the daily grind. Mostly though I stared at Darlene. She caught me a couple of times and tossed me a self-conscious smile before looking away. I was raised a proper gentleman and I know it's rude to stare, but when dames go for the guy on the other end of one they don't seem to mind so much. I was sipping my drink when she locked onto me with her beautiful hazel eyes. Brother can she do things with those eyes. Then, just like that, she turned to Cesar and I lost her. I watched them for a while and even the way she absently stirred her drink while talking to him was sexy. She could swizzle *me* that's for sure.

After a long wait our frazzled server arrived with a tray full of happy hour fare that Mikey had ordered. Artichoke dip with little toasted bread slices. Beef nachos with lots of sour cream and guacamole but not a lot of beef. And of course a big plate of Buffalo wings. I don't remember, but Congress must've passed a law that Buffalo wings have to be on happy hour menus. The freckle-faced redhead finished by dropping a pile of paper napkins on the table and asked if we wanted another round. I enviously eyed the beers the other guys were having and considered switching from scotch and soda, but the girls seemed suitably impressed with the big-boy drink so I stuck to my guns.

"Scotch soda, honey," I said stealing a quick glance at Darlene.

Our server disappeared just in time for me to get a load of two new arrivals on the patio squinting into the setting sun and looking for a place to park. I got another shiver and was sure this one was going *up* my spine. Or was it? Okay, I guess maybe it could've been going down. Damn it, can't the Mayo Clinic figure this out?

I couldn't quite make the guy standing behind her but the gal in the doorway cut an imposing, unmistakable figure. It was Vicky Mannheim. Vic's been known to tip a few after hours but this was a surprise since she usually works until seven or so, especially on Fridays. Restaurant chefs and managers like account reps who work late on Fridays. That's when they finally figure out they didn't order enough product to make it through the weekend. Vic's always there for them. Not me, I make my own rules and figure maybe next time those jokers will be more careful. I call it tough love for customers.

Anyway, it was a surprise to see her. And a surprise she didn't come to join us. Or even notice us.

Vicky did spot the only empty table on the patio and started moving in that direction. That's when I finally caught sight of the guy she was with. He was a short, soft little man wearing a long, black raincoat that tried without success to make him look tall and hard. As I mentioned before, Vic's a big girl and that's why I couldn't see him at first, but now my blood ran cold as I tracked the two of them across the deck. It was Mark Westerling.

Conner had spotted them as well and beat me to the punch. "Well, well, well. What do you suppose those two are going to talk about?"

I could see suspicion in Dan's eyes so he must've borrowed my thought. Vic and Westerling don't usually pal around. Or do they? The thought crossed my mind it was a date, and that struck me as funny but then got real creepy, real quick. If they had a roll in the hay, there'd be nothing left of Westerling but his glasses. Besides, they're both married. Anyway, it was a safe bet this was no social drink and that's when suspicion bloomed into full-blown paranoia.

"Vic's in on this," I said out loud without meaning to.

I guess I must've had a long face because when I turned back everyone at the table was looking at me like my dog just died. Which was weird because she just did.

I had to put down my golden retriever, the lovely Rita, last week when she got pneumonia. She was fifteen and had a good life but I cried all the same. Chucky doesn't cry much but losing Rita caught me with my gloves down. The lady vet was a sweetheart though. I was carrying on and scared some kids in the waiting room so she gave me a shot of tranquilizer that must've been for a Saint Bernard. It worked I'll tell you that. And she didn't even charge me for it.

Anyway, I was aiming to have another drink and make my way around the table to Darlene but right now I just wanted time to myself. It was hard to figure what was going on or how I fit in. I could've stayed and tried to sort things out but there was too much to think about, and I was too tired to do the job. I stood up and pulled out my wallet to get my American Express Rewards

Gold Card but Mikey held up his hand to stop me.

"I got this one, E.C. Get some rest this weekend."

I threw one last look Darlene's way as I started to slalom through the tables. Her eyes were slitted with worry and I'm pretty sure what I saw on her face was genuine concern. Although it could've been gas from the nachos. I knew that was part of *my* problem for sure. Tui's cheery goodbye on my way out didn't put a dent in my mood and I stepped outside into the fading light. Manning's is one of those places that pipes their music outside the front door, I guess on the theory that classic rock will make you hungry. Usually I ignore it but tonight the O'Jays were ringing in my ears as I started the search for my Subaru.

They smile in your face, all the time they want to take your place. The back stabbers. Baaaaack stabbers.

Now the arena is crowded with lots of people in tattered peasant clothes and animals of all sizes and shapes. Horses, sheep, pigs, dogs and cats running in circles. The crowd roars as the bull comes closer. He looks impossibly huge. He charges anything that moves and gores them with his horns, but somehow they all escape unharmed and run away. Suddenly his eyes lock on mine. I look down and see a red and gold cape draped in front of me and feel betrayed by it. I'm the only one in the arena now and the bull is bearing down on me at full speed. I scream but there's no sound.

At the last second, I jump aside and the bull follows the cape as I pull it behind me with my right hand. I can smell him and feel the anger as he passes. There is a murmur of approval from the crowd but only for a moment. The bull turns and is upon me again. I switch the cape to my left hand and lead him through once more. I see his right horn is much longer than the left and sharpened to a point. This time there are muted olés.

Suddenly, I am no longer the target of the bull's rage. Men on very tall horses draped in shiny armor have now entered the arena and the bull is chasing them. The scene swirls around me in slow motion and I watch as the bull tries to gore the horses while the men stab long spears into his neck. He looks confused and tired and a strange pity washes over me.

A bullfight is not an equal contest between a man and a bull, it is a tragedy.

4

The morning sun found its way in through moth holes in the mini blinds. I blinked my eyes open and when I checked the clock it was exactly seven forty-three. I must've been having a real swinger of a dream because I'm usually up before six, so that rattled me. I never remember my dreams and can only hope this one involved Darlene and lacy lingerie, but I don't think so. Or me with my fingers wrapped around the Jerk's throat squeezing the life out of him. Somehow I knew that wasn't it either. Whatever it was I didn't feel rested at all.

Relying on force of habit and muscle memory, I made my way to the kitchen and waited numbly for my trusty Mr. Coffee machine to help me out of the stupor. My head was pounding, which told me I'd had a couple more scotches when I got home last night, but when I tried to piece together the details it didn't work. Or seem worth the trouble.

I was sitting at the kitchen counter and well into my second cup when the fog finally lifted and yesterday's events started to come into focus. I opened my laptop and saw an email from Mr. Jonathan J. Girard, MBA. Knowing it would probably ruin my Saturday, I reluctantly clicked on it.

It was addressed to "Team" like they always are. God forbid Girard would use our real names but when you're counting heads you don't want to get too personal. Besides, he sent it to all of four people and that would've involved a lot of typing. The email itself was short which I was grateful for. A couple of sentences in I realized it was the exact same drivel he spouted yesterday afternoon, and that he'd been reading this email word for word.

Jack Girard is a guy who probably uses a teleprompter when he's telling mom he loves her.

Mr. Coffee sensed my foul mood and made a gurgling noise to get my attention. He meant well, but a third cup this morning would've turned me into a bundle of nerves. More so than I already was. He looked sad when I turned him off but I knew he'd be up and ready to do his job tomorrow. Mr. Coffee is a morning person. I'm not.

Against my better judgment I opened the attached memo. The title line read: *Departmental Reorganization to Maximize Customer Acquisition and Retention.*

The coffee I threw up in my mouth tasted especially bitter.

It was tough sledding through the business lingo but the message was clear and it roared through my pounding head like a freight train. Unless we can somehow stop this reorg, Dan, Scott, Vic, and yours truly will be playing the food distribution version of *The Hunger Games.*

I had a pleasant moment imagining Girard as President Snow, and Darlene and me as Katniss and Peeta. My mind jumped to the last movie, whatever Mockingjay part that was, when the rebels execute Snow, and Katniss and Peeta make love. I don't think that's really in the movie but it should've been. I was lost in that scene when my cell phone started buzzing.

My phone used to have a ring tone. It was The Doors and it was pretty cool.

Hello, I love you, won't you tell me your name? Hello, I love you, let me jump in your game.

I should've told you this up front but I don't have a smart phone. Chucky doesn't carry devices smarter than he is. I use a phone to make phone calls and I have a flip phone that does the job just fine. But a few months back it stopped playing The Doors and I couldn't figure out how to get them back on stage. Maybe Jim Morrison was too high but whatever happened the damn thing just buzzes now. I saw on caller ID it was Scott Sorenstam.

"Hey Scott, we missed you last night at Manning's."

"Yeah, I needed a drink but Tamlynn had a soccer game. Besides, I wanted to tell Dot about the reorg and cry on her shoulder."

Scott wears his emotions on his sleeve so he probably did cry on hers. I could tell from the tone of his voice he was still shook up. Truth is I was too.

Fear is a funny thing. If you don't feel it at least a little you won't know what hit you until it's too late. That's served me well in some tight spots. Like the Costco parking lot for example. But feel too much of it too much of the time and you'll end up in a basket. I've seen that too. Fear doesn't own Chucky, it's the other way around, so I figured it was my job to prop Scott up. No sense having a group panic attack.

"We're going to be fine, Scotty," I assured him. "How did Tamlynn's game turn out?"

Girard calls him Scotty but I'd never called him that before, and I wasn't sure why I did just then. I guess I was trying to be reassuring in a big brother kind of way but the awkward silence on the other end told me he didn't want a big brother, or my brand of reassurance.

"They lost," he said finally. "We're not supposed to keep score at her age but we all do. It was 17-2."

I ignored the soccer debacle, which let's face it was pretty bad even for 7-year-olds. I'm no expert but obviously they need better organization on the back line. I mean, who's coaching these kids?

Plowing ahead, I tried to do a little damage control.

"For starters this isn't a done deal yet, Scott. Once Summerhill leaves after the team building the whole thing may blow over. This reorg makes as much sense as my grandma after she had that series of small strokes. When Girard figures out sales are going to go down, not up, he'll change his tune."

"I don't know, E.C. They seem dead serious about this."

I knew he was right and felt a creeping sense of dread, but I couldn't show him my cards or it would be game over. I was groping for the right thing to say next, which definitely would not be Scotty, when suddenly I knew what to do. Sure I killed a few brain cells last night, but I've got more to spare than most people and when the engine upstairs starts firing on all cylinders I can go from zero to sixty in six seconds flat. I don't know much about cars but I think that's good.

"They're dead alright, but not serious," I said with a little Groucho Marx flourish, using my eyebrows for full effect even though Scott couldn't see me. "I've been thinking it over and here's what we're going to do. You and me and Dan and Vic need to meet Monday morning and come up with a plan. We've got to convince the Jerk this will hurt sales. And it will. Maybe we can get a few of our big accounts to back us up. If we're all on the same page and hit Girard in the mouth he'll probably cave. And then, well, who knows?"

I started strong but ran out of gas and Scott knew it.

"Okay, that sounds like a good idea," he said without sounding like it was a good idea.

"Great, I'll call Vic and Dan and set something up for ten at Starbucks in Oswego Village Monday morning. You got any conflicts?"

"Nothing I can't move. See you then."

I was about to hang up when he doubled me over with a shot to the midsection.

"By the way, Dan called last night and told me Vic and Westerling were at Manning's. I've never seen them together outside work. You know what that was all about?"

I wish I did, Scotty.

"Nope. Probably nothing." I kept my tone real casual. "Have a great weekend and I'll see you Monday."

"Yeah, bye."

I sat and stared at my phone for who knows how long thinking about Vic and Westerling. What the hell *were* they talking about? I've been down my share of dark alleys and they don't scare me much, but my mind started down one now that made even Chucky afraid. Vicky is United's best associate by a wide margin. We all know that. And Westerling knows better than anyone how much money she piles up on the bottom line. Stands to reason the more accounts she works the happier the suits are going to be. But what could that mean? And what could those two be cooking up? I was thinking maybe I'd find out the hard way when the O'Jays reappeared to ask me a musical question.

What they doin'?

Something was eating me and I had a feeling it was going to eat a lot more of me before it was through. There was plenty to be scared of down that dark alley, so just to be safe I backed out real slow and easy. When I called Vic's cell it felt like I was parachuting behind enemy lines. And going from a dark alley to jumping out of a plane felt plenty weird. Anyway, she didn't pick up which is not like her. She usually works a half day Saturday and has a hair trigger answering her cell.

"Hi, this is Vicky Mannheim, Associate Sales Director of United Food Distributors. I'm on another call. Please leave a message after the beep and I'll get back to you in a jiffy."

Jiffy? I rolled my eyes for nobody's benefit and left a message for her to call me back. If I'd texted, I'm sure I would've gotten an immediate response. But I don't text. I don't speak that language and don't want to learn.

I tried Conner next and he picked up on the third ring.

"Hey E.C., what'd you do with the rest of your Friday night?"

"Not really sure, Dan, but I know drinking was involved," I said wearily.

"Same." He sounded tired too. "But here's a news flash. I think Darlene's sweet on you, dawg. She pulled me aside after you left and wanted me to check on you later to make sure you were okay. I guess I got pretty hammered and forgot. You okay?"

Anyone over thirty who uses the term "dawg" should be put to sleep, but my heart was doing back flips inside my ribcage because of what he just said so I let it go.

"Except for this stupid reorg, everything's jake," I said unconvincingly. "You?"

"Yeah, I'm okay. It is what it is, Mr. Poole. It's the same game, just another system is all. And like Girard says, we'll figure out how to game the system."

Something struck me funny about what Dan just said. He's not usually a glass-half-full guy and he sounded almost upbeat about the reorg. I hastily shoved that thought in the upstairs file cabinet and explained my plan for a Monday meeting to get our act together. He was all in.

"What about Vic?" he asked.

Both of us had the image of Vic and Westerling at Manning's

branded on our brains but didn't bother discussing the obvious.

"Left her a message. I'm sure she'll be there."

I wasn't sure of that at all.

"What've you got going today, E.C.? Any plans?"

"Couple of errands to run and then I thought I'd watch the Oregon game at Buffalo Wild Wings. You want to join me?" I asked knowing he wouldn't. Dan's an Oregon State fan and he hates the Ducks.

"No thanks, I feel like I might be coming down with something. Think I'll just stay home and take it easy."

"Smart. See you Monday, bro."

I threw in the "bro" to rib him about saying "dawg" but he missed the irony so I just hung up. How long I sat there after the flurry of calls is anyone's guess but there was something real fishy going on with this reorg that I couldn't reel in.

I was just about to throw a Jimmy Dean Sausage Biscuit in the microwave when my phone started buzzing again. They say breakfast is the most important meal of the day and that's why I always start with a Jimmy Dean Sausage Biscuit. I love those things. I guess I love having diarrhea too.

"Hey, E.C. What's shaking?" Vic said in her sunny top o' the morning voice. I had planned on playing my hand slow but when I heard that voice I threw all the cards on the table.

"What do you think about this reorg, girl scout?"

I call her girl scout because she is one. Or was one. She grew out of her uniform that's for sure but never really left the service if you know what I mean. She was born for it. Hell, I bet she sold more cookies than the rest of her troop combined. Vic probably holds the all-time record for moving Samoas. Those are the big sellers, right? Do people even buy the other ones? I sure don't.

Anyway, I call her girl scout and she likes it.

"I think it's stupid," she said abruptly.

That caught me off guard and my engine stalled.

"Well, uh, yeah. It's bound to be stupid if Girard has anything to do with it," I sputtered.

"Guaranteed," she giggled. "At bare minimum we're going to waste a lot of gas zig-zagging around the whole region."

I guess one thing on the plus side of this reorg is bigger mileage checks, but that won't mean much unless they plan on reimbursing me while I look for a new job. It also occurred to me that Vic knows I know about her and Westerling and was blowing smoke to keep me guessing.

"True," I stated flatly. Then as casually as I could muster, "I saw you and Mark at Manning's last night. Did he spill any beans?"

If she knew that I knew what I thought I knew, well, I didn't know.

"Not really. We didn't talk about it much."

Right. And I'm the Duke of Earl.

"He has a nephew who wants to get into sales and was wondering if I would mentor him next summer. I met him last week. Super nice kid."

Sounded plausible enough but I wasn't ready to swipe my card and buy that line. You don't swipe much anymore of course, what with all the chip readers, but I wasn't ready to do that either. And what's the deal with that? I like chips as much as the next guy, just not in my credit cards. Anyway, maybe what she was saying was true, but I've got a pretty good nose and it didn't pass the smell test she and Westerling had a drink and the reorg didn't even come up.

"Well he couldn't find a better role model than you, girl scout."

"Thanks, E.C.," she said modestly. "I listened to your message and I think a coffee meeting sounds like a super idea. I have to swing by Olive Garden in Aloha at nine so I might be a few minutes late. They're doing a complete tableware reset, dishes, glassware, flatware, the whole shebang."

Vic and I both knew that would probably be a thirty-grand order so me and Dan and Scott would be a lap behind her this quarter before we even ordered a latte.

"That's awesome, Vic. Good hit. Enjoy the rest of your weekend and I'll see you Monday."

Before I closed my laptop, I noticed the last two lines of the email in bold type reminding us of the team building Tuesday and the sales meeting Friday when Girard plans on shuffling the deck. I had the whole lousy situation in my head and was starting to drown in a whirlpool of this morning's conversations when the microwave dinged and threw me a rope. My sausage biscuit was ready so I shut down my brain. I was hungry and right now there were a lot more questions than answers. Like why do Jimmy's Sausage Biscuits taste so good?

5

I turned the shower off and stood there for a minute letting the water roll off my back. And some of my troubles too. I finally opened the sliding door, made a mental note to book some "me time" at that day spa in Lake Oswego, and toweled off. I suppose people might get the wrong idea if they saw me there but I'm pretty comfortable in my own skin, especially if it's been recently exfoliated. Besides, they've got some real tomatoes handing out the terrycloth robes.

By the time I laced up my old pair of Nikes it was after ten. Maybe it was the shower, or maybe it was the biscuit, but I was starting to feel better about things. I was pleased I'd set up the Monday morning meeting. That was a good place to start. There was plenty more to learn but I didn't have enough information yet to sort this out. And there was nothing I could do about it until next week anyway. I promised myself I was going to run a couple errands, enjoy lunch and the Duck game, and forget about this mess until Monday.

I hopped in the car and headed down the hill, weaving my way through the sprawl of apartments and condos in Mountain Park until it opened onto Boones Ferry Road. It was Saturday morning and traffic was already heavy when I turned right on Kruse Way and angled west to I-5. As soon as I hit the on-ramp I knew I'd made a fatal mistake, but there was no turning back now. I mean I could, but it would be illegal. And I just qualified for a safe-driver discount with Farmers.

Like most cities, Portland freeways were designed in the '60s and '70s and easily handled the load back then. Now they don't.

They're just a real popular place where everybody's in a hurry to get nowhere and wait.

The stretch between Lake Oswego and Wilsonville is usually sluggish but today it was stop and go. Mostly stop. Looking around at the mass of crossover SUVs that were my fellow inmates, I noticed little "O" flags on many of them and suddenly realized what the problem was. It was game day. The Oregon Ducks were playing their hated rivals, the Washington Huskies, in Eugene, and kickoff was at one. Normally the drive takes about two hours. These people would be lucky to catch the second half.

What's the deal with those little flags anyway? I went to U of O for a year and a half and had a good time. Probably too good. I finished a few years later at Portland State so I'm really a Viking, but I still like watching the Ducks. Mostly because they tend to score a lot and their uniforms are cool. But watching a game and rooting for them is one thing. Dressing in school colors, running little flags up your antenna, using a duck call, tailgating for five hours, and generally acting like somebody hit you in the head with a hammer on game days is another. Especially if you're fifty.

Anyway, it took me twenty minutes to crawl five miles to the Wilsonville exit and by the time I hit the off-ramp I was giving serious thought to rooting for the Huskies. My destination was Costco but I needed to swing by the office to check on a delivery for City Bar & Grill, my best account. The United Food Distributors headquarters is only a quarter mile from Costco and right on the way. Finally free of the freeway duck flock, I let out a sigh of relief as I pulled up to the loading dock. When I stepped out of my car a cheery "Hola, amigo," rang out.

The slender figure and friendly face of Cesar Castillo suddenly appeared at Bay 7. There are eight bays in the United dock and

I've stopped trying to figure out how they decide which one to use. Whenever I ask Cesar about it he just smiles and points to his temple like the shipping system is rocket science. Maybe it is. It's over *my* head that's for sure.

"What're you doing here, my friend?" I asked, forgetting he works on Saturdays.

"Working, E.C. What're you doing here?"

"Sorry, Cesar. Just swung by to check on a drop ship for City Bar & Grill. They've got a couple of weddings and a big orthodontist convention this weekend, and they need a truckload of product."

Cesar went to check his computer so I parked my rear on the dock and tried to think about anything but the reorg. I settled on orthodontia. How much fun could an orthodontist convention be? Conventions of any kind are cruel and unusual punishment in my book, but a convention of orthodontists? Jesus. What are the breakout sessions for that one like?

"We're loading it right now, E.C. Should be there by noon."

"Perfecto!" I said giving Cesar a thumbs up.

I'm pretty sure perfecto is Spanish for perfect, but walking back to my car I felt like an idiot for saying that to a Hispanic man. As I opened the door I looked up and caught sight of something that stopped me in my tracks. Across the parking lot near the office door was Dan Conner. The guy who was supposed to be sick today. He was standing beside a silver Dodge Durango talking to a man I'd never seen at United before. He was tall with olive skin and long thin sideburns, wearing wrap-around sunglasses. A cigarette dangled from his lips and a wisp of smoke curled up around his collar and over the top of a black fedora. He looked like a real grifter. I didn't like him.

Dan must've made a speedy recovery. Or he lied to me. I hadn't been spotted yet and considered shouting hello to see how he reacted but decided instead to process the information first. Maybe it meant nothing, but I like to know who's making friends with my friends.

I slipped into my car and headed down Parkway Avenue, my mind spinning the tumblers on a lock I didn't have the combination for and couldn't pick. Not yet anyway. By the time I pulled into the Costco parking lot a couple of big questions needed answering. Why was Conner so upbeat about the reorg when I talked to him this morning, and why did he lie about not feeling well? And who was that city slicker he was talking to? Okay, that's three questions but I had exactly zero answers. My uncanny sense of danger was telling me there was trouble ahead, and there was. Big trouble. I shuffled in the front door of Costco and flashed my membership card.

I hate Costco. I hate all big box stores but I hate Costco the most. As far as I can tell the scam works like this. You have to pay to play. You can be a regular member for $60, but I bought the "executive" membership for $120 because I'm a sap and the girl who sold it to me looked like Gwen Stefani. Anyway, you pay a tidy sum for the privilege of playing bumper carts with a crowd of skinflints just so you can save a couple of bucks on cheap toilet paper. One-ply toilet paper. The kind you need to be extra careful with. And, on top of that, you have to buy a package of six dozen rolls that won't even fit in the trunk of your car.

Costco is truly survival of the fittest. That part I like because I'm pretty fit. Fitter than most of the people who shop there anyway. Costco sells lots of health food and exercise equipment but from the looks of the other shoppers nobody buys much of it.

And all those big bodies and big carts sure don't make it easy to navigate the aisles.

So yeah, I hate Costco but I paid the damn fee so I come about once a week to try and get my money's worth. Shampoo and dish soap were my mission today. After a couple of wrong turns and a minor fender bender with a grandma who growled at me, I found the shampoo I was looking for. Costco carries a couple of name brands but most of the stuff is their private label Kirkland. It's all Kirkland this or Kirkland that. I'd bet a C-note at even money that half of everything Americans use nowadays is Kirkland. Poor Amway must be getting killed.

I conservatively estimated the gallon container of "3-in-1 shampoo" I selected would last me two years, which is also how long it will take to recoup my membership fee since I probably just saved a quarter. Eyeballing the giant bottle I wondered what three things are in my shampoo and why it's a plus they're all in there together. And why I even use shampoo is something I need to consider since I'm basically bald. I put the shampoo in my cart.

Lady luck must've been blowing on my dice today because I turned a corner and nearly T-boned the dish soap display. It was enormous. My work done, I wrestled a box of dish soap the size of a dishwasher in the cart and headed for the front end.

It doesn't matter what day or time you come to Costco the checkout lines are a mile long. After fifteen minutes I realized I should've bought some Kirkland whisky for a little toner. It's probably rotgut stuff, but Chucky will do what he's gotta do. Anyway, after I finally got my receipt checked by the storm trooper at the exit and broke out into the warm Indian summer weather it felt like I just busted out of the joint. I wouldn't know but that must feel good. At least until the dogs catch up.

Loading the giant containers into my trunk, I started to wonder why Indians have different summers than the rest of us. I mean summer's summer, right? Unless you're in South Africa or Peru or something. Then summer's winter. Or winter's summer. Whatever the case, I had bigger fish to fry so I pointed the Subaru in the direction of Beaverton and Buffalo Wild Wings. It was quarter to one and almost time for kickoff. And I was hungry.

When I finally found a spot in the crowded parking lot it occurred to me if I'm hungry I shouldn't be going to Buffalo Wild Wings. They have plenty of big screen TVs alright, and beer, but the food would get you chopped in the first round. It's one of United's big accounts so I shouldn't say that, but it's not mine it's Scott's. I mean, the food isn't bad it just isn't very good. They give you a little paper tray of wings, your choice of a hundred different sauces that somehow all taste the same, a flimsy plastic fork that couldn't poke holes in Jello, and a piece of toilet paper for a napkin. Probably the Kirkland one-ply. How is this a thing?

It was only ten after but the game was already underway. The Ducks had won the toss and were driving. When I squeezed onto the last empty stool at the bar a big roar went up from the crowd. I looked just in time to see a 330-pound lineman lifting a 200-pound running back in the end zone like he was a newborn baby. Six-zip Ducks. I shook my head in amazement. I mean, I know these linemen have to be in game shape, and they could sure put the hurt on me, but God some of them are fat.

The game was a seesaw affair and by the time my wings and second beer arrived it was halftime and Oregon was up 21-17. By the sound of it, there must've been quite a few Oregon State fans in the house because the Huskies had been getting some full-throated support.

I'm not sure how they get along in the wild but in sports bars Beavers and Ducks don't play nice in the pond. And it's not just because they're in-state rivals, it's a culture war. There are probably a few exceptions, but basically everyone who goes to U of O watches MSNBC and everyone who goes to Oregon State watches Fox News. Also, the Oregon cheerleader uniforms are hot and Oregon State's are not. Simple as that.

The boneless wings at BWW have a weird texture but are easier to eat than the bony ones, so I ordered a dozen of those with Kickin' Honey Garlic sauce. Chucky can stand the heat so I gave some serious thought to having the Jammin' Jalapeño or the Mango Habanero, but I didn't want my head to sweat and the morning after can be uncomfortable. Especially with one-ply toilet paper. I also considered the Asian Zing and Caribbean Jerk, and then toyed with the idea of a dry rub seasoning. Honey BBQ is too sweet and Parmesan Garlic sounds like something they'd put on your never-ending pasta bowl at Olive Garden. I finally settled on the Kickin' Honey Garlic because it combines a little heat with a little sweet. That's right where I wanted to be. Also, I was just plain exhausted.

The Huskies charged out of the locker room and took the game by the throat in the second half. By the time I polished off the last of my third beer, the third quarter was over and the Huskies were up 34-24 with the ball to start the fourth. The Beaver fans were having a fine time and I saw a couple of big Duck dudes sizing them up for a fight. I didn't want to have to break glassware over anybody's head but it was something to keep my eye on.

Washington was in the red zone facing third and five and tried an out pattern to pick up the first down. An Oregon corner read the play perfectly, stepped in front of the Husky receiver, and it was a pick-six the other way. Suddenly it was 34-31 after the PAT and now the Duck fans were the ones doing the dancing. When Oregon recovered an onside kick and set up shop in Washington territory the place went nuts. I could hear well enough from the stall in the men's room but wished I was out there to see it. Maybe the boneless wings weren't such a good idea.

When I finally got back to the bar, the Duck's drive had stalled and they kicked a chip-shot field goal to tie the game. After that, neither team could move the ball and with less than a minute to go the Ducks had possession inside their own five with the score still knotted. Most coaches would take a knee and go to overtime but that's not the Duck's style. Maybe the offensive coordinator saw something in the Husky defense, or maybe he just has some muy grande cajones, but the quarterback faked taking a knee, rose up, and threw a perfect strike to some skinny speedster who took it all the way to pay dirt for the Ducks.

Crazy game. And despite the discomfort downstairs I had a pretty good time. For the better part of three hours the reorg hadn't even crossed my mind. Until I pulled into my driveway and killed the engine.

6

Something hit my front door like a brick and I bolted upright in bed. Every muscle was tight and my right hand was reaching for the nightstand drawer, ready to bring some heat if it was a crook. Or the cops. But I don't have a gun. I don't even have a drawer in my nightstand. Anyway, when I realized it was just the *Sunday Oregonian* and the paperboy's fastball was high and outside, the tension slowly drained out of my body. Very slowly. Like anti-freeze when they do those radiator flushes so your car is winterized.

I'm probably the last person in Portland who still takes the paper version of the *Oregonian*. But I only get the Sunday paper because the weekday editions could double as Kirkland toilet paper. I get the feeling it won't be much longer until newspapers disappear altogether. Then we'll all have to live in those cable news bubbles, and social media bubbles, and other bubbles as well, listening only to people who think like us telling us what to think. I guess most folks already do.

Not Chucky. I like to feel my news, not just read it. I've been to the *Oregonian* website, which they call *OregonLive* to make it sound exciting, and I hate it. First of all, everything now is "breaking news". In my book, breaking news is when Jesus comes back to straighten out his dad's mess, not a winter storm that might drop a few flakes on the Sylvan overpass. What's worse is all the stories are two sentences long with links that say "Read More". Yeah, I'd like to read more. Put it in the story. I shouldn't have to work so hard for my news. All that clicking and scrolling makes me dizzy. Besides, when you're on any of those so-called news sites it's only a matter of time before you swallow the click bait and end up on the hook. I'm not necessarily complaining mind you. I like staying current with the most daring dresses worn on the red carpet, but that ain't news.

Anyway, I got my Sunday paper. I made a mental note to give the paperboy some spring training and shambled to the kitchen to see what Mr. Coffee had to say. He was hissing that happy noise which meant I was almost saved, so I parked myself at the counter and made the mistake of opening my laptop. Bad habit opening laptops. There on my screen was the attachment I didn't read yesterday morning, and the title was glowering at me like a boxer during weigh-in before a prizefight. *Sales Stagnation and Competitive Dynamics.*

I knew I was going to have to give it the once-over, but I figured it could wait for later so I poured myself a cup of joe and ran last night's highlight reel in my head.

When I got home I had thought about calling Darlene to see if she wanted to grab dinner and a movie, but my stomach was still doing a tumbling routine after those boneless wings and four pints of beer so all I could think about was a nap. By the time I woke up, it was six thirty and I figured Darlene had probably washed her hair and was settling in to binge-watch *Game of Thrones.* And you definitely don't want to bother anyone binging on GoT.

I still wasn't ready to wrestle with the reorg and needed something to eat so I zapped a Marie Callender's pot pie and cracked a Coors. Not Coors Light. That's for people who just want to drink something ice cold that goes down easy but still gets them buzzed. I drink the original Coors Banquet Beer myself. Because it actually tastes like beer. Oregon's always been uptight about booze, so me and my college buddies used to drive to Idaho back when 18-year-olds could buy beer there. And we always bought a case of Coors. Looking back, driving five hundred miles to buy beer was really stupid, but I still like the taste of Coors.

I remember flipping on the TV, like you do when you're home alone on a Saturday. I usually watch sports or reruns of *Chopped* so I don't watch that many movies at home. I'm not even sure why I pay for Netflix. They have too damn many movies to choose from. I'm sure a bunch of them are Oscar winners, or Oscar nominated, or Oscar worthy, or whatever, but I've never heard of them and I'm not going to waste my Saturday night on a weepy chick flick. Like I told you before, Chucky doesn't cry much. Besides, I realized I was out of Kleenex and forgot to get more at Costco.

So when I do watch movies I usually watch action-adventure. That's my favorite genre. I like action. I like adventure. You do the math. It's hard to go wrong with Liam Neeson but I watched all three *Taken* movies last month in one sitting. Bruce Willis is a tough guy who reminds me of me, but I guess I thought the reorg might make *Die Hard* too close to the bone. I never get tired of the Impossible Mission franchise and almost pulled the trigger on *MI-3*. And there's that other one where he hangs onto the side of a plane, but I got hassled by a couple of Scientologists the other day so I wasn't in the mood for Tom Cruise.

I'm also a sucker for James Bond, especially the old ones with Sean Connery. That man *is* 007. Period. Pierce Brosnan was cool but doesn't quite measure up, and Roger Moore was too snarky. I know it was the '80s but those wide lapels and short ties made Bond look like a pimp. Timothy Dalton was lame, and who knows who the guy was *On Her Majesty's Secret Service*?

Who cares? At least he got to make out with that dame from the Avengers. God she was hot. And I know I'm supposed to like the new Bond movies with Daniel Craig but I don't. Too dark and depressing. Plus the guy is absolutely ripped and that makes me a little uncomfortable.

So in the end I decided it wasn't a night for Bond and fell back in the arms of an old friend, Jason Bourne. I love those movies. I can watch them over and over and over again. Last night I chose the original *Bourne Identity,* mostly because of that scene where he cuts the chick's hair. That's one of the sexiest scenes in the history of Hollywood. And the haircut turned out surprisingly well didn't it? Kind of shaggy and layered perfectly. I don't think Treadstone had a beauty school but Bourne can sure handle the scissors. Anyway, it proved to be a good choice and had kept me from thinking too much.

So that was it for my Saturday night home alone. I suppose I could've watched *Home Alone* but that would've been really sad. And I hate that movie.

I should've been thinking about giving Darlene a haircut, but I couldn't shake the image of Daniel Craig's six-pack abs and knew I needed to hit the gym. Sunday's my workout day and that's when I keep the chassis of this muscle car looking good. I packed my bag and was just about out the door when my phone buzzed me back inside.

"E.C., this is Mercedes. Got a minute?"

Mercedes Rolle is the Executive Chef at City Bar & Grill. With thirty-eight high-volume restaurants in Oregon, Washington and California, Pacific Restaurant Concepts is the big dog in our yard. And City Bar & Grill is their crown jewel slinging hash to the tune of almost ten million a year. It's my biggest account by far.

Mercedes made exec chef the hard way. She's a tough customer but keeps her cards on the table. She and her husband and five kids live halfway to the Oregon Coast on a farm outside Vernonia. On top of putting in sixty-hour weeks her commute is about an hour and a half each way. I can't figure how she does it. Not the commute, the five kids.

"Hey Chef. Just heading to the gym to pay the wages of sin. What's up?"

"We got a new regional VP, Johnny Scarpetti. He called yesterday, last night actually, and wants a vendor audit. All line items. Everything."

She sounded tired. And what she was saying sounded fishy because we had done a full audit for PRC less than a year ago. I guess fishy is something you smell but that's how it sounded.

"New bosses always want to flex in front of the mirror," I said casually, trying to hide a sense of foreboding that was creeping in like a sticky fog.

"Tell me about it," she sighed. "Scarpetti ran the Seattle ops for the last seven or eight years and I hear he's as mean as he is smart. Sorry to bug you on Sunday, E.C., but he wants the audit done by noon Friday so I thought I'd better give you a heads up."

"No worries. You can call me anytime. I'll get rolling on it this afternoon. If I don't die at the gym that is," I offered weakly. "How's life on the farm?"

"Brad and I are taking the brood mushroom hunting. Swing by the restaurant, there might be chanterelles on the menu next week."

I smiled and shared a chuckle with myself because of course I'll swing by the restaurant. I swing by City every week. Most weeks I'm there twice.

"Will do, Chef. Happy hunting."

Kids were screaming in the background so I couldn't tell if she said goodbye before hanging up, but I wouldn't have heard it anyway because something she said sent me down another dark alley. This new guy Scarpetti must know the numbers from the last audit are all pretty fresh. Maybe he's trying to shine somebody's shoes but I had a feeling there was more to it than that. A feeling like an old friend whispering in my ear.

I've heard the name Scarpetti before, but where?

When I pulled into the parking lot of 24-Hour Fitness I was still chewing on the call from Mercedes and couldn't swallow what I was thinking. It's a Sunday and I had to make four fast laps around the lot before I fought off an Audi Q5 and finally squeezed into a spot about a mile from the door. Maybe the long walk will be my workout.

I decided to put the reorg puzzle back on the shelf for a couple hours, but you don't take a high-horsepower brain like mine straight to neutral. You need to downshift. Besides, there was another important question that needed answering. Like why is a gym open 24 hours? I mean, who works out at three in the morning? That's just weird. Or is it so people can work out for 24 hours straight? I was doing the math on how many 5-Hour Energy drinks it would take to pull that off when the husky girl at the front desk interrupted my calculations.

"Mr. Poole. Nice to see you again," she said with a faintly-disapproving air. "It's been a while hasn't it?"

I did a quick check to my left and right to make sure there weren't any dames within earshot, and glancing at her nametag, I started to do a little damage control.

"Well, Terri, this must usually be your day off because I'm in every Sunday like it's church. But I *have* been working weekends lately so I've been getting a sweat at the office. Mostly core work but a little lifting too."

She gave me a tired smile like she's heard it all before. And she probably has. Truth is I haven't been in much since the morning after St. Patrick's Day when I threw up on the elliptical. The New Year's resolution was going pretty well up until that point. My personal trainer, a muscle-bound Swede named Tomas, called me twice a week for a couple of months and laid the guilt on pretty thick. But Chucky does what he wants when he wants so I told him to back off. I also told him I tore my Achilles playing rugby. Against New Zealand. In the World Cup. Maybe he got a new job modeling for statues or something, but he stopped calling. Anyway, I shot Terri a grin and made my way to the locker room.

The men's locker room at 24-Hour Fitness is not a place for the faint of heart. I guess I got good genes, so stripping naked and showering in front of a bunch of preening pretty boys doesn't bother me much. Maybe it does them. Still, I'm usually in a hurry so dressing and showering at home saves time. I shoved my bag in a locker and headed out to the floor. There were plenty of lovelies working the ThighMasters, and I usually spend a few minutes pretending to stretch so I can take their full measure, but not today. I needed a good workout. And I needed to get the reorg out of my skull.

Things didn't go according to plan because an hour later I was dripping sweat and my heart was pounding like a ticking time bomb. That always happens after Zumba class, but somehow this was different and I couldn't quite put my finger on it. Not my pulse, the problem. Seeing Vic and Westerling together, and then Conner lying to me, stuck in my craw. And now this Scarpetti guy and the audit at PRC. Not sure what to make of it yet but it reminded me I had exactly five days and four hours to figure Girard's game. And who else was in on it.

Driving home I got a lightning bolt out of the blue and just about rear-ended a Subaru Crosstrek. Those economy models aren't as sturdy as my Outback so that could've been ugly. But my brakes bit just in time and saved that tin can. It had finally come to me where I read about this Scarpetti character. He was in the *Portland Business Journal* a couple of weeks back featured in one of those executive profiles they do. You know the ones where they try to make some stuffed shirt seem like a real swell?

Who are your role models? My dad. *Oh, you mean the only greedier son of a bitch than you?* Who would you most like to meet? Steve Jobs. *Good luck with that. He's dead.* What are your passions? My wife and three beautiful children. *Yeah? Name them.* How do you spend your spare time? Memorizing scripture and playing the piano. *No you don't. You watch your hedge fund and play fifteen-handicap golf. And you tell people you're an eight.*

When I got home in one piece, I hurried up the stairs and fumbled with the key in the lock. Good thing I hadn't emptied my recycling in a month because after a thorough search I found just what I was looking for near the bottom of the bin. The crumpled issue had a couple of lines under the masthead that read *Giovanni Scarpetti Named New Regional Vice-President of Pacific Restaurants Concepts, page 18*. When I opened to page eighteen I got that chill in my spine again. And I was sick of trying to figure out which direction it was going.

There was a bunch of fine print about Scarpetti's professional accomplishments, little pearls of wisdom about the restaurant business, and his turn-ons and turn-offs, but I wasn't interested.

I was staring at the airbrushed photo and trying to pick my jaw up off the floor. The gaunt face and features, the olive skin, the long thin sideburns. It was him alright. It was the guy I saw Conner with in the United parking lot yesterday. When he was supposed to be home with the flu.

"You dirty double-crosser," I mumbled to myself and yanked the page out. Now things were starting to add up and I didn't like the total. Actually, I didn't have all the numbers yet so it would be more of a subtotal. Whatever it was I didn't like it. I hadn't stuck around for the goodbye kiss but Conner and Scarpetti were acting awfully chummy. He's the new regional and they're auditing me. And Vic's cozying up to Westerling.

It was starting to feel like a game of musical chairs and I'd be the one left standing when the music stopped.

7

I didn't want to raise eyebrows with this off-site meeting so I made a brief appearance at the office and spent time chatting people up in the hall. Talking louder than usual too. Things were going smoothly, but when I walked in my office around a quarter to nine and sat down I was staggered with a hard right to the chin. There it was sitting on my desk. A copy of *Who Moved My Cheese?* I blinked hard to make sure my eyes weren't playing tricks. They weren't, and to make matters worse there was a Post-it note signed by the Jerk.

Savor the adventure and enjoy the taste of new cheese!

"Enjoy the taste of a knuckle sandwich, asshole."

Something told me I shouldn't have said that out loud, and when I looked up Mikey Willard was standing in my doorway grinning.

"Thank God it's you," I said thankfully.

"You have a bad attitude, Mr. Poole, and I think you need to be *corrected.*"

He drew the last part out exactly like that creepy butler in *The Shining.* The guy who kills his wife and twin girls with an axe for getting a little sassy. I don't have kids, and I'm sure they can get under your skin, but that seems pretty harsh. I mean, how could you kill a couple of sweet little girls with an axe? Teenagers sure, but little girls? Come on. Anyway, I love that movie.

"Girard's in the warehouse raising hell so you're safe."

"What's he doing in the warehouse? I didn't think he knew where it was."

"He must've read one of those books about management by

walking around. He's pretty pumped about this reorg and is out there slapping backs."

I didn't know what to say to that so I said, "I don't know what to say to that."

Mikey smiled. "The pickers were playing some old Run DMC and Girard actually tried to moon walk. I guess he thought we were bonding."

Pickers are the guys and gals who fly around the warehouse building loads for the trucks. You have to see it to believe how fast they can put together a pallet. Sure they make mistakes once in a while but not very often. It's hard work and Mikey and Cesar like to let them have as much fun as they can, which usually means cranking the music. I shuddered at the thought of Girard trying to boogie to *Walk This Way*.

"You know what he says then?" Mikey asked with both eyebrows raised almost up to his receding hairline. "Why don't you show us some of *your* moves, Michael? I'm sure you've got more rhythm than me."

"Can you believe that?" he pleaded with both hands outstretched. "Even for him?"

I think I may have mentioned that Girard's a racist but did I forget to tell you that Mikey's black? All I could do was shake my head. Sometimes I need to check the sign on the door just to make sure we're not working at Dunder Mifflin.

"Hey, Mikey. Here's a copy of *Who Moved My Grits?* Girard left it for you," I said waving the book at him.

Mikey gave me a big grin and laughed through his teeth like he was letting air out of a balloon.

"Already read it. See you around, E.C."

I got no business trying to guess how hard it is to be black in

America, or brown, or just plain different. So I don't. Can't be easy though. I'll tell you one thing, Mikey's got more class in his little finger than Girard will ever have. Not that he'll ever have any. I guess that's how Mikey shrugs it off. I couldn't.

I needed some gas for the Subaru and it was almost nine thirty, so I packed up and headed for the ten o'clock at Starbucks. I considered stopping by the break room and shredding *Who Moved My Cheese?* but decided I'd better leave it on my desk in case Girard stopped by. It felt like leaving books or magazines on the coffee table so when guests come over they'll think you read *Atlantic Monthly* or *The New Yorker*, or the *Collective Works of William Shakespeare*. Sure, we all look at the cartoons in *The New Yorker,* those are hilarious, but who reads *King Lear?* Seriously.

There's a Starbucks right by headquarters. Hell, let's face it, there's a Starbucks right by everything and at United we call that one headquarters. I wanted to keep this little affair on the QT though and the Starbucks by the office would be crawling with United employees. Sure, in Starbucks you can get lost in the noisy privacy of a big café, but it was more the optics I was worried about.

It was ten 'til when I swung into the Oswego Village parking lot and found a spot right in front, and when I walked in I spied Scott Sorenstam at a table with his back to me. I'd recognize that pencil neck and wispy blond comb-over anywhere. Why do guys do that? Do they think dames are that stupid? Or desperate? Anyway, it was Scott alright and he was patting the hairdo into place and finishing up a phone call when I tapped him on the shoulder.

"Sure. Sure. I'll call you when I know more. Yeah, bye."

He laid his phone down on the table, looked up and said hi, but I was locked on his Caller ID. It read John J. Girard. Not sure how many seconds ticked off but I must've looked like I'd seen a ghost.

"You okay, E.C.?"

"Yeah, fine." I snapped to and slapped on a friendly smile to hide the horror movie running inside my head.

I moved around the table to face him, looking for telltale signs of guilt in those soft features and watery eyes. I can usually read Sorenstam like an open book but this time all I could see was the cover.

"You need a refill?" I asked moving toward the long line at the counter.

"No, I'm good. Thanks."

I was grateful the line was long because it gave me time to catch up to my racing mind and pull it over to the side of the road, and by the time I was third in line I had my heart rate down to something manageable. I still couldn't quite make heads or tails of it but figured I had the goods on everybody now. They were trying to make a monkey out of me. All three of them. I decided I'd keep my cards close to the vest and play it real cool when I got back to the table. There are times when I want to keep things to myself and this was one of those times.

Just when I thought I was about to slap some cash on the counter and get a triple-tall latte underway, the two attractive middle-aged dames in front of me blew up the operation. Even though they'd been standing in line for five minutes, neither one of them was ready to order. How does that happen? Don't get me wrong, I love dames and us guys have plenty of quirks that must drive them right off the cliff, but they're *never* ready to order.

And then at the end of the transaction it comes as a complete surprise they're being asked to pay. This isn't a soup kitchen, ladies. Get your money out.

Anyway, after staring at the menu board for eternity and asking too many questions about gluten, high-fructose corn syrup and soy milk, they finally ordered a classic coffee cake. To share. And yeah, heated. The platinum blonde who seemed to be the ringleader of this duo wanted a Venti caramel frappuccino and was just a little too loud when she passed on the whipped cream. For chrissakes, you're not drinking coffee you're having a milkshake. Why not have *extra* whipped cream? Get some of those fancy sprinkles too, sweetheart.

The redhead she was with, who was wearing a skirt that was too short and too tight but pulled it off alright, stepped up to the plate and ordered a grande, skinny, half-caf, 155-degree latte with two-and-a-half pumps of vanilla. I wanted to grab her by the shoulders and ask how in Sam Hill she came up with that. In part because her sweater was off the shoulder and she had really nice shoulders, but I also wanted to know. Was it a slow process of elimination that took years and hundreds of trips to Starbucks or did she just wake up one morning and know?

Finally, after fumbling through their purses and then arguing about who was going to buy the coffee cake they paid. Separately of course. Then after more fumbling to reorganize the purses they slowly made their way to the pick-up counter where the blender was already buzzing with the milkshake.

One more thing. Women have a lot of stuff to carry around, more so than men, and I got sympathy because purses are a complicated environment, but couldn't they move away from the cash register before the rearrangement? Or is it a reorg?

Anyway, I finally ordered my triple-tall latte, and just for laughs asked for it at 161 degrees. I expected that to get a rise out of the cashier but she just nodded, scribbled on my cup with her Sharpie, and stuck it in line behind the redhead's. The one with more writing on it than the *Dead Sea Scrolls*.

When I got back to the table Conner was there but Vic wasn't. She said she'd be late so she could bag her Olive Garden elephant, and she was. I was worried Dan would have to run the gauntlet at the counter, but I forgot he hates Starbucks so he had a giant cup of Dunkin' Donuts coffee in front of him. He claims he's saving money but I think he actually likes Dunkin' Donuts coffee better. He also likes donuts.

"Feeling better, big fella?" I chirped, slapping him on the back.

Conner craned his neck to make eye contact and the blank stare told me he didn't remember handing me that line about feeling under the weather.

"It's Monday," he shrugged. "Other than that I feel fine. Why?"

"When I asked if you wanted to watch the game Saturday you said you were coming down with something. Said you were going to stay home. You missed a good one."

A look showed up on his face I hadn't seen before. He should've owned up to the con game he ran and apologized, but his cheeks got red and he gave me a crooked smile like he was hiding something. Dan's harder to read than Scott but his puffy cheeks get red when he's excited or mad or embarrassed. Or when he drinks. Then they get really red.

"Turned out to be nothing but I did take it easy Saturday. Sue took the kids out shopping and to lunch so I grabbed a little shuteye and caught the second half of the game. Unbelievable. The Ducks have to be the dumb luckiest team in college football," he sighed shaking his head.

I just smiled. Obviously he decided to double down on the lie and that was a bad bet.

Sorenstam was texting somebody and hadn't heard a word we said. It crossed my mind it might be Girard again but figured he'd be more careful than that. Dan started checking his phone too so I kicked back, sipped my 161-degree latte, and sized them up. The latte was probably 158, maybe 157 by now, but it still burned my tongue when I sucked through the little hole in the lid. I hate that. I knew my tongue would feel funny all day.

At quarter after ten Vicky Mannheim bounced in the door. She spotted us immediately and was wearing an ear-to-ear grin when she arrived at the table. She has a happy face anyway, but with a thirty-grand sale she looked even happier. Still, unless I missed my guess there was more to it than that. And Chucky doesn't miss very often.

"Hi, boys. Which one of you dolls bought me a mocha?"

I was about to take the rap when Scott looked up from his little screen and without missing a beat said, "Thought you might be another ten or twenty, Vic, and nobody likes a cold mocha. Let me get you a hot one."

He started to stand but Vic put him back in his place and bopped him on the head. Which required a hasty comb-over repair. "Kidding. Be right back."

I turned to watch her head to the counter and my jaw dropped. I couldn't believe what I was seeing. There was no line. Nobody. That *never* happens at Starbucks. Well, sometimes it does at those little kiosks in grocery stores but never the big ones. Anyway, it's just Vic's luck.

"How'd the Garden reset go?" I asked half-heartedly when she got back. I really didn't want to know.

"Corporate must be sitting on a pile of cash. They bought the whole book."

Dan and Scott perked up because they both have Olive Garden accounts and if one Olive Garden does something they all do it.

Dan popped the obvious question, "How much?"

"Thirty-seven."

Dan gave her a thumbs up and we all nodded our heads but nobody said anything. Most of the time we live on line-item sales moving food and paper trying to keep our noses above water. When you land a new account, or score a reset like Vic and write a bunch of smallwares and tablewares, or if you're really lucky kitchen equipment, that's a big bump in quarterly sales. Everybody pretends to be happy for you when it happens but nobody really is.

"So, what about this reorg?" I asked abruptly so Vic didn't have time to take a victory lap.

I scanned the table looking for someone to give me a tell but came up empty. Still, I figured whoever stepped up to the plate first might be the rat. It was Conner.

"What about it, E.C.? I've been thinking it over all weekend. There's nothing we can do."

You can have your buddy Scarpetti give you my best account. That's something you can do, Danny Boy.

Vic chimed in next. "The memo didn't say how they're going to shuffle the accounts did it?"

No, but Westerling holds the deck and he probably told you.

"I guess that'll be a fun surprise at Friday's meeting," Scott added sarcastically.

Yeah, unless you and Girard are dealing the cards.

My mind was chasing its own tail so I paused and took a deep breath before opening my trap. Even if I couldn't trust any of them I needed to play this straight and see who blinks.

"Listen, this reorg is supposed to be about boosting sales, right? And they think they're going to do that by having us at each other's throats. They'll probably cut costs too by getting rid of one of us, so that's a win-win for them, but then there are less people doing more work and plenty of dissatisfied customers. And then fewer customers." I put my palms out and raised my eyebrows to sell the logic.

"We've been through this before," Dan said with a heavy shrug of his lumpy shoulders. "After the dust settles it'll still be the same game."

I started thinking maybe Dan really doesn't sweat this and just wants to get on with it. Or maybe he's got his ducks lined up already. Although in his case I guess it would be beavers. But I don't think beavers line up for anything. Maybe the front door of the dam at happy hour but that's probably it.

"I don't think so, Dan. This game is different. You ever seen *Glengarry Glen Ross?*"

"No. Why?"

"Anybody seen it?" I asked glancing around the table.

Vic shook her head no but Scott raised his hand slightly and mumbled under his breath, "Yeah. Good movie but not a good one to watch if you're in sales."

It is a good movie. I don't think it made bank at the box office but the critics loved it. And I think Pacino got an Oscar or Golden Globe or something. I wouldn't watch it with the kids though unless you're okay with them hearing a lot of bad words. Really a lot.

"Forget the fact that the Jerk would be perfect in the Pacino role," I said without taking my eyes off Conner, "there's a scene where Alec Baldwin makes a speech to shake up the sales team. He tells them the company's offering rewards for annual sales. First prize is a Cadillac Eldorado. Second prize, a set of steak knives. Third prize, you're fired."

I paused to let them consider that.

"They're selling real estate not food but the game is the same. Watch the scene on YouTube. That's what they're doing to us."

I turned to meet Vic's gaze and her eyes were filled with what looked an awful lot like confusion mixed with concern.

"Don't you think you're overreacting a little, E.C.? Gloria will be here tomorrow and we're probably going to hear a lot more about this from her. Maybe we should see how it plays out first."

"Maybe I am, Vic, but this smells bad."

Something *did* smell bad, which was a strange coincidence, but then I noticed Vic had one of those artisan breakfast sandwiches Starbucks crows about. Must be the bacon and gouda because that cheese is really stinky. I don't know what's artistic about that.

"If we don't tell Girard we think this is a stupid idea he'll steamroll us," I continued, holding a finger firmly under my nostrils to keep my stomach in place.

Now Dan, Scott and Vic were all staring at me like I just got cancer. Even if they agreed with me, they sure weren't spoiling for a fight with Girard. Not that I blame them. They've all got mouths to feed. I briefly considered taking their advice and just going with the flow, but Chucky doesn't go with the flow. I'm pretty strong in the water so I don't need to worry much about the flow, or the current, or the tide, or whatever else water does.

I probably could've been a Coast Guard rescue swimmer except my ear canals are abnormally small and get really plugged up. My mom had to take me to the doctor every year at the end of summer to have them drained.

"Look, I don't want to get anyone in hot water," I said, "but if we all stick together and kick up dust, I think Girard will have to listen. If it's only one or two of us, we're toast."

"What exactly are we protesting, E.C.?" Scott asked plaintively. "Their right to make business decisions without consulting us first?"

My head was starting to hurt holding thoughts that were too big for it, but I couldn't stop now.

"Sure they've got the say-so, Scott, but for starters our customers are going to wonder what the hell we're doing if suddenly they all have a new sales rep. What do we tell them? And we're going to live in our cars if we've got accounts all over the region. Turning the bonus pool into a game of cutthroat means nobody's playing on the same team. It's cash not a Cadillac, but we all know what the third place prize is. Or should I say fourth?"

All three of them were still staring at me but now it didn't feel like pity. The talk at the table turned to who might get who's accounts, and it was the first time I'd seen any of them really interested in the discussion so I just sat back and listened. My mind drifted to those animal shows where lions fight each other for the privilege of devouring some slow-footed zebra. Only this time I was the zebra. And those tasty internal organs they wanted first crack at are my accounts.

After about ten minutes they'd apparently had their fill and turned their hungry eyes back in my direction. Scott awkwardly stood up while draining the last of his Grande Americano.

"Sorry, E.C. I got to hit it. If you guys really think meeting with Girard will make a difference, I'm in."

He patted Vic on the back and fist bumped Dan on his way out the door.

"I've got to go too," Dan said scowling at his phone. "Looks like Red Lobster got shorted this morning and Chef Sebastian's pretty steamed."

I was thinking about how lobsters must feel when Vic reached across the table and put her hand on mine. I've noticed before but Vic's got big hands. My hand completely disappeared under hers and that felt uncomfortable. I'm not exactly short on equipment in the engine room if you know what I mean, but still.

"Don't lose too much sleep over this E.C. Whatever happens we'll make it work. And we'll all still be friends, right?"

I smiled weakly as she departed.

I've got a theory about you and your friends, Vic.

"Peace out, girl scout," I said holding up the V-sign but feeling no peace.

I tried to see things from their angle but it didn't work. Sure they've all got problems, but so do I. Are we really friends? I wonder. Yeah we *act* chummy but I don't know these people that well. And who was it that said you keep your friends close and your enemies closer? Michael Corleone in *The Godfather*, right? Pacino again. Man he's had some juicy parts. I thought he was over the top in *Scarface,* but other than that great stuff.

Anyway, Vic's words were still ringing in my ears when the O'Jays cut her off and started asking me that question again.

A few of your buddies, they sure look shady. Blades are long, clenched tight in their fist. Aimin' straight at your back, and I don't think they'll miss. What they doin'?

8

I watched them all leave the parking lot before I chucked the rest of my latte in the can and headed out the door. I had a busy day on tap myself. Monday's always are. Usually I hate that but today I was grateful for something to take my mind off the reorg and so-called friends. While I made my rounds, I took inventory of the situation and by the time I got back to the office about four I was giving serious thought to getting in line and going with the flow. Until I spotted Vic in Westerling's office that is. With the door closed. I couldn't make out what they were saying because the door was closed, but Vic was behind Westerling's desk and they were both hunched over his laptop pointing at something. And I don't think it was what the stars of *The Big Bang Theory* look like in real life.

I cursed softly when Vic suddenly looked up and caught sight of me. Obviously I should've conducted my surveillance from a safer vantage point. Chucky doesn't usually make mistakes like that. They can get you killed. Or at least spotted. She gave me a quick wave, which caused Westerling to look up and see me too. He didn't wave. Trying to appear casual, I fired off a two-fingered salute and strolled down the hall to my rat hole.

That description fit alright because when I walked in the door I saw some rat had put *Who Moved My Cheese?* on top of my in-box. I could've sworn I left it on the corner of the desk, and that made my spider sense tingle. I was wondering who moved my *Who Moved My Cheese?* when I caught a faint whiff of perfume. I looked up to see the fine figure of Darlene Camper snuggled up against the doorjamb like it was her lover. I was jealous.

"Hey, slugger. I was worried about you over the weekend. You seemed kind of upset when you left Manning's. And you didn't say goodbye. Everything okay?"

"I'm fine, doll," I said with as much bravado as I could muster. "I guess this whole reorg thing has me tied up in knots."

She looked skeptical so I decided to press the bet.

"You believe me, don't you?"

"I believe anything you say," she said sweetly.

There was no point filling her pretty head with all the dirty details so I decided to keep my story simple and skin deep. But I couldn't seem to put any words together because Darlene's sweater dress had my tongue tied up in knots. I love those things. Tight sweaters were a great invention but making a whole dress out of that stretchy, clingy material? That's genius. I don't know who came up with the idea but they should get the Nobel Prize for Fashion.

Maybe she read my mind, or maybe it was written all over my face, but she raised her eyebrows and smiled.

"Like the dress?"

"Sure do, babe. But it's not the dress it's the dresser."

"Thanks," she demurred. "See ya."

I could've sworn I caught a wink but couldn't be sure. She spun on her high heels and strutted slowly down the hall. It was a sight to behold, but I was kicking myself for saying something so stupid. I mean it sounded like I was complimenting a piece of bedroom furniture instead of her. I sighed and watched the heels disappear around the corner at the end of the hall.

Shaking my head to snap out of it, I opened my laptop and checked email. Buried in the usual pile of order requests, shipping notices, and offers to save fifteen percent on my car insurance, was a not-so-friendly reminder from Girard about the team building tomorrow and Gloria Summerhill's thesis. Knowing I'd have to read at least some of that business school BS tonight, I sighed and started to pack up my briefcase. Letting out a loud groan, I threw *Who Moved My Cheese?* in with the rest of my stuff and headed for the elevator.

I had a half-dozen stops to make before I could knock off, so it was almost seven and a little dusky when I pulled in the parking lot of the lovely Westview Townhouses. Maybe they were lovely forty years ago but they're not anymore. And I'll grant you they all face west for the most part, but there's not much of a view. On top of that, the landscaper must be legally blind and the parking lot needs work. I just about planted my face stumbling over one of the deep cracks in the asphalt jungle and cursed under my breath.

Safely inside my standard two-bedroom, one-and-a-half-bath condo, I dumped the contents of my bag on the counter and damned if *Who Moved My Cheese?* didn't come out on top of the pile. I considered cracking it open for a few laughs but cracked open a Coors instead and headed for the shower. Most days that's the only way I can wash work off my skin and out of my head, and I sure needed today out of my head. My mind was such a mess that what I really needed was one of those power washers they use to get the mold off the siding of our townhouses. Although even that doesn't do the job. The mold and mildew at Westview is really bad.

Anyway, by the time I'd drained the hot water heater I felt like a new man. The fact that I couldn't get *Back Stabbers* out of my head and was singing it in the shower bothered me, but I took a long pull off the luke-warm Coors and dried off. I made a mental note to keep my beer in the refrigerator while I shower and threw on my favorite sweats. Actually, it was more tugging than throwing. They looked pretty snug when I checked the mirror but I always do my wash in hot water so they must've shrunk.

I hadn't thought about dinner, and was too tired to cook anyway, so I tossed a Stouffer's Salisbury Steak in the microwave and took a load off at the kitchen counter. My mind had wandered off somewhere when I realized there was a noise coming from the microwave that microwaves shouldn't make. I jumped up like a cat but my catlike reflexes weren't catlike enough and the loud pop told me I had major cleanup to do. Sure enough I did. But it was just one more layer on top of the lasagna last time I forgot to cut those little slits in the film, and the bean burrito before that, so I figured it could wait another day. Maybe I can borrow the power washer. Probably I'll just buy a new microwave.

Once I picked all the shards of film out, I dumped dinner on a plate and popped another Coors. You can eat Stouffer's dinners right out of the plastic tray, and I've done that a time or two, but those little compartments separate the steak from the macaroni and cheese and I like to mix them up. Chefs talk about flavors marrying, and I'll tell you what, the sauce from that meat and the cheese in those noodles make a happy couple. Sauces probably shouldn't look so shiny but it sure tastes good. Just for the hell of it I checked the ingredient list on the box, and wished I hadn't.

By the time I was done, it was pushing eight and the brooding fall light outside my windows set the mood for what lay ahead. Fighting the urge to pop another Coors and check Netflix, I opened my laptop and scrolled down to Girard's email. I shut my eyes when I clicked on the attachment, hoping it would disappear, but when I peeked it was staring me in the face like some English teacher who just assigned *The Catcher in the Rye* for the weekend.

A sunny weekend. I had a dried prune who did that once and I still hate her. And the book too. I had no idea what Salinger was talking about. "Don't ever tell anybody anything. If you do, you start missing everybody." What the hell does *that* mean? Anyway, there was the thesis of doom staring me right in the face.

Sales Stagnation and Competitive Dynamics.

I cracked another Coors.

Gloria Summerhill is no dumb blonde. People say she's the smartest thing going at United Food. Some say she's even smarter than the CEO, Raymond B.D. Stoddard. And he's plenty smart. Got an ulcer to prove it.

The big cheese has been with the company for thirty-four years. He started out as a forklift driver in Topeka and worked all the way up to the big office in Houston. The stock has tripled since he took over so he must have a big brain. His head's way too big for his body, that's for sure. I only met him one time at a sales conference in Fort Lauderdale when he was still an executive VP. He said hello and called me by name, but that wasn't such a tough trick since I was wearing one of those big conference badges with my name on it. He knew how to be polite when it benefited him, but was the kind of guy who'd ask you a question and not stick around for the answer because he didn't give a damn.

Anyway, he's a smart guy and if you give him half a chance he'll tell you so. But this Summerhill dame, she's got him beat I guess. He stole her away from Microsoft a year ago and word has it he had to pay a pretty penny to get her. Old man Stoddard can pinch pennies better than most so she must be smart. And she sure can write a thesis. One hundred and thirty-eight pages of thesis. I'm a pretty speedy reader so I figured I wouldn't waste more than an hour to pick up a few juicy tidbits I could sprinkle in the conversation tomorrow. And have time for one last beer before bed. I was scrolling hard and on page fifty-nine when I realized I didn't understand a thing she was saying and there weren't going to be any tidbits. Juicy or otherwise. She likes to use the word sclerosis I can tell you that.

The sales team is the heart of any organization. Only through rhythmic effort does blood flow to the other organs and limbs to keep the body alive. Without the dynamism of competition, and the defibrillating effect of change, sclerosis of the sales function is inevitable and eventually the lifeblood of business – profit – will dry up and the patient will die.

Who writes crap like that? Except Salinger maybe.

Her whole thesis made it sound like business is flesh and blood and she's a doctor. A doctor of sales. She sounds like a quack if you ask me. I googled sclerosis and it means abnormal hardening of body tissue or excessive resistance to change. Yeah, that adds up. But if sales is the heart and sclerosis is the problem can't we just cut back on red meat and dairy and exercise more? Maybe put in a stent or something?

By the time I hit rock bottom and couldn't scroll anymore, it was after nine and I'd come up empty looking for lines to feed Summerhill. I thought to myself maybe she likes cheese and chuckled. I closed my laptop and picked up the copy of *Who Moved My Cheese?*

Another beer probably wasn't a good idea with the day I had coming up, but I'm usually short on good ideas, so I grabbed the last frosty one in the fridge and twisted off the cap like I was wringing Girard's neck. I've got pretty strong hands but this cap must've been one of those bottling machine mishaps. The cap was too tight and I could tell immediately I'd done real damage to that sensitive little bridge of skin between my thumb and forefinger. Like I told you before, I'm a bleeder, so there was a lot of blood.

Anyway, after going through a dozen sheets of Kirkland paper towels I had it pretty well under control and could finally handle the book. I've read *Who Moved My Cheese?* before and it's a load of mouse crap. There are lots of these books around and they all try to make cost-cutting reorgs sound like a day at the beach with Darlene. Some people get jazzed up about that sort of thing, but I'm not buying it. These reorgs are just a smoke screen for suits who want to take a hatchet to head count and suck more blood.

I spent a minute or two imagining what Darlene would look like at the beach. I know most guys prefer bikinis but I'm not most guys. Don't get me wrong, I like bikinis well enough, but I'm more of a one-piece guy and Darlene would look mighty fine in one of those suits. Anyway, leaving a little to the imagination isn't a bad thing. Chucky can take it from there.

So in case you haven't read *Who Moved My Cheese?* I'll give you the lowdown. There are these two mice, Sniff and Scurry, and two tiny people, Hem and Haw. They spend the whole book running around a maze looking for cheese. That makes sense and should be the end of the story. But it's not. And to back up a little, Sniff and Scurry are good handles for mice but who names their kids Hem and Haw? Anyway, they all go to Cheese Station C for a place to eat. Cheese Station C used to have a lot of cheese. It wouldn't be a cheese station if it didn't have a lot of cheese, right? But then, I guess because life was too good, the Big Cheese decides to move all the cheese to another station. They call it Cheese Station Z or something. That's probably not right, but it did remind me to check Netflix for *Ice Station Zebra*. I love that movie.

So Sniff and Scurry find the new cheese station without any trouble. They're mice. That's what they do. But the tiny men run into some walls. One of the two, Hem or Haw I'm not sure which, has a good attitude about the cheese being moved and finds the new cheese. But the other one has a bad attitude and decides to just wait around for Cheese Station C to open back up. The little corporate bootlicker who found Cheese Station Z wants his buddy to find the new cheese cafeteria too, but figures he should have to sweat for it. So he leaves some screwy clues on the walls of the maze to help guide him.

Change Happens. Anticipate Change. Monitor Change. Adapt to Change Quickly. Change. Enjoy Change! Get Ready to Change Quickly and Enjoy it Again.

Seriously, this is supposed to help a friend out? What a pint-sized asshole. We're going to ruin your life now so deal with it would be better advice. But the real genius of the book, unless you're lactose intolerant, is how it uses moving cheese as a metaphor and makes the whole thing so understandable. Anyway, in case you don't speak mouse, the screwy clues mean that anticipating change is like getting ready for cheese to move. Or monitoring change means you need to smell the cheese to see if it's getting old. I'm not making this up. And enjoying change means you should savor the adventure and enjoy the taste of new cheese. And that's about the long and short of it. Mostly short I guess. I glanced down and the neon yellow Post-it note on the cover caught my eye.

Savor the adventure and enjoy the taste of new cheese!
Best, Jack.

What a lousy, stinking rat I thought. Also, I wondered why people sign everything now with just "best"? I *really* hate that.

Is writing "best wishes" too much trouble? I also hate it when people write "cheers". You're closing a letter or email, not making a toast. And you're probably not British. Stop it.

Anyway, it was almost eleven when I finally climbed into bed, and I was no more ready to face tomorrow than when I rolled out this morning. I hemmed and hawed about what time to set the alarm and finally settled on six straight up. After killing the lights, I stared up at their last glow in the fake stucco ceiling. And then I got mad.

Keep moving the cheese you assholes.

That thought ran through my head a few times before the screen went black.

9

If you're eating a continental breakfast you're in one of two places. You're sitting at a table for two in a sunny sidewalk café somewhere in Europe sipping espresso in the company of a pretty dame. In that case something good is probably about to happen. Or, you're sitting at a big round table in a cheesy hotel conference room somewhere in America gulping crap coffee in the company of co-workers. In that case something bad is definitely about to happen. Guess where I am.

I've been to The Continent. Spent a couple weeks in Paris a long time ago with my ex-wife, Sybil. We had a few continental breakfasts but it rained a lot, we were broke, and most of the time Sybil was either sad or mad. So there's that. Me and her were on the rocks and we split up not long after we got back stateside, but I liked Paris just the same and knew someday I'd go back. The next time though it'll be with the right dame. Someone who dresses up like those French women do. Who wears high heels to lunch, drinks good wine, and once in a while smokes a cigarette she holds between the tips of her fingers that gets covered in red lipstick. Someone like Darlene.

But I'm in a Courtyard by Marriott conference room and a world of trouble. United has a big event space that would hold all the people for this team-building exercise but Girard wanted to take it off-site. Big wigs like to take things off-site. They must think it makes torture seem like a vacation. I got lost for a minute thinking about torturing the Jerk when a voice from behind reminded me I was in the buffet line.

"You waiting for that cantaloupe to get ripe, Poole?"

I turned to my left to find Doug DeLash, the United Food Quality Control Director. He looked up from my nearly empty plate and grinned ear to ear.

"This whole buffet is product I'd personally reject so I can assure you that's as ripe as it's going to get. Maybe you'd like some of these moldy berries instead." He swept his hand over a bowl of questionable looking blueberries.

"Oh, you mean like the berries *you* bought and I sold Houlihan's last week?"

Doug didn't take the bait. He just smiled with an air of casual indifference to quality that quality control directors really shouldn't have, looped around behind me, grabbed a croissant off the end of the table, and made a beeline for the far end of the room. Doug could do a better job controlling quality but he's an okay guy and I was thinking I could do worse than be his table buddy for the next few hours, so I loaded some of the cantaloupe and better-looking blueberries on my plate, grabbed a muffin, and tailed him. But when he parked at a table near the front I could see Westerling there. And Vic right next to him. He was showing her his phone and she was nodding her head and whispering in his ear like there was something to be real confidential about.

Westerling's nephew must be a special kid if those two are spending this much time setting up a summer internship.

I took a bite of bran muffin and scanned the room for another place to sit. Really I was looking for Darlene. When I spotted her she was at a table front and center with two empty seats next to her. My feet started moving without me asking, but when I was halfway there it dawned on me that one of those empty chairs had Gloria Summerhill's name on it, and the other had Girard's. He thinks Darlene is his girl Friday and always wants her nearby to wipe his nose. The way the Jerk treats Darlene doesn't seem to bother her much, but it doesn't sit well with me. Sorenstam was sitting on the other side of the table talking on his phone and that didn't sit well either.

Uh oh, Jack, your shoes look a little scuffed up. Can I shine them for you?

I was just about to throw in the towel and sit with Sue Ann Pennington, Marta, and the rest of the marketing department hen party when a life preserver landed in the water beside me. A life preserver with a Spanish accent tied to it.

"Hey, E.C. Slum with us man."

I whipped my head around and spied Mikey and Cesar all alone at a table in the back right by the door. Perfecto. The back of Girard's bus was right where I wanted to be today. Those two are good company and being by the door makes it all the easier to slip out and take those emergency calls from customers. You know the ones, the ones you get when you call yourself. That's a standard move out of the conference playbook and everybody does it.

"Didn't see you guys. Saved my ass." It felt like they really did.

"You're too white for this table but we'll make an exception in your case," Mikey mumbled through a mouthful of scrambled eggs.

I spotted Dan Conner stand up, answer his phone, and walk briskly towards us and the door. He was smiling and nodding so it must not have been a fake call. Or an unhappy customer.

Oh, that's great news Johnny! I'll take real good care of you and PRC.

I considered tripping him as he brushed past me but that

didn't seem like the right move at a team building. Just then Cheryl Wong, the United Human Resource Director, stepped up to the podium and the lights dimmed. It was five after nine and time for the first torture session to begin.

Cheryl Wong, like a lot of HR directors, is outwardly pleasant, dresses conservatively, chooses her words carefully, was born without a sense of humor, and is anal retentive to the extreme. You have to be a special breed of cat to think "on-boarding" new employees and walking old ones out with a box is good work. But somebody's got to do it I guess. Cheryl is also about five feet tall and you could barely see her head over the podium. It looked like the microphone was wearing glasses and a silver-gray wig. The screen behind her came to life and the opening credits for a blockbuster PowerPoint presentation started to roll.

"Good morning," she squeaked.

Of course she was too close to the mic so we were all stunned by a powerful blast of electronic feedback. Has an amateur public speaker ever *not* done that?

"Welcome," she continued, oddly unperturbed that everyone in the room was covering their ears. "Ms. Summerhill and Mr. Girard are unable to join us until lunchtime so we're going to begin the exercise. Everyone please close your laptops. And turn off your cell phones."

From my vantage point at the back of the room I could see a hundred shoulders slump in unison. No fake phone call could save us now. Unless you could sell a medical emergency this room was our prison for the next eight hours. I gave serious thought to faking a stroke or appendicitis or something but figured it wasn't worth the fare for the ambulance ride.

Just to soften us up with a hard body blow before hitting us in the mouth, Cheryl ran us through a fifty-minute PowerPoint on sexual harassment in the workplace. This is standard HR stuff these days and we've all heard it before. I know companies don't want lawyers on their case but frankly I don't see the point. I like to play a good game of grab ass as much as the next guy, but only if the gal at the gate hands me a ticket to the ballpark. Most guys get that. But some guys don't and no PowerPoint presentation is going to rewire their Neanderthal brains.

When she got to the part about different cultures and how some men think it's their job to grope dames, especially Latinos, Cesar choked on his Rock Star and actually spit some out. Half the room turned around to see what was happening so I patted Cesar on the back and Mikey gave them all a thumbs up that everything was okay. We spent the next five minutes with our heads down avoiding eye contact so we wouldn't come unglued.

When the show was finally over, Cheryl directed a couple of the banquet servers to hand out a hard copy of the PowerPoint. The same PowerPoint she just read verbatim in a monotone. And the same PowerPoint we have a copy of in email. I was sorry a perfectly good tree had to die, but at least now Mikey and Cesar and I had paper to play hangman.

At this point the warden granted us time in the exercise yard. Obviously the underripe cantaloupe and moldy blueberries weren't a good idea so I headed straight for the men's room, weaving through a throng of co-workers all furiously working their phones with their thumbs. In the next millennium, if global warming doesn't fry everyone, humans are going to have huge thumbs. We'll have no necks and big eyes, and really big thumbs. Maybe we won't even need fingers anymore. But opposable thumbs need something to oppose so I guess we'll keep those.

Anyway, I waited for everyone else to leave the men's room before I left the stall because I didn't want anybody to know it was me making the place unpleasant. So I was a little late getting back to the table. I knew immediately that my subterfuge didn't work when Mikey looked up and grinned as I sat down.

"See a doctor, man."

I've been meaning to make an appointment, but I still had some choice words teed up for Mikey when Cheryl stepped back up to the microphone and I lost my chance. The feedback wasn't as bad as the first time, and after it subsided the midget judge handed down our sentence for the rest of the morning.

"After lunch we're going to break into groups and do some role playing. Then if we have time there's a really fun trusting exercise we'll do."

It was scary she actually thought it would be fun.

"To make the groups work we're going to mix and match your personality types. Maybe some of you have done this, but before we break for lunch you're all going to take the MBTI," she said triumphantly like we're supposed to know what the hell MBTI means.

When my MBTI hit the table it said in big, bold letters right on top it was the Myers-Briggs Type Indicator. Somebody must've cuffed me with that blackjack before because now it rang a bell. The MBTI is one of those phony gimmicks companies use to figure out who you are and what you're good at. Sure, they could actually talk to you and learn who you are and what you're good at but that would require actually talking to you. So they do this instead.

Mikey and Cesar were already busy filling the thing out and having a pretty good laugh about something so I figured it might not be so bad. And I might as well get it over with. Just so you know, the MBTI is basically four stupid questions and each of your answers gets you tagged with a letter. It makes sense this stupid thing goes by an acronym because the whole point of the exercise is to figure out what acronym best suits you. Which is really stupid.

Are you outwardly or inwardly focused?

That depends on whether there's a dame in the room or not. After I got to the bottom of the first one it looked like I was an "I" for introversion. Not an "E" for extroversion. I do prefer a slower pace, tend to think things through, and I'd rather sit back and watch than be the center of attention, so I'm definitely an "I". Sue Ann must be an "E". Maybe two of them.

How do you prefer to take in information?

I must prefer "sensing" because I like to keep my facts straight and my feet on the ground. Hard for me not to. I like solutions not problems and don't mince words when I want to get my point across. Being intuitive, imagining possibilities and enjoying fancy ideas for their own sake all seem like something dames do, so I'm no "N" for intuition. That left me a straight-up "S" for sensing. Seems like intuition should be an "I" but introversion already took it so I guess they decided to use the last letter of the word instead. Myers and Briggs are obviously smart people.

How do you prefer to make decisions?

In the end I got a "T" for "thinking". Sure I've made a few decisions without thinking it through and things didn't turn out so good. Like the time I tried singing *Bad to the Bone* at the Tiki Room karaoke night. I can carry a tune as well as the next drunk guy but I guess I'd had a few too many that night. I had no idea how vicious karaoke fans can be. Yeah I was bad, but it's not like they paid a hundred bucks for a ticket to see me. Or a ticket-handling fee either. Jesus.

Anyway, I've stepped in it once or twice before but so what? Most of the time Chucky keeps his wits about him. I can shoot holes in flimsy arguments and lean on cold, hard logic before I call heads or tails. Harmony, forgiveness, empathy? Those things are for suckers and they also get you an "F" for "feeling". Should be an "S" for suckers but "S" is already taken too. I felt good with the "T".

How do you prefer to live your outside life?

This one was tougher than the rest. They said if you like things settled and think people should show up on time and play by the rules, and you like to know where you're going and how to get there, then you prefer "judging" and get a "J". That sounded like me. But if you like to keep your options open and play a little loosey-goosey with the rules sometimes, and you can handle a big-league curveball and take things on the fly, well then you prefer "perceiving" and you're a "P". That sounded like me too. Tough call between the "J" and the "P".

Suddenly I became aware of the time and when I looked up I saw Cheryl collecting the questionnaires. And that everyone was finished but me.

"Need more time, E.C.? Maybe more letters?" Mikey was obviously pleased with himself and couldn't resist twisting the knife. "Maybe you *prefer* to not make decisions at all?"

"Asshole," I hissed as Cheryl closed in on us.

Out of time, I slapped myself with a "J" and turned in my paper to the teacher. Chucky can play pretty fast and loose so I definitely could've been a "P". Actually it would be nice if the quizmasters allowed you to be a "JP", but the MBTI is strictly a four-letter deal so I decided I'd just have to live with the "J". Anyway, I was getting dizzy with all the letters buzzing around in my head and didn't really give a damn.

When I added it all up I was an "ISTJ". That put me up in the top left corner of the chart, whatever that means. Nothing would be my guess, but the little box up there said I'm responsible, sincere, analytical, reserved, realistic, systematic. And hardworking and trustworthy with sound practical judgment. They whiffed on me with the hardworking part but the rest of it fit. Mikey said he came out with an "ESTJ" which means he's most of the things I am but a lot more friendly. And Cesar is an "ENFP" if there ever was one. Playful, optimistic, enthusiastic. That's Cesar alright.

Our Miss Wong had just finished collecting all the test papers when suddenly the double doors behind us swung open. Backlit by the atrium, there stood none other than Jack Girard and Gloria Summerhill, the King and Queen of Reorg. Maybe they were waiting for a skinny boy in a short tunic with a long trumpet to announce their presence because they lingered at the door long enough for all eyes to land on them before slowly making their way to the front table. It came as no surprise that Sue Ann actually stood up and started clapping. A few other toadies followed suit but almost everyone remained seated. There was just enough polite applause for a good par save at a golf tournament and an audible murmur followed the two through the room.

Cheryl stepped up to the mic and we all cringed waiting for the feedback. Somehow she managed to avoid it and announced the royal arrivals without butchering their names. It's pretty ironic that an HR director can't keep people straight or pronounce their names right, but she does that a lot and we all think it's funny. Except when she calls me either Ellis or Charles which

I don't think is funny at all. Anyway, the Jerk and the good doctor weren't ready to speak yet so Cheryl showed us mercy and wrapped up the morning session.

"It's not quite noon so they're still getting lunch set up," she said unapologetically. "It will be served in the Aspen Room which is down the hall on the right. Please be back here at one fifteen sharp for the afternoon session. Thank you."

This time she triggered the feedback turning *off* the mic.

10

There was still the matter of the blueberries and I had to make another pit stop, so by the time I got to the Aspen Room the buffet line was out the door. Mikey and Cesar were almost to pay dirt and motioned for me to join them, but I waved them off and grabbed one of those stupid little one-gulp water bottles and drained it to calm my gut. I thought it would be better to let my stomach settle before trying my luck at the buffet. And besides, nobody likes a line-cutter and ISTJs don't cut lines. ENFPs might do it but not ISTJs.

It was half past noon when the line finally petered out and I bellied up to the buffet. Conference buffet lunches are all pretty much the same and this perp walk was a lineup of the usual suspects. Fruit salad. *A colorful blend of underripe fruits.* Green salad. *A festive out-of-season mix featuring spring greens, slivers of red cabbage, and wilting, whitened romaine.* Salmon à la King. *Sorry little fillets of frozen, farm-raised Atlantic salmon swimming in an ocean of corn-starch-laden cream sauce.* Arroz con Pollo. *Overcooked chicken chunks and haphazardly-cut bell peppers hiding in gummy rice with the barest hint of chili and cumin.* Sautéed vegetables. *Mostly squash and zucchini steamed into submission with too much garlic.* And cookies. *Stale chocolate chip and oatmeal raisin most likely.*

I was still feeling iffy downstairs so I played the buffet real easy and went for the rubber chicken and green salad with ranch dressing. Maybe too much ranch dressing. What is it about ranch? Most folks love it and I do too. Maybe it's the buttermilk, or maybe the secret blend of fresh garden herbs, but it just tastes good. And you've got to admire its versatility. It's a dressing. It's a dip. It's a sandwich spread. Fancy foodies look down their noses at lowlifes who like ranch but I'll bet they have a jar in the back of their refrigerator for when they're alone.

Anyway, it was now ten to one and people were filtering out of the Aspen Room to freshen up and work their phones. I found an empty table and hunkered down to eat what felt like my last meal before making the long walk to the chair. I stay on the right side of the law for the most part but if things hadn't broken my way in life that condemned man could've been me. Right now I could taste what a man's last meal would feel like. And feel what it would taste like. Except it wouldn't be Arroz con Pollo and a soggy salad. I'd open with some Oysters Rockefeller or a crab cocktail, probably a tableside Caesar, definitely a bone-in New York with loaded baked potato, and maybe even a tableside Bananas Foster for dessert. Now *that's* a last meal. I'm not sure they offer tableside service on death row but I'd be fine if they just plated it all in the kitchen.

After I picked through lunch I swung by the john one more time to be safe, so when I got back Girard and Summerhill were already standing by the podium and the lights were going down. The Jerk laughed at something Gloria said, but not like he meant it, and then stepped up and adjusted the microphone. He's not much taller than Cheryl Wong so there wasn't much adjusting to do. We all braced for the feedback but he didn't start talking right away, he just stood there swinging his head back and forth, chin up and out, surveying the room. Reminded me of Mussolini in those old WWII film clips. It felt like we were Italians who just want to ride scooters and make love, and Girard is the psycho about to drag us into war.

After fumbling to get some notes out of his suit pocket, he finally started talking, except the mic wasn't on so we couldn't hear him. Which was fine by me. Even from the back of the room you could tell Girard was getting red, and people started laughing nervously which only made him more red. He had his arms outstretched and was looking around frantically for somebody to blame when Cheryl rushed up and flipped the little switch at the base of the mic that would've been obvious to anyone but the Jerk. The one labeled "on-off". He leaned in to start over and we were treated to the best feedback of the day.

When he finally regained his composure, Girard tried to brush off the snafu.

"Last time we do this at a Marriott," he said sarcastically with a sneering smile.

He turned to Summerhill and for her part she followed the script by laughing a little too hard. I watched the young Marriott banquet manager in the back of the room shift nervously in her chair and force a smile. She knew he wasn't kidding and the next time United Food does one of these things it'll be at the Crowne Plaza. I'd bet a Benjamin she's secretly thrilled.

"I'm really sorry Gloria and I couldn't be here for the morning session but I'm sure Cheryl did a great job. She always does."

It was clear from Girard's clipped tone of voice he blamed Cheryl because he made an ass of himself with the microphone. He gave her a hard look and continued.

"Before we start the afternoon session I'd like to introduce someone who really needs no introduction."

"Then don't," Mikey said under his breath.

Girard swung his right arm out and almost backhanded the guest of honor before pompously announcing, "Ladies and gentlemen, the Executive Vice President of Sales and Marketing for United Food Distributors, Gloria Summerhill."

Having managed to duck the punch, Summerhill stepped up and she and Girard attempted a show of corporate unity by hugging. Sweet idea, but the hug was so awkward it looked like an arranged marriage of two Mongolian children. Displaying his usual lack of self-awareness, Girard stepped away with a smile and Ms. Gloria Summerhill, MBA, assumed the position at the podium. She wasn't bad looking, at least from a distance. The platinum blond hair couldn't be real but was certainly well-coiffed, and well-tailored. The snug tweed pantsuit she was wearing looked like it set her back a few hundred bucks. She was pretty fit too I would say, and she's quite a bit taller than Girard, especially in heels, so the microphone had to be adjusted for real this time.

"Thank you so much, Jack." She threw a quick nod in the Jerk's direction. "When I was at Microsoft I used to come down to Portland quite often but it's been a while and great to be back. And what a beautiful fall day." It had been pouring rain all morning so Summerhill was trying her hand at sarcasm. She giggled and paused. "I guess the weather is why I'm a little rusty making a speech."

Most stuffed suits adhere to the open-with-a-joke rule of public speaking and I assumed that was her best shot. There was a smattering of forced laughter, but Cesar, Mikey and I just stared at each other in stunned disbelief.

"Seriously, I know you are anxious about the upcoming reorg so I wanted to take a few minutes before you start your afternoon session to get into the who, what, when, where, why and how. And of course give everyone the chance to ask questions."

Girard's eyes swept the room with a menacing glare. It was obvious he wanted no questions asked, and wouldn't allow any even if one of us was stupid enough to try.

Summerhill slapped a thick pile of paper on the podium, slipped on some stylish readers, and devoted the next twenty minutes to sucking out what little air was left in the room. I was shocked she didn't use the word sclerosis, but she *did* make it perfectly clear I was a lonely stone tree in a petrified forest of sales. She delivered the monologue with a polished, icy air and whenever she tried to smile it made the hair on the back of my neck stand up.

I'm petrified alright. Petrified I'm about to lose my job.

It was a little after two when she finally finished, and as promised, asked for questions. She cocked her head and raised her eyebrows as if to say *try me.* I'm not shy with dames and wouldn't mind getting under Girard's skin so I thought about it, but why drag this out any longer than necessary? When there were no takers, she reached out her right arm to invite Girard back to the podium. Basking in a muted round of applause she stepped aside with a creepy smile frozen on her face. The Jerk knew we all had questions. Plenty of them. But he also knew nobody would dare cross him in front of Summerhill. He liked it that way and took the opportunity to rub salt in our wounds.

"Gloria, I'm sure the only question anyone has is how soon we can get started."

I've been in my fair share of fights and had a few wounds to show for it, but I've never had anybody rub salt in one. The toughs I run up against pack a roscoe not a salt shaker. And even if they did it would be stupid to stick around the scene of the crime just to season dead meat. Still, I'll bet it doesn't feel very good.

Girard wasn't done.

"I wanted to save something for last. A little surprise," he said doing the Mussolini thing again. "The company wants to roll this reorg out slowly, which is smart, and Gloria has chosen the Portland region for the pilot. It's really quite an honor. We're going to show the rest of the company how it's done."

Girard turned to Summerhill, nodded and smiled. "Thank you."

Gloria mouthed a thank you back at Girard and I threw up a little bit in mine.

Cesar shook his head and muttered, "Que montón de mierda."

I can order a cerveza or dos, and locate the old el baño when it's muy importante, but I don't speak much Spanish. I didn't need a translator though to figure out that Cesar just called all that a load of bullshit. Girard was still posing and preening but seemed to be wrapping things up. He called Cheryl Wong to the podium and couldn't resist a parting shot at the poor woman.

He sneered at her while tapping the mic. "Hope it works better for you than me."

Girard patted Cheryl condescendingly on the back, took Gloria Summerhill by the elbow, and with every bit as much pomp and circumstance as when they arrived escorted her off the stage and through the room. As they neared the door the happy couple passed close by our table and the Jerk tossed a particularly evil grin my direction. I volleyed back a cold stare.

Even while I was staring down Girard, I managed to get a closer look at Ms. Summerhill. Gloria Summerhill is no spring chicken. Sixtyish I'd guess but a well-preserved dame. She's no stranger to the tanning bed that's for sure, and gravity hadn't beat her yet. She looked like the kind of older woman who could teach you a few things. I thought about that for a minute and decided it might not be a bad idea to take a couple of classes. Just to brush up. And not for credit or anything, strictly audit. But I've got a different dame in my head. And a strong feeling there's plenty to learn in *that* classroom.

The Jerk turned and gave a half wave to the room, then he and the good doctor of sales disappeared around the corner and down the hall. Gone were the King and Queen of Reorg. All pomp and no circumstance.

Warden Wong granted the inmates another break and on my way to the men's room I made a mental note to check Netflix for *Back to School*. I love that movie. Didn't win any Oscars but Rodney Dangerfield was hilarious. And the Vonnegut cameo killed me. Maybe I'll put together a Dangerfield double-feature next weekend and open with *Caddyshack*. Is that wrong?

By the time we were back in the cell block it was twenty after two and desperate people were pounding coffee and cookies to try and stay awake. Cesar was the only one I could see who wasn't but he'd had enough Rock Star today to fuel an Apollo moon shot. When Cheryl fired her monotone machine back up it was obvious no amount of caffeine or sugar was going to help. She proudly announced that groups had been formed based on our MBTI results and we were going to do a role-playing exercise. Then she pulled out some papers and treated us to one more taste of feedback reading her notes.

"Institutional change is something we all have to face. Coping with change is different for everyone but the one constant is that we all need a support group. Together we can adapt and thrive in any new environment." Cheryl droned on for a few minutes sounding like a shot-up plane losing altitude before finally finishing with, "Alone we will struggle and some will perish."

Perish? What are we role-playing, Climbing Everest?

I paid little attention to the monologue but caught just enough to get the game. Cheryl had put together groups so that each one was a different alphabet soup. I guess there were a few too many ESTPs and INFPs, but you'd expect that. And apparently ISTJs like me are a rare breed. But you would expect that too. Anyway, who cares?

Cheryl and some banquet servers started handing out assignments and when she made her way to our table in the back I sweetly suggested that me, Cesar and Mikey would make a good group. I pointed out we had a good balance of letters, and Cheryl gave me a menacing, mechanical smile. Except for the frumpy body, plain face, and stupid glasses, she reminded me of one of those pleasure units in *Westworld* who got her wires crossed. She handed me my group assignment, turned abruptly, and marched briskly back toward the front of the room. I got lost for a minute thinking about pleasure units and what a great concept that is. And what a great movie *Westworld* is. I filed another mental Netflix note, but knew I had to start actually watching movies and checking them off my list. I was way behind.

When she got back to the podium, General Wong gave us our marching orders. I drew Group D duty. Mikey ended up in A and Cesar in E, so I bid my comrades in arms farewell and trudged to boot camp in the far corner of the room. I had a bad feeling in the pit of my stomach about Group D, and it couldn't possibly be the blueberries anymore. When I was close enough to eyeball my table I knew why my stomach pit felt bad.

First of all Darlene was nowhere in sight. Girard must've called her out to wait on him hand and foot. And Summerhill too.

And why is it that only one hand and one foot get waited on? That makes no sense. Worst of all though, Mark Westerling and Sue Ann Pennington *were* in sight and sitting at the Group D table.

I guess you don't get to choose who you go into battle with but I sure don't want Westerling and Sue Ann in my foxhole. If foxholes are even that big. I'm not sure they have a standard occupancy but foxes aren't very big so I don't think all three of us would fit anyway. Rounding out the Group D roster were Lucinda Morrison, who works in accounts receivable, Ken Bushnell from purchasing, and Dina Perry, the Social Media Coordinator.

I can't figure out why a foodservice distributor needs a social media person. I'm pretty sure the United Food Facebook community is used exclusively to beg for babysitters and sell concert tickets. And excuse me for saying so, but anyone who follows United Food on Twitter needs their head examined. Anyway, Dina's got it pretty easy.

Cheryl dropped off a bundle of envelopes with our names on them. Mine said "Ellis" and Sue Ann, who had assigned herself the job of Group D den mother, made a point of saying it extra loud when she handed me mine. And for Sue Ann that's really loud.

"Thanks Suzy Q," I grumbled as I ripped open the envelope.

Each group had been assigned a problem to solve and each of us a role to play. In this deeply moving corporate tragedy, our manufacturing company needs to downsize and is closing a plant. I'm supposed to be the manager of the smaller plant that's closing and Dina is my assistant manager. Lucinda plays the part of the main plant manager and Ken is her assistant. Sue Ann is to be the HR director, and in the starring role of company president is none other than Mark Westerling. Cheryl had told us that the roles we play are based on our MBTI results and the exercise is intended to take us out of our comfort zone and make decisions differently for the benefit of the company. I'd been out of my comfort zone since breakfast so this should be a snap.

Westerling spoke up, adjusting his glasses and trying to get into character best he could.

"Okay folks, we've been bleeding red ink for three straight quarters and it has to stop. We need Lucinda's plant to pick up production slack for E.C.'s, and we need a workforce reduction of thirty percent to get back to black."

"You mean fire a bunch of my people, right Mark?" I asked rhetorically but cheerfully.

If Westerling had thought I was going to make this easy he knew what he was in for now, and wore a pained expression for a little too long before taking a deep breath. He was probably still sore about last Friday and looked like he might want to continue the fight, but wisely thought better of it.

"This is an exercise, Poole. Let's just solve the damn problem and then we can get on with our lives, okay?"

He was actually making sense for once. So as much as I like to crawl under that snake's skin I simply nodded. But it was the kind of nod that isn't a yes or a no.

My role-playing profile said I'm emotional and empathetic. I guess that means I'm supposed to get worked up about my people losing their jobs. I would be plenty mad if this was real, but it wasn't and all I wanted right now was for it to be over. So I settled on a strategy of agreeing with whatever anyone else said no matter how stupid it was. I figured that would get this over sooner, and also eat at Westerling. That's a win-win. Problem is the rest of Group D was taking this thing seriously and I lost a full hour I'll never get back listening to Sue Ann play camp counselor while Lucinda and Dina argued about head count. Westerling was brilliant in the role of asshole boss and he managed to bludgeon Dina into submission whenever she tried to save somebody's job. Only Ken seemed to fully grasp how asinine this exercise was and he and I amused ourselves by exchanging occasional eye rolls.

It was now ten to four and we were supposed to be sprung from the joint in ten minutes. But no soap. First, the group "presidents" had to give a summary of how their "team" solved the problem. They all gave long speeches explaining their brilliant solution, thanking everyone in the group and their mother. Marlee from payroll actually did thank her mother. It felt like watching the Oscars, except there was no orchestra to drown people out and chase them off stage.

It was after four thirty when the cell doors finally opened and we could taste the sweet fruit of freedom. And breathe the sweet smell of disinfectant in the Courtyard by Marriott atrium. My brain died hours ago, but the thought of going home, cracking a Coors, and watching the Blazer game gave it a jump. Until I spotted Girard and Summerhill and Scott Sorenstam, that is, talking about who knows what. And Vic Mannheim and Mark Westerling both glued to his phone. Again. And Dan Conner glued to his while showing us the white man's overbite and dancing Gangnam-style to something somebody said.

And Darlene Camper walking straight at me.

11

"You free for dinner tonight, big guy?"

That stopped me cold. And made me hot. Can you be both at the same time? I'm already at sixes and sevens about the spine chill thing and now this. It'd have to wait for another time though because right now Darlene was front and center and close enough to kiss.

"What'd you have in mind?" I offered weakly while trying to locate my breath.

"*I'm* not asking, silly. That's *your* job," she said with arched eyebrows and a hint of a smile. "Why do *I* have to be the one to pull the trigger?" Her gaze hit me with the force of a punch. Then she delivered the real one. "Jack and Gloria want the sales team to join them for dinner at Manning's."

I didn't feel the full impact because I was fixed on her lips. Darlene can be hard to read, and right now her smile reminded me of the Mona Lisa. Saw that paint swirl at the Louvre when I was in Paris with Sybil and it doesn't help to be up close. Not that they let you get close. They don't. And it's not a very big painting to begin with which is disappointing, especially since you have to walk two miles of hallways to get to the room where it's hanging. I mean the Mona Lisa is what everyone comes to see, right? Why not put it in the lobby where you buy the tickets? Then you can skip the rest of the crap. Anyway, when you zero in on the smile you really can't tell what that dame is thinking, and right now I couldn't tell what Darlene was thinking either.

"Six o'clock. Don't be late."

She touched the tip of my nose with a long red fingernail and broke into a bigger smile, then turned and strutted away waving goodbye with her hips. The charcoal pencil skirt she was wearing helped say so long, and together with the fitted white blouse made a pretty package. I was thinking about tearing open packages on Christmas morning when the dinner invitation finally found my chin. It landed like a ton of bricks.

"Damn it," I cursed under my breath, but maybe not under far enough.

Girard spun around and caught my eye. He flashed a nasty grin and before turning his attention back to Gloria casually asked, "Will we see you tonight, Poole?"

"Oh, yes sir," I snapped back, giving an exaggerated thumbs up he couldn't see.

Of course he knew the answer before he asked the question but did it just to torture me. He tortures people for sport and likes it. There's a rumor around the office he's into the Beaverton S&M scene. And that he likes getting it as much as giving it. It crossed my mind that Gloria Summerhill could give him all he wants. I could definitely see her in one of those latex catsuits with a whip.

If it's pain you like, Girard, I'll give you some. Getting spanked by Summerhill might hurt so good but you won't like what I dish out.

I chuckled to myself but not for long. The image of Summerhill and Girard stuck in my brain was making me sick, but I had a date with doom in an hour and it was going to take a while to scrub it out. It was rush hour and would be risky, but I needed a shower bad so I made double-time to the Subaru and raced home.

It was only five after six as I turned into Manning's parking lot, so I breathed a big sigh of relief. I was looking forward to seeing Tui's mug, but he wasn't at the door which made me sad.

The hostess was cute though, so I didn't mind following her to the table. It was a big round in the middle of the dining room with a view of the fake lake, and I was not surprised to see Sue Ann and Westerling already there. And not at all surprised to see Vicky sitting right next to Westerling. Scott and Dan were there as well and sharing a laugh about something. I didn't care what. Girard and Summerhill were fashionably late of course, so I relaxed and patted myself on the back for making the call to go home and shower. I still couldn't get the image of Jack Girard in a leather thong out of my head though, and that was something I was going to have to deal with.

Vic turned to me wearing that million-dollar sales smile.

"You look fresh as a daisy," she observed sweetly. She of course meant it. She always means it and that makes her hard to rib so I played it as straight as I could. Which wasn't very.

"Thanks, Vic. ISTJs like feeling fresh."

She giggled and I saw Scott smirk. We've worked together for three years now and I still can't tell if he likes me or hates my guts. My gut tells me he hates my guts. But not as much as Westerling.

"How did you like the team building, E.C.?" Sue Ann asked as if it was a question of how much, not if.

"Loved it."

I was just about to follow up with another snide remark, but stopped short when I saw the hostess out of the corner of my eye approaching our table with Gloria Summerhill and the Jerk hot on her heels. Show time.

"Hello everyone," said Gloria breezily.

Everyone breezed a hello back, some more breezy than others. I lost the game of musical chairs and had an open seat next to me, so I stood to help Gloria with her chair. I'm no expert but I could tell her perfume wasn't cheap. She patted me lightly on the arm and whispered a little thank you, which gave me the jumps. Girard took his spot a couple seats down from me and wasted no time with hellos or polite conversation.

"Sorry for the short notice about dinner. Gloria's got an early flight out tomorrow and wanted the chance to talk to you all directly about the reorg."

As usual he was not sorry. The Jerk *likes* jerking us around. Which makes sense I guess.

"Let's get our orders in and then get down to business shall we?" He was looking around the room with his right arm up like he could conjure a waiter out of thin air.

"Jack, we don't need to be in such a hurry. Maybe people would like a drink first."

I got the distinct impression Gloria Summerhill wanted a drink first.

"Well, then let's get *that* started," he said still waving his arm and snapping his fingers. He was actually snapping his fingers. Who does that?

Back in the day when I was a waiter at Joe's Grotto in downtown Portland, I worked the floor with a guy named Jon. Everyone called him Slim. Which he wasn't. One night we were slammed and some tinhorn jerk in Slim's section was waving his arm and snapping his fingers. Slim, who was carrying dinners to another table, wasn't a guy to take trouble from anyone. He moved the plate in his right hand on top of the three stacked up his left arm and walked over to the guy's table.

"What's this mean?" he demanded, snapping his fingers right in front of the guy's nose. "I don't know what this means."

The guy could only manage a weak comeback.

"My soup's cold."

When I was at Joe's we served our soup bowls on a plate with a paper doily liner. And you could still smoke in a restaurant. Without missing a beat, Slim pulled a Bic lighter out of his waiter's jacket with his free hand and lit the doily on fire. Didn't say a word. Just gave the sniveling sap a hard stare and walked off to sling his hash. I saw plenty of things at Joe's that made me laugh but that was the best.

I wished Slim was here to deal with Girard but at least nobody in a Manning's apron had come running. The Jerk was starting to stand up and raise hell when out of nowhere a huge brown man appeared behind him, laid a big mitt on his shoulder, and gently lowered him back in his seat.

"How can I help you, sir?"

While Girard was blustering about the drink order, Tui, never breaking eye contact with him, made his way around the table to me. I stood up with a big smile on my face and got a bone-crushing bear hug for my trouble.

"E.C., I'm so happy to see you."

"You're pretty good with names, Tui. How'd you remember?"

Tui stood back and grabbed my shoulders to size me up.

"How could I forget?" He sounded wounded.

By this time the whole table was staring at me and Tui.

"Everyone, this is Tui. He runs the joint," I said, turning to face the group.

Tui giggled and shook his head no. I sat back down while making a sloppy gesture around the table.

"These are my partners in crime at United Food."

I guess crime does pay for some people. But these people aren't my partners.

Tui knows Scott of course and gave his shoulder a quick squeeze as he made his way back around to the Jerk. I could tell Sorenstam was relieved he didn't get the bear hug treatment. Tui also recognized Dan from last Friday's happy hour and gave him a little wave, then motioned a server over.

"Very nice to meet you all. Thank you *so* much for coming to Manning's," Tui said. He put his arm around the young lady and continued, "This is Debbie. She'll take good care of you."

With that Tui disappeared back to the front desk leaving everyone at the table wondering what the hell just happened.

Debbie wasn't quite as sunny as Tui, but who is? She was pleasant enough and went about her business with an air of confidence, taking the drink order and then reeling off the daily specials without fumbling the ball. Sue Ann Pennington drinks about a gallon of Diet Pepsi a day, maybe more, but I guess she hadn't hit her quota because that's what she ordered. Scott asked for a Pellegrino with lime. I thought he'd have a beer but I guess the stool pigeon wanted to fly straight tonight. Me and Dan and Vic all *did* order a beer, and so did Girard. Gloria Summerhill asked for a Grey Goose martini up with a twist. She already seemed like a big-city socialite but that sealed the deal. Westerling said he was fine with tap water. That figured.

Girard started flapping his gums about the reorg, but I was already lost in the menu. Since I'd passed on most of that miserable buffet I felt like I could eat a horse. Come to think of it, that was probably what was in the Arroz con Pollo. But that would make it Arroz con Caballo. I don't see how that could be any worse. Anyway, I was hungry.

The crab mac and cheese caught my eye. So did the chicken pot pie. But since United was picking up the tab tonight I decided on the steamed artichoke appetizer, a field green salad, with ranch naturally, and the rib-eye steak with a side of potatoes au gratin. Might do dessert too. I started to wonder why they bothered to call them field greens. I mean, where else do greens come from? But suddenly I realized that Girard was still talking, and this time to me in particular.

"You with us, Poole?"

"Sorry Jack, I guess I'm a little hungry," I said closing the menu.

Of course I wasn't sorry. But I *was* hungry.

Girard looked like he was ready to start throwing punches but just then Debbie arrived with our drinks and I was saved by the bell. I gave him a big grin to piss him off and took a long pull on the IPA.

What's the big deal with IPA anyway? I think it stands for India Pale Ale but it sounds like somebody gave a beer the Myers-Briggs test. IPAs are all hazy and hoppy and made by some craft brewery in some renovated warehouse district somewhere, but so what? Seems like there's a thousand of them now. When I started hitting the sauce, which was before I was old enough, there were a bunch of American lagers and that was that. If you wanted something special you ordered a Michelob. Which was just an American lager in a curvy bottle that cost more. Back then a beer was a beer.

Anyway, getting a dinner order from a party of eight takes longer than it should, so by the time Debbie finished and marched off to punch it in, I figured Girard had forgotten all about me. And he had. Carefully wiping some foam off his mustache with a middle finger he waded right back into the reorg.

"We're still working on the client lists and ironing out a

few wrinkles in the bonus plan, but we'll get you up to speed on Friday," he said nodding at Westerling. Turning to Summerhill he added, "And we'll be ready to rock and roll on Monday." Then returning his glare to the rest of us said, "I'm sure you all read Gloria's paper, and my memo, so let's go around the table and give us your thoughts."

Sue Ann was on Girard's left elbow and he thumbed her to bat leadoff. She'd probably make a good lead-off hitter at that. Sue Ann has a small strike zone and seems like she'd be the kind of batter who could take a pitcher deep into the count and work some walks. Spray the ball to all fields too. Plus she's obviously got good speed and could steal you a base or two, and move up on a hit-and-run or fielder's choice. Anyway, she was up first.

"I really don't think I have any questions, Gloria. You and Jack have done an *amazing* job of explaining everything. And your thesis was *brilliant*. Thank you so much for choosing us to roll this out. We're just *super* excited."

Sue Ann of course really *was* super excited and Summerhill forced a smile.

"Well, Suzanne, I've got a lot of skin in this game and I need a region where we can get started on the right foot. Jack runs a pretty tight ship here so I know I can count on him to get it right."

Sue Ann was so thrilled to be in the presence of corporate royalty she didn't notice Gloria got her name wrong. It wouldn't have bothered her if she did. She was busy beaming at Girard, who was beaming at Gloria. I was beaming because my artichoke had arrived.

Next up was Conner. Dan doesn't like these affairs much and had beads of sweat on his upper lip and a wrinkled brow to prove it. He took a big swig of his beer before taking a big swing for the fences. Dan would not be a good lead-off hitter. He'd probably bat eighth.

"Yeah, it's pretty darn exciting to be first out of the gate with this, Mrs. Summerhill."

Dan was trying to be prim and proper but Gloria Summerhill isn't married. And she wasn't amused.

"It's Ms.," she said curtly, "but you may call me Gloria."

Dan was sweating bullets now and stammered to continue. "Sorry. Gloria. I, uh, do think it's going to take a few weeks for our customers to get used to the new system, but after we iron things out I'm sure it'll be a big success. I've already talked to some folks in the field and they seem pretty excited about it."

Yeah, like your friend Johnny at PRC right? You sweaty bastard.

Summerhill seemed annoyed by Dan's comment.

"Well it's all about communication, Don. If we do our jobs right then this reorg should be invisible to the customer and it will be a seamless transition."

She was talking to Dan not Don, but was looking straight at Girard who nodded and shifted uncomfortably in his chair. I peeled the last leaves off the artichoke and smiled to myself. I hadn't guessed how much heat Summerhill would bring today and seeing Girard sitting in the hot seat made me happy. So did the artichoke heart. I like the leaves well enough but let's face it there isn't much there to chew on. The heart's where the getting is good, especially smothered in a bunch of garlic aioli. I love that stuff. It's like mayonnaise only better.

I was making a mental note to try steamed artichoke with ranch dressing next time when Westerling stepped up to the plate. I expected he'd have a hardball question or two for

Summerhill but he just put both palms up and shrugged. And then through those pursed thin lips delivered a cryptic line that made my blood run cold.

"I think we've covered everything. I'm all clear if you are."

"Yeah, we are," Girard said smugly and turned to Vicky.

Summerhill, who was sitting between me and Vic, eyed her closely and said, "You're the star of the team, Valerie. I expect you'll lead by example and show these boys how it's done."

I could tell Vic was uncomfortable with that comment. So was Girard. He doesn't like dames smarter or tougher than he is, which is pretty much all of them, but especially dames like Gloria Summerhill and Vicky Mannheim. Sue Ann must've liked the remark because she was beaming again. But Sue Ann is always beaming. She'd be beaming if her dog got run over. I could tell Westerling didn't care. About the remark, not the dog. Dan and Scott had pretty good poker faces but I was sure it didn't sit well where they sat. Vicky *is* our superstar, so Summerhill's little dig didn't bother me one bit. I got no problem with a dame being better at her job than me. I was on the floor because Summerhill was now 0-for-3 on names.

"Thanks, Gloria," Vic said timidly while slipping furtive glances to us boys. "This will be a challenge for us, and I'm a little worried about travel time, but we're just going to have to use our cars as offices. We'll make it work."

More than we already do you mean? And yeah you'll make it work just fine honey because you and Westerling have it all figured out, don't you?

Summerhill grabbed Vicky's arm in a show of female solidarity and dished out another one of those thin smiles that don't do anything to cover her cold heart.

"I know you will."

Now it was my turn in the barrel, but just then Debbie arrived with a tray of soups and salads and bought me more time. I was the only one who ordered an appetizer, which had earned a glare from Westerling I guess because it will bankrupt the company. It didn't make me Mr. Popular with the rest of the table either because they all had to wait for something to eat. Girard didn't like it for both reasons so he was *really* steamed about my artichoke. Debbie was still working her way around the table but the Jerk didn't wait for everyone to be served and was already chomping on a mouthful of field greens when he glared and nodded for me to continue the charade.

"Sorry to be the fly in the soup, Gloria," I said, "but I don't see how this will be invisible to our customers. We've been calling on the same accounts for years."

Sue Ann and Scott had both ordered soup instead of salad and were peering into their bowls suspiciously when glamor girl cut me off at the knees.

"Maybe you didn't read my thesis, Elliot, but in order to break the stasis of sales stagnation and reap the benefits of competitive dynamics there must be a shock to the system. I thought I made it perfectly clear in my remarks this afternoon that some personal pain must be expected for there to be company gain. And we all want that, right?"

Right, honey. We do the work and you palm the greenbacks.

"No pain, no gain," I parroted with an emphatic nod of my head while shoveling a load of lawn clippings in my mouth.

Stasis? What the hell is stasis? I was half in the bag last night, but I don't remember reading about stasis in her stupid book report. Plenty about sclerosis, sure, but no stasis.

What really grabbed me though was that she whiffed on my name too. How do you manage that? We're supposed to be your A-team to launch this reorg and you can't get *anyone's* name right? I can see slipping up on one or even two but all of them? Maybe she did it on purpose. Maybe she just doesn't care. Either way she's one rotten iceberg of a dame that's for sure.

Nobody paid much attention while Scott anchored the relay race with a milquetoast monologue about Summerhill's thesis and Girard's memo. I guess at least one person actually read them. By the time the entrées hit the table it was almost eight and I was having trouble keeping my ears open and eyes from crossing. The medium-rare rib-eye hit the spot though. Westerling ordered the rib-eye too but his was medium-well. Chucky likes his steak bloody. Okay pink, but still. Just after we tucked in, Tui stopped by the table to check on things. I gave him a thumbs up and couldn't resist poking Westerling in his rib-eye when Tui asked him how his dinner was.

"Done enough for you, Mark?" I asked cheerily, starting to work on a fork full of gooey, cheesy potatoes. Which tasted amazing. Everything should be served au gratin in my book. Westerling glared at me and returned to sawing the shoe leather in front of him.

After dinner Vic and Westerling were buzzing and whispering with Summerhill on one side of me, and Scott was button-holing Girard on the other. Dan was checking his phone a lot. I thought about asking Sue Ann to dance just for something to do, but Manning's doesn't have a dance floor and you can't really dance to Enya. I mean you can but who wants to? I suppose I should've paid more attention to what was said but I was focused on my pumpkin swirl cheesecake. And I got the feeling it wasn't going to matter anyway. It had been a long day and I felt like dirty wash in the wringer.

When I finally got to my man cave, I headed directly for a long hot shower. I still smelled pretty sweet from my shower before dinner but now I needed to wash the whole night off. Jack Girard's sneering arrogance. Gloria Summerhill's condescending corporate crap. Conner's double-crossing. Sorenstam's sucking up. Mannheim and Westerling stacking the deck. Tui's cologne. All of it.

As the warm, wet blanket of steam rose up to surround me I let my mind drift. This was no accident. Somebody wants me gone. Hell, maybe several somebodies.

The horses have disappeared and a long line of men holding barbed sticks with ribbons dangling from them are marching into the ring. I'm holding the sticks as well. The bloody bull charges the men and they each in turn somersault over his back while plunging the sticks between his shoulders. This scene unfolds in slow motion until finally the bull turns to face me. Several barbed sticks hang from this back and fresh rage shows in his eyes. Now it's my turn and fear overwhelms me again as the bull lowers his head and begins to charge. I see nothing but the long right horn and let out another soundless scream.

I am certain I'm going to die.

12

When the bird chirping finally registered I realized I had left the window open all night. It was a murky morning, fall was in the air, and my bedroom was an icebox but I was covered in sweat and the sheets were soaked. I know one good reason for that being the case but I was alone. I must've been doing some serious tossing and turning, though, and now I just felt tired and empty. A cup of strong coffee and a cigarette might set me straight but I'm all out of smokes. Because I don't smoke.

After I dropped out of college I worked graveyard in a can factory with a bunch of salty characters who all smoked. I wanted to fit in, so one night I bought a pack of Pall Mall straights and chain smoked a couple on a fifteen-minute break. Threw up in the parking lot. I haven't touched one since, so this morning coffee would have to do.

I couldn't shake the cobwebs out, so maybe I didn't need that nightcap after all. Two cups of joe and a shower didn't do much to change things, and I was starting to like the idea of calling in sick and crawling back into bed. I've got some PT in the bank and the thought of taking a day to sort this out didn't sound half bad. But guys like me don't get sick very often, and when we do we don't cry about it. And it wouldn't look good if I'm loafing on easy street while this reorg is about to go down. Besides, why should I give any breathing room to whoever's trying to cook my goose? That would be silly. I figured nobody could even *take* my goose let alone cook it if I was there to do something about it.

I don't back down from a fight and started to get worked up while I was pulling on my Dockers and United Food polo shirt.

Mr. Coffee had one more cup to sell, and I was in no big hurry, so I took a load off at the counter and opened my laptop. There was nothing to sweat over in email and I was starting to feel a little better. But while I was checking orders I felt the wind shift on me and my sails starting to flap.

I'd be a fool to not see what's happening and Chucky's no fool. I'm getting the shaft.

If this was a game of Texas Hold'em, and I was eyeballing the other stiffs at the table before the flop, I'd have Dan pegged for a pair of jacks in the hole. Scott with queens, Vic sitting on the "big slick" ace-king, and Girard with two bullets. And me peeling the corners of my cards back and staring at a 3-7 off suit. I've never actually played Texas Hold'em but I've watched the World Series of Poker on ESPN a few times and I'm pretty sure you're supposed to fold that hand.

Anyway I cut it, the deck was stacked against me and it felt like I was living on borrowed time. There's a point in some fights when one guy's taking a beating and his corner knows it's over so they throw in the towel. Or the referee steps in. Some palookas are too stupid to know how to box, but too tough to go down, and they'll get themselves killed if somebody doesn't stop the fight. Is that me I wondered?

I don't remember leaving the house or getting in my car, but I was still wondering about that while I was stuck in morning rush hour traffic on the Terwilliger Curves. Most people who quit on life don't have the guts to do themselves in, they just keep going through the motions like something's bound to change. Most of the time it doesn't. Sure you might be one of those lucky bastards who wins the lottery but you'll just blow that wad and end up worse off than before. Hard to believe, but statistically true.

Lucky and stupid seem to go hand in hand.

Anyway, that's how I felt right now. I didn't have the guts and was just going through the motions. Having finally made it downtown, I was waiting for the elevator up to City Bar & Grill and shook my head in disgust. At myself. The sandy-haired dame in the polyester pantsuit riding the elevator with me must've sensed my mood because she shot me one of those *are you okay?* looks. I flashed a weak smile and leveled with her.

"Rough day. And it only just started."

She smiled back an *I'm sorry*. When the doors opened on the seventeenth floor she strode into a big law office like she owned the place. It was the kind of snazzy office full of big plants and stuffed suits that takes up a couple of entire floors. I thought maybe she was a deaf-mute lawyer because she hadn't said a word, but that didn't add up. There might be deaf lawyers around but there ain't any mute ones, that's for sure. I watched her disappear and nodded to myself. She could be a real skirt if that pantsuit was a skirt. And she'd lose those bent-frame glasses with the square lenses. Didn't those go out in the '80s?

It was a bright, sunny morning and the dining room and bar face east, so when the doors opened on the thirty-ninth floor I stumbled into the elevator lobby and straight into a laser beam that blinded me for a moment. I patted my breast pocket looking for my Ray-Bans but cursed softly when I realized I'd left them in the car. City Bar & Grill sits near the top of the U.S. Bank tower at the north end of downtown Portland. Big Pink they call it. It's big alright, and looks sort of pink when the sun hits it just right, so that's fair. But I'm red-green color blind so I really wouldn't know. Anyway, the restaurant takes up most of the floor and through the picture windows you can see the whole city, the Willamette River, the Columbia River, and the Cascade Mountains. Mt. Hood takes center stage when the weather is nice and Mt. St. Helens is right there too, at least what's left of her since she blew her top.

Anyway, City has a nice view. They serve breakfast, lunch and dinner seven days a week and it's a real popular place. Locals and tourists come in droves for lunch, happy hour, and dinner but it's mostly businesspeople doing that power breakfast thing in the morning. It was nine fifteen and the joint was already jumping. Having regained my eyesight, I skirted the busy dining room and used the service entrance to the kitchen, walking into a beehive of activity and noise familiar to anyone who's ever worked a big restaurant. Orders being shouted out by the Sous Chef and repeated by the cooks. Pots and pans rattling. Food sizzling at the sauté station. The hood system sucking air. Spanish being spoken here and there, and of course a few choice words. In the middle of it all I spotted Chef Mercedes talking to her Sous Chef and I carefully made my way through the scrum.

"Morning, Chef. What's cooking?" I asked, wishing for the thousandth time I could take back words I just said.

Both her and the Sous, a young Hispanic man with a fierce expression but kind eyes who goes by the name Javier, turned and gave me a blank stare. Chef Javier is too polite to ask me if I'm an idiot, and too busy to stick around for my answer, so he wheeled back to his line, grabbed a handful of tickets from the chattering printer, and started barking orders at his crew. Mercedes silently took me by the elbow and maneuvered us to her tiny office at the back of the kitchen. When we got there she shut the door and dropped wearily into her wobbly eggshell office chair. She waved me to the cheap banquet chair I've perched on more mornings than I can count. It was not even nine thirty, she'd probably been at work for a couple hours, and already looked exhausted. It's a hard life being a chef. I took a deep breath and counted what few blessings I still had, which didn't take long.

"Do you ever get tired of saying stupid shit?" she asked tiredly.

Obviously she hadn't forgotten what was cooking.

"Nope. It's a gift, Chef. I like to share it with the world."

She sighed and shook her head. Mercedes Rolle is what they call petite in the world of women's wear and really quite beautiful, but the loose chef coat and baseball cap make her look more like a Little League pitcher. Cute, but the kind of kid who would sit you down with an inside fastball if you were crowding the plate. And steal your snow cone after the game. We spent the next twenty minutes performing our well-worn routine going through the City order guide. She fired off line items and quantities like a machine gun while I pounded the keys on my laptop like a guy pounding keys on a laptop. Anyone who didn't know the lingo would swear we were speaking a foreign language. And I guess we were.

"Is that it, Chef?" I asked, peering over the top of my screen when she seemed to finally run out of bullets.

"I think so," she said closing her laptop. "I probably forgot something but when I remember at three in the morning I'll call you and you'll run it down here, right?"

She was kidding of course, and wearing a crooked but very sexy Mediterranean smile that I don't get to see often enough, but she and I both knew I'd do it if she called. The account's that big. As I was standing up to go she suddenly flipped her laptop open again and held up a hand.

"Hey, wait. What the hell happened to the price of kale this month? It's almost three bucks a pound."

I sat back down. I know kale is a tiny fraction of her food cost, and so does she, but chefs get squirrelly when prices jump.

"Well, most of it comes from China and in case you haven't heard we're in a little trade war with them. That and the fact that every restaurant in America uses it in every dish on their menu so there's less to go around. You know Mickey D's has it in a salad now, right?"

She rolled her eyes and stood up.

"Yeah, and it's worse for you than a fucking Big Mac. That's how *they* roll."

I love it when Chef Mercedes swears. I've heard her dress down cooks with a blue streak that would peel the paint off a Dodge Ram pickup. That might bother some guys but not me. I could listen to her swear all day and all night. It's like opera or something.

She walked me back through the mayhem in the kitchen and we emerged into the bright light of the spacious dining room. You couldn't have asked for a prettier fall day, and even though I'd seen it a hundred times I was struck dumb for a minute staring at what's left of Mt. St. Helens with both Mt. Adams and Mt. Rainier peeking over her lovely headless shoulders. But not as dumb as I was struck when my eyes landed on a table by the window where Dan Conner was laughing at something his breakfast companion just said. Something Johnny Scarpetti just said.

"What the fuck?" I blurted out before catching myself. I don't usually swear but I don't usually have to watch my co-workers selling me out either.

Mercedes was about to say goodbye and already turning back toward the kitchen.

"What the fuck is what?" she said returning to my side and trying to follow my stare.

Oh my god, I thought, she said it again. That was twice now in one day. I'm not sure what it is that gets me. She makes it sound like *foke*. Like an Italian movie star or something. Like Sophia Loren or Gina Lollobrigida would say it. Maybe that's it. Anyway, I grabbed her arm and pointed at the table by the window.

"Isn't that your new boss, Scarface?"

"It's Scarpetti. And lower your voice," she said lowering her voice.

"Right. Sorry. And what's Dan doing here with him?"

"Well you'd know better than me but it looks like they're having breakfast."

Normally I'd take that bait and play the line a little, but after the "what's cooking" thing I decided to lay off. Besides, I had a four-alarm fire in my gut that was out of control and I was standing there with no hose.

"You want to meet him?" she said excitedly with her hand on my back, starting to steer me into the dining room.

"No. I can't. Not right now," I sputtered, backing up against her gentle pressure. "I'm late for a meeting at that new place in the Hamilton Hotel, Cosa Nostra."

That part was true, but Chef Mercedes knew it wasn't the real reason. Especially when I didn't head straight for the elevators and kept pressing my line of questioning.

"Has Scarpetti mentioned anything to you about United? About me?"

The crooked smile had vanished from her face and was replaced by squinting eyes and something that looked an awful lot like concern.

"Not really, no. Just the vendor audit. You're working on that, right?"

I'd gotten a start on the audit Sunday afternoon, but it's football season and the Bears and Packers were having one of those bruising NFC Central battles, so that's as far as I got. Which wasn't very. The score was 13-10 Chicago late in the third and what was I supposed to do? You can have your West Coast offenses and pass-happy scoring fests but I like smash-mouth football, thank you very much. Defense, blood and guts, three yards and a cloud of dust. That sort of thing. Late in the fourth, the Bears' nose tackle arm-swam through a double team, pancaked the fullback trying to block him, and drove the Packers quarterback into the turf. Broke his collarbone. And the Bears won 16-13 on a last-second field goal. How fun is that? Anyway, I'd forgotten completely about the audit.

"I'm on it, Chef," I said cheerfully, peeling my eyes off Conner and Scarpetti for the first time since I spied them. "I'll have it for you Friday morning, maybe Thursday if I can stop running for a few minutes."

"Friday's fine. Gotta go."

With that she disappeared back into her kitchen kingdom, leaving me with a cold loathing feeling and that hot fire still raging in my gut. I shot one last look at Conner and Scarpetti, who were laughing again, and headed to the elevators for the long descent into parking lot hell.

"Fuck you, Dan," I said out loud while waiting in line to buy my way out of the Smart Park. I tried making it sound like Chef Mercedes but it came out all wrong, so I tried it again in my own voice. Louder this time. By now I was at the booth and the look from the attendant told me he thought I meant him. I handed him a sheepish grin and a ten-spot, holding up my hand to say keep the change as I pulled out into sunlight and heavy traffic.

The Hamilton Hotel is in the Pearl District and just a short drive from Big Pink. I was stuck in gridlock trying to cross Burnside Street and cursing myself for not leaving the car in the lot and walking. Nice day. Pretty girls. Stupid move. When I finally broke loose and found a spot a couple blocks from the hotel I parked more or less near the curb and hot-footed it into the lobby. I was already twenty minutes late. The Hamilton had only been open a couple of weeks so the valets at the door were a little too friendly. That'll change, I thought. And when the mousy girl at the reception desk looked up and saw me she practically squealed with delight.

"Welcome home to the Hamilton. How can I help?"

She delivered her lines from the corporate script with the phony enthusiasm of an up-and-coming actress trying to land a part in a two-bit movie.

This ain't home, sweet lips, and I don't need your brand of help.

"I'm looking for David Eastman. He's the GM of the new restaurant. And I'm running a little late."

"Oh, David, yes," she said with a mousy smile. "Cosa Nostra is right around the corner to your left and through the double doors. He's expecting you."

Okay, I guess she was helpful. But she really did look like she should be dating Sniff or Scurry.

Eastman was expecting me twenty minutes ago and I knew I should've called, but I had Conner and Scarpetti laughing and Chef Mercedes swearing on my mind. And there was nothing I could do about it now anyway. Besides, even if I landed this account it would probably be somebody else's next week so who cares? I followed directions and found myself standing in a big, empty room that looked a lot more like a construction site than a restaurant. Power saws were buzzing, the smell of fresh paint was thick in the air, plastic curtains everywhere, and workmen moving around real slow like they were getting paid by the hour. Which they were. The joint was supposed to open in three weeks so they must be right on schedule. Which like all new restaurants means way behind schedule.

"Hello, I'm David. You are E.C. I take it?"

I tensed like a cat because the voice snuck up on me. People have found themselves in a world of hurt sneaking up on me like that but thankfully this time I was able to keep my catlike reflexes in check.

"Yes. Yes, E.C. Poole. Pleasure to meet you," I said extending my right hand. "Sorry I'm late, traffic was a bitch."

David Eastman winced slightly at the word but kept perfectly still. He was a small elegant man who stood proudly erect, wearing perfectly tailored beige linen trousers and a cream-colored silk shirt. He took my hand gently with a weak smile and I could tell immediately I should've described traffic as something other than a bitch.

"No problem. I've got plenty to keep me busy as you can see." He made a sweeping gesture with his right arm, never breaking eye contact.

I was standing there wishing I wasn't such an ape, but I was grateful he let me off the hook and bowed my head by way of apology.

"Let's talk in the lounge. It's nearly finished and it should be a little quieter in there."

He graciously pointed the way and we walked briskly through the dust and din, and into a room that looked like something straight out of *The Godfather*. It took my eyes a minute to adjust, but what came into focus was all very clubby, even for a steakhouse. There was a lot of dark wood, walnut or mahogany maybe, gleaming brass everywhere, and plush leather booths and barstools. Italian leather would be my guess. And the walls were filled with old sepia-toned photographs. There were plenty of wise guys in pinstriped suits chewing on cigars and mugging for the camera, and a few of the Rat Pack. I've heard Sinatra was Sinatra because of the mob so that made sense, but I only had eyes for the big picture on the far wall. It was a photo of Sophia Loren riding on the back of a scooter wearing a little black dress with strappy high heels, her beautiful bare arms wrapped around some Italian pretty boy.

I was imagining Sophia saying *foke* and must've been staring at her too long because David finally asked, "Lovely isn't she?" with a slightly annoyed but bemused look on his face.

"Yeah, they don't build 'em like that anymore do they?" I replied with maybe too much gusto.

He gave me an odd smile and murmured an answer I couldn't quite make out. Whatever it was, I could tell once again I'd offended David Eastman's delicate sensibilities and decided maybe it was time to stop acting like a teenage boy and do my job.

"Will Chef Weatherspoon be joining us?"

David was more than ready to get down to business, and his eyes became sharp.

"Chastain regrets not being able to be here. He is visiting two farms on Sauvie Island to source products for his menu."

"Which farms?" I asked idly.

"Fettering's," he answered haltingly. "Yes, Fettering's I think. And Goose Meadow I believe it was."

I've never been to either one but still nodded convincingly like I'd grown up there. Sauvie Island isn't far from town and has a lot of farms. Hell, lots of farms aren't far from town, and I suppose I should know more about farms if I'm supposed to be selling chefs on the United Food farm-to-table program, but seeing vegetables in the ground just doesn't do much for me. I'm more of a table guy than a farm guy.

Fact is, I've only been to Sauvie Island a couple of times and that was for the nude beach. It's a pretty beach on the Columbia River but the people sharing the sand with you aren't. And why is that? Do only chubby middle-aged Frisbee enthusiasts like to get naked in public? Whoever they are, they sure don't like guys wearing shorts and a tank top and bringing a camera to their nude beach, I'll tell you that.

Anyway, David proceeded to explain what Chef Weatherspoon wants to do with his menu and it all sounded screwy to me.

"We will serve steak of course, but Chef insists his menu will have a plant-based focus and that all ingredients without exception will be one hundred percent organic and sourced from suppliers with sustainable practices."

You're going to have a plant-based focus? It's a steakhouse, Dave. How can you have a plant-based focus and serve big slabs of red meat? That's stupid.

"That's smart," I said, again nodding but not so convincingly this time. "Diners are looking for that now, especially in Portland, and United has got a killer farm-to-table program. I'd like to run it by Chef when he's here, but I can show it to you now if you've got the time."

He agreed and we took a seat in one of the booths where I gave David my standard fifteen-minute spiel. I was trying to keep my eyes locked on him and sound earnest, but I couldn't help stealing a glance or two at Sophia and he knew it. God, she was hot. How can anyone make riding a Vespa look that sexy? I'd sure like to be that lucky paisano whose ribs were her handlebars. Anyway, when I was done, David neatly stacked the farm-to-table brochure and price lists I gave him, and then escorted me through the restaurant mess to the lobby.

"Thanks for your time, David. Sorry again I was late," I said offering him my card.

"Again, no problem," he replied handing me his. "I will give your information to Chef Weatherspoon and I'm sure he'll contact you soon. Good day."

He disappeared back into the dust and noise before I could say goodbye. I threw a quick wave and smile at the front desk girl, who now somehow looked even more mousy. But to be fair my eyes were still full of Sophia Loren.

"Goodbye, Mr. Poole. I hope we'll see you again," she squeaked.

Nice work remembering my name, toots, but not likely. I'm about to get the axe and won't have the bankroll to sleep in your fancy beds, that's for sure.

"Sure thing," I said on my way out the door.

My pace slowed to a crawl as I headed back to my car and I got lost again trying to sort things out. From one angle this was cut and dried, but when I changed the angle things got messy and wet. Mostly, I was still wondering how the hell you can have a plant-based steakhouse and tried to set the odds for how long Cosa Nostra would keep the doors open. But my mind kept tugging me back to City Bar & Grill. And Dan Conner. And Johnny Scarpetti.

It was almost one when I passed a little hole-in-the-wall Middle Eastern grocery that I remembered has a pretty good falafel sandwich, and I thought putting something in my stomach might make it stop doing backflips. Besides, I love falafel sandwiches. Not the falafel, that's just a deep-fried ball of chickpeas, it's the tahini sauce that gets me. I love that stuff.

As I licked the last drop from my fingers while I fumbled for my key fob, it occurred to me that tahini sauce might be the best thing I had going for me right now. And that wasn't good.

13

I made a couple more stops on my way back to the office so by the time I pulled into the United parking lot it was almost four and the sun had buried itself behind a bank of dark clouds. I was doing my job alright but my heart wasn't in the game. It never really is, but usually I can fake it well enough so my customers can't tell. Pauline McAfee, the owner of Pauline's on Broadway, asked if I had the flu when I stopped in to see her. I said yes to get her off my tail. And the chef of Tivoli Trattoria, Nguyen Thant, told me I looked sad and needed a girlfriend. "You sad. You need girlfriend," he told me, scolding with a wagging finger and a gap-tooth smile. He was right. So I spent the rest of the trip back to Wilsonville thinking about Darlene. And how a Vietnamese cook ends up as the chef in a glitzy Italian restaurant.

When I got back to the office, I wasn't in the mood to talk to anybody so I took the back stairs up to my glorified cube. The break room is on the way so I grabbed a cup of joe to fire up my engine and input all the orders I had. The first thing my fired-up engine did was ask why a foodservice company can't put decent coffee in their break room. Portland Roast sounds good but it isn't. It's United's economy blend that we sell to diners and dives and it tastes like battery acid. Not that I've ever tasted battery acid but I imagine it's pretty bad. I guess United doesn't make enough money to give us a decent cup of coffee. And trust me, cream and sugar don't help. But maybe that's because they only give us non-dairy creamer and some nasty artificial sweetener. I decided to give our office manager a piece of my mind next time I saw her and headed down the hall.

The late afternoon sun was peeking through the clouds and shadows were getting long in the hallway. I rounded the corner and caught sight of Vic in her office with Westerling again. That's not a surprise anymore, but Girard being with them sure was. Vic and Westerling looked like they were pitching the Jerk on something but his back was to me so I couldn't tell if he was buying or not. I took a step back. This time I was a little more cagey and set up my stakeout from a perch where nobody would be the wiser. Westerling was scowling at his laptop but Vic was fired up about something and shaking a finger at Girard like he was a kid who broke a living room lamp playing baseball inside the house. Not that I would know what that's like.

Westerling looked up suddenly which gave me a start. His mouth was moving fast and he swung his laptop around for Girard to see. The Jerk moved close to Vic's desk and leaned in to get a better look. I couldn't make anything out from my angle but when Girard stood up straight, threw out his arms, and started shaking his head, I figured the sales pitch didn't go over so well. I'm in sales so I can usually tell. By this time Girard was almost at the door, and Vic had her palms up and eyes open wide. I had no interest in getting busted this time, so before the Jerk opened the door I hightailed it to my office wondering what the hell *that* was all about.

I dropped heavily in my chair with an exaggerated groan and slowly opened my laptop. I needed a stiff drink, but I had a lot of orders to input and probably wouldn't make it out of here until after six. Mostly though I had a real bad feeling. It could be the coffee, but more likely it was because I couldn't put two and two together about the meeting in Vicky's office. It was actually two and one but I couldn't put that together either. Math was never my best subject. Is Girard in on the game Vic and Westerling are playing? Maybe he put them up to it. He's calling the shots for sure, but it looked like they threw him a curveball he couldn't hit. Are those two trying to squeeze everyone else out and the Jerk didn't like the idea? That didn't fit either. Any way I sliced it there wasn't a happy ending to the story for me.

I finally finished the last order and slammed my laptop shut. I winced and checked to make sure it wasn't broken. The last thing I wanted to do right now was ask Westerling for another one, but the dice rolled right and it powered back up. I closed it gently this time and struggled more than usual to zip up my Patagonia all-weather jacket. It looked good when I tried it on in the store, and I don't doubt it will keep me warm and dry in all weather conditions, but for three hundred bucks it sure seems like I should be able to put it on without a fight.

Anyway, I finally zipped up, turned out the light, and headed for the elevators. And as luck would have it I found myself walking side by side with Dan Conner on his way out.

"What'd you think about dinner last night, E.C.?"

I was thinking more about his breakfast with Scarpetti this morning and getting hot under the collar. I've got a temper that can get out of hand at times, but I'm able to keep it under control when I want it that way. And I wanted it that way right now.

"The steak was cheap and overcooked but the potatoes were good. Very cheesy," I answered with a weak smile and a shrug.

Conner gave me a withering sideways look.

"The conversation, asshole. I know what the food's like at Manning's."

I paused before answering because I was sure there was a smart way to play this, but I just couldn't think of it right now.

The elevator doors opened which bought me some time and I settled on a strategy of bobbing and weaving before I hit him in the mouth.

"Well, Summerhill's a piece of work isn't she?" I said. "She'd throw her grandmother under the bus if it got her another step up the ladder. And she didn't seem all that chummy with the Jerk either."

"Yeah I got that too," Dan said nodding as we got off the elevator and moved through the darkening lobby. "If this reorg doesn't work, heads are going to roll that's for sure. And Girard's might be the first."

Dan's Mitsubishi Outlander started to beep and we walked together toward the noise. When we got there he put his hand on my arm and gave it a squeeze.

"We'll get through this, E.C. We're all in it together."

Yeah, sure we are Danny boy. You and Scarpetti, and Vic and Westerling, and Sorenstam and Girard. And me. I get all warm and fuzzy just thinking about it.

Just as Conner opened the car door I decided to throw a hard left jab. Let's see what he has to say about his lovey-dovey breakfast with Scarface. It might not help but it might be fun.

"Hey Dan, I was with Chef Mercedes at City Grill this morning and I saw you and the new PRC veep having a bite. What's his name again?"

"Johnny. Johnny Scarpetti. We go way back. I'm glad they shipped him down to the Portland market. He's a smart cookie. He'll make some good changes here."

"Is that what you guys were talking about?" I asked holding the car door open so Conner couldn't slip my collar. "What kind of changes is he planning?"

Dan somehow managed to tug the door shut. Normally he wouldn't be able to do that but I was only using twenty percent of my strength because I didn't want to make it too obvious. Thirty tops. But sometimes I don't know my own strength, and right now I could've ripped that door off. It's a Mitsubishi after all. Anyway, as Conner started the engine he let the window down, craned his neck out, and gave me a parting shot.

"We've got big plans. I'll tell you about it later but I gotta run. G'night E.C."

By the time I climbed behind the wheel of my Subaru I had two things figured. Conner and Scarpetti are in cahoots for sure. You don't need to draw Chucky a map for that. Also, Dan's Outlander may not have a higher safety rating or get better gas mileage than my Outback but it looks better. I mean, all these crossover SUVs are pretty much the same but his Mitsubishi looked a little like a Lexus. Not the RX, that's too big, but like the UX or maybe the NX. Anyway, it looked better than mine.

I wanted to get home and the car was running, but my mind was the only thing in gear right now. You can't tell what a stew tastes like until it cooks for a while, and this reorg was still a bunch of meat and potatoes, and vegetables, and whatever else you put in a stew, sitting on the kitchen counter of my mind. Still, the big picture was slowly coming into focus and I was starting to see how the chips stacked up.

Here's what I did know. That was too many metaphors and they don't belong together. And Vic is the goose who lays the golden eggs at United. There's another metaphor, but it's true, and we all know it. And now she's got Westerling in her corner and Girard on his heels. Conner's probably running second, because if he has Scarpetti, he has PRC too. And nobody's going to mess with PRC, not even Girard. Sorenstam's a little harder to figure but I've got him made as a mole. He's the one with Girard on speed-dial and gave him the goods on what went down at our coffee meeting. Me? I'm the patsy.

I was nodding my head in agreement with myself when a sharp rap on my window made me freeze and reflexively reach for the artillery under my arm. Except it wasn't there. Because, as I've mentioned before, I don't own a gun. Sure I'd be handy with one if I did, but when you've got hands that should be registered weapons you don't need a gun. Besides, Wilsonville isn't a high crime area so I just take it nice and easy. But when I looked to my right out the window all my practiced calm went right out the window. My heart skipped a beat and my eyes got big so I could take in the whole picture. It was Darlene.

By the time I got out of the car and stood face-to-face with her she was giggling. I have that effect on dames so I'm used to it, although this time it could've been because I had trouble getting my seatbelt off. The damn thing's been sticking lately and I haven't had time to worry about it. Plus I hate going to the Subaru dealer for service. I don't know much about cars and they know it. I always feel stupid when they tell me I need a part I've never heard of, and I always buy it. Maybe this time I'll just buy a new Mitsubishi.

Anyway, it was starting to drizzle and Darlene's auburn hair was glistening in the soft light of the parking lot and her lips looked dewy and moist. She wasn't wearing a coat and her blouse was starting to surrender to the elements. I considered wrapping my jacket around her to keep her from shivering, but I have such a hard time with the zipper it didn't seem like a good idea. Especially after the seatbelt. So I settled on the next best thing.

"You're cold, baby. Hop in and I'll give you a ride to your car."

It's right there, silly," she said pointing at the Toyota RAV4 directly in front of my Subaru. "But I'll hop in for a second. I want to talk to you."

I made a mental note to add the RAV4 to my list of potentials as I scrambled to open the passenger side door. It felt good to see her settle into the seat as I gently closed the door after her. I could make a habit of this I thought. A long habit. Maybe now was the right time to pop the question. About dinner I mean. That thought brightened my mood as I climbed back in the driver's side but I decided to put a date with Darlene on the shelf for now. I was saving her for something special, and this wasn't it.

"What's on your mind, doll?"

"What's on *yours* is the question, buster bub."

My mom sometimes called me buster bub and hearing Darlene say it felt weird. Back home it usually meant I was in trouble. And maybe I was right now because the bedraggled beauty in the front seat was staring at me with eyes that strongly suggested I come clean.

Should I tell her everything? Do I know everything? Hell, do I know anything? Can I even trust her?

"What's on my mind is you, baby," I said with a half smile and a friendly leer.

She stabbed the tip of my nose with her finger.

"Why don't you put your money where your mouth is?" Settling back in her seat she added, "You know exactly what I'm talking about."

I did. And I decided there wasn't much downside to spilling the beans. Besides, I was crazy about this broad and maybe, just maybe, she could help. I felt the weight of her gaze but took some time gathering my thoughts before I finally turned to face the beautiful music.

"I think I'm done at United, sugar."

Darlene frowned and I saw a fire in her eyes start to flicker.

"Why? What do you mean?"

"Look, you know better than anyone Girard doesn't like me. He doesn't like my wisecracking. He doesn't like my sales numbers. He doesn't like that I'm taller than him, and bigger than him, and smarter than him. And I'm pretty sure he's still mad at me for hitting him in the family jewels with a lawn dart at the company picnic last year."

"Well, if you're so big and smart why would he fire you?"

The question dripped with sarcasm and those gorgeous hazel eyes had turned cold and almost black.

"Sorry, I didn't mean to get puffed up. If I was so smart I would've asked you out a long time ago." I hadn't planned to say that but thought it might break the ice. She stayed still and silent, playing me with a perfect poker face.

"Besides, I don't think they're going to fire me. They won't have to. Summerhill served Girard the opportunity on a silver platter with this reorg and he's probably going to give me just enough rope to hang myself. Everybody else is set up real nice. Vic's the golden goose, and she and Westerling have been joined at the hip since last Friday. You saw them at Manning's."

"Maybe they were having a drink, E.C. Did that ever occur to you?"

That could've been a joke I suppose, but there wasn't any laughter in her voice. And no compassion either. I started to wonder if the goose is golden too, or if it's just the eggs, but I had more important matters at hand.

"Maybe."

Her hard stare made me realize I didn't have any choice now but to show her all my cards.

"I've seen Vic in Westerling's office twice, and he was in hers this afternoon. With Girard. She's the top sales dog so why wouldn't they give her the pick of the litter with accounts? And Dan's best buds with the new head of the Portland region for PRC, Johnny Scarpetti. I've seen them together twice, including breakfast today at City Bar & Grill. That's my best account. What am I supposed to think, doll?"

I continued to rattle on but Darlene had sunk back into her seat and was staring straight ahead out the windshield. The drizzle had turned to light rain and it was dark now. I turned on the lights and wipers so she could see better.

"Who put all those bright ideas in your thick head? People have meetings. It's a business. So what?" she said with more than a hint of exasperation creeping into her silky voice. "And from what I hear, Dan and Scarpetti were childhood friends."

"So it would make sense that Dan takes over my best account, wouldn't it?" She just shrugged, so I answered my own question.

"Well it makes sense to me. And Scott's been awfully chummy with Girard lately. I caught him on the phone with the Jerk ratting on me and Vic and Dan when we met to talk about the reorg. Scott's a stoolie the way I figure it."

Suddenly Darlene spun in the seat and leaned toward me with her eyes blazing and her nostrils flared. There was something about her face that wasn't the same. Probably the eyes and the nostrils but I couldn't be sure.

"You got it all figured out do you? Well, you sound paranoid to me. And what about Mikey and Cesar? Are they in on it too?

Do you think maybe they'll short some of your orders to make you look bad?"

She was asking questions but didn't want answers. At least not from me.

"Don't forget Sue Ann. She's probably going to slip you some phony deals to sell that you can't deliver on. And what about me? Am I one of the suspects too? I'll tell you one thing, you sure make it hard for people to be on your side."

She was glaring now and her eyes tore at me like claws. I wanted to tell her how beautiful she looked when she was mad but figured this wasn't the right time.

"Easy, babe. I'm just stacking up the facts."

"Sounds to me like you're making up what you're stacking up," she said reaching for the door handle. "I like you, E.C. I could fall for a guy like you. At least what I thought you were."

It was raining hard now and the windshield wipers were slapping time to my heart pounding. She had the knockout punch all lined up.

"Oh hell, I don't know who you are. You like to play tough guy, but I don't think you're so tough. You're complicated that's for sure. I like that, but the one thing I never figured you for was a quitter."

Darlene opened the door and stepped out without a glance back. I tried to say something but no words came out, and she slammed the door on us before there ever was an us.

With that she was gone and the car was full of silence and the smell of her perfume. I watched her strut through the driving rain and get in her car, and I kept my eyes glued until she disappeared from the parking lot. Then I just sat there listening to the wipers. And the rain.

I don't remember much of the drive home. My headlights were punching holes in the dark as I slowly climbed up Mountain Park, numbly watching the white lines on the road slip under my car. All I could really see was Darlene's face. I tried to think of something else but it didn't work. Chances are I'm going to lose a good job, and that's not the end of the world, but I just lost a good dame and that hit me where it hurts. I wanted to chalk it up to lousy luck, but I knew luck wasn't the problem.

Just my luck, but the seatbelt gave me a hard time again after killing the engine. I hesitated before opening the door, dreading the dash across the parking lot to my flat. Damn rain. I hate the rain. A lot of Portlanders will tell you they like the rain. And they mean it. I guess they like getting soaked to the bone, but I don't. Anyway, in spite of the zipper I was grateful for my Patagonia jacket. The rain was coming down hard now splattering the pavement like spent bullets, but I made it to my doorstep with only wet pant legs and squishy shoes to show for it.

When I shoved my key in the lock, stepped inside, and slammed the door behind me, it felt like I was getting thrown in the slammer. And shuffling to the kitchen felt like the long walk to the electric chair. I threw my keys on the counter and a Stouffer's Meat Lovers Lasagna in the microwave for my last meal. It's got more meat than the regular lasagna, and if it's the last thing you ever eat you want that, but I didn't care. All I needed was a priest to say last rites and they could pull the switch.

After glumly shoveling the lasagna down the hatch, I stepped outside on the balcony with three fingers of scotch. Okay, maybe four. It was still raining, but it felt good peppering my face and I stared down at the parking lot watching the light dance in the puddles. I gulped down a finger and leaned on the railing.

So this is death, I thought. I sure felt dead and buried, except I wasn't dead. Or buried. I felt alone too. Why is it that nobody's around when you hit the skids? Nobody likes a loser I guess. Or a quitter.

Maybe Darlene's right. Maybe I am a quitter. It sure would be easy to kiss the concrete and all my troubles goodbye. Hell, it probably doesn't even hurt that much. Just a few seconds in the air, a body bag, some yellow tape, and that's all she wrote. Except I live on the second floor, so I decided I'd rather finish my drink than drive myself to Urgent Care with a sprained ankle. On top of that, United just changed insurance carriers and I've got a high deductible and out-of-pocket. And it's the out-of-pockets that'll kill you.

After another couple fingers I wondered do I really care if I live or die? If life is so damn important what does it mean? For some reason the image of a bullfight flashed through my brain and I shivered. I've never been to a bullfight. I don't know if I'd like it, but something about it makes me want to go. I finished the last finger of scotch and wondered if it's really *how* you live or die that's important. Anyway, I guess the good thing about being dead is you don't give a damn anymore.

When I laid down in bed it was still raining hard and I listened to it beat against the window for what felt like a long time.

Sorry Darlene, I guess I am a quitter.

Somehow I'm still alive but now it's deathly quiet, we are completely alone, and the bull is staring at me. Trying to tell me something I can't understand. I'm holding a much smaller cape now, and a sword. I slowly bring the cape up and point the sword at him to show I'm ready. The bull is weak from the spears, barbed sticks, and endless charging, and looks uncertain. In spite of myself, I wave the cape and spread my arms to invite his charge. The crowd roars as the bull rushes me. It's the moment of truth.

As always, I lose my nerve at the last second, jump away, and stab the bull from the side. He falls dead but it's nothing more than the brave action of a coward and I'm ashamed. The bull deserves a more honorable death than that. I'm straddling the carcass and listen to jeers rolling down from the top of the arena in waves. Never can I make out faces in the crowd but this time I see Darlene's. It's contorted into an ugly mask of disgust and she's yelling at the top of her lungs.

Does honor mean nothing?

14

I don't know how long I laid in bed sweating. It was maybe ten minutes but felt like an hour. I couldn't shake the image of Darlene in the car last night. There were veins bulging in her throat and that beautiful face was all twisted. It was the first time it wasn't very nice to look at. I sank back into my soft, damp pillows and they tried their best to soothe me. But it didn't work. Darlene was gone and there was no doubt about it. No birds broke the morning silence, but the day had dawned clear as a bell and looking out the window I could see all the way to the Coast Range buried in low-lying fog. The hills looked far away, but not as far away as Darlene had gone.

Somehow I made my way to the shower, got dressed, and ended up at the kitchen counter but don't remember how. Halfway through my second cup, Darlene's bitter words still rang in my ears and those icy eyes haunted me.

"You think I'm a quitter too?" I asked Mr. Coffee out loud.

He didn't answer. Mr. Coffee doesn't talk much but sometimes I wish he did. I could use some advice right about now. He did gurgle but even that sounded like disappointment.

I had no stops to make this morning, which is unusual, and I wouldn't have made them if I did. What's the point? I sat at the counter and slowly worked my way through a Jimmy Dean Sausage Biscuit, but somehow even that didn't taste very good, so I shoved the plate aside and opened my laptop.

I didn't bother with email this morning but it still took me a while to find what I was looking for. And for once it wasn't what the stars of *JAG* look like now or why Marisa Tomei never got married, it was my resume. I can never find my own stuff because I've got too many folders and I name the documents something stupid. I would've used the search function but you can't use the search function when you don't know the name of the damn thing you're searching for. You'd think I'd name my resume "E.C. Resume" or maybe just "Resume". I mean who else's would it be? But I didn't. As it turns out, I called it "Life of Chucky" and ended up sticking it in a folder titled "United Food P&P". Don't know why I'd put my resume in there but it could've just been a mistake. I'm pretty sloppy dragging and dropping.

Anyway, it took me a while to find, but now I was staring at my resume and wondering how I was going to sum up my stint at United in one short, snappy paragraph. I shook my head to try and kick-start brain activity but that backfired. Too many fingers of scotch last night.

I hate resumes. Reading other people's resumes is kind of funny but writing them isn't, so I decided to read my own and build some momentum for the task at hand. Maybe there's a rhythm to my professional life that will make United seem like it was part of a master plan. Besides, reading my own resume should be funny, and I sure could use a good laugh.

Right off the bat, the "Professional Objective" had me chuckling.

Seeking the right fit with an established company where I can put my passion, experience, and demonstrated skills in sales to work. Looking for a good culture, fair compensation with incentives, and opportunity for advancement.

Who wrote the rule that every resume has to start with a load of crap?

Right fit? *What, am I buying a suit?* My passion for sales?

145

Sales ain't my passion, baby. A good culture? *We're talking about profit-crazed companies, not the Moose Lodge.*

It makes it sound like a mail-order bride looking for a sugar daddy. And then the cover letter is just a longer version of the same crap. The objective is to get a job. Everybody knows it. End of story.

Scrolling to the bottom of the page, my first job made me laugh out loud, which helped.

Joe's Grotto Seafood Restaurant – Server, Trainer, Shift Leader. Gave impeccable service in critically-acclaimed, high-volume seafood restaurant. Maintained high average checks by leveraging product knowledge and upselling. Often tops in monthly wine sales.

I was a waiter for chrissakes. And a liar. For starters, I never trained anybody new and we didn't have shift leaders. Joe's was busy alright, but the critics never gave us any love. We had no idea what our average checks were and I was top wine salesman exactly twice. Which is not very often. When you're just starting out you try to make it sound like your first job was important. That's fair enough, but after a few years it's time to call a spade a spade, so I deleted everything but Joe's Grotto and server and scrolled up to the next job.

Continental Fancy Foods – Director of Operations. Managed all aspects of a consumer food-products company with an extensive product line doing nearly one million in annual sales. Sold top accounts directly and exhibited at national food and gift shows. Reported to the CEO.

Yeah, I was the operations director alright. Chief cook and bottle washer is what I was. Continental Fancy Foods was a pet project for the rich wife of a rich husband who got rich buying and selling commercial real estate. Jesse Wilhelm was her name and she fancied herself a gourmet chef. I guess some of her rich friends at her rich parties told her how good her food was and she thought that's all she needed to go into business. What she needed was half a brain. She was pretty enough, and nice enough, but a hamburger short of a Happy Meal if you catch my drift.

Anyway, the "extensive" product line consisted of a flourless chocolate torte, three different soups, a chicken liver mousse, a country pâté, a caper tartar sauce, and a nasty cocktail sauce that tasted like ketchup mixed with strawberry jam. All of them were called "Jesse's World Famous Such and Such", they were co-packed by a company in Idaho, and ended up costing an arm and a leg in the few gourmet groceries and upscale delis that were stupid enough to carry them. Didn't matter how the products were displayed they just sat there. I think we did maybe four hundred thousand in sales the last year before going belly up. That's nearly one million, right? And we lost over thirty grand. Sure I made some sales, and I did go to a few fancy food shows, but mostly I just ate the chicken liver mousse out of the can and got drunk in hotel bars.

So that one was all a bunch of BS too, but I decided to leave it as is. Fluffing your resume a little here and there isn't a crime. And besides, Jesse died a couple years back so what are they going to do, call her?

There was plenty else to clean up if I was going to be straight about it, but I didn't bother. There were surely more laughs in store with what Chucky did next and I couldn't wait to get to them.

Integrated Office Solutions – Leasing Agent. Led Portland office sales team and was a top leasing agent for three straight years.

More bull. IOS was a big company that sold and leased Ricoh copiers, with a big sales team, but I didn't lead anyone. In fact I was the rookie salesman in the Portland office. I never was the top agent but I never was the bottom one either so that part was technically true. What a lousy job that was. Almost everyone who wants to break into sales starts out selling copiers. You buy a cheap suit at Men's Wearhouse or a cheap dress at Ross for Less and go bang on doors. You get paid peanuts, probably a tiny commission, and maybe even have a bonus plan you'll never cash in. Mostly you spend your day in a cubicle cold calling businesses and getting hung up on. That's what I did. Cold calling hardly ever works, but once in a while somebody would pick us out of the phone book and call us. I guess it sounded like a good idea to solve their office problems by integrating them. Whatever that meant. Anyway, that was a rotten couple of years.

Sticky Buns – Owner. Ran successful breakfast franchise for two years. Acquired by venture capital firm.

Yeah, I bought a restaurant franchise alright. I borrowed five thou from a bank at some crazy interest rate, and another five from my sister Karen to get up and running. And it wasn't really a restaurant, it was a food cart. Back before food carts were all the rage. My timing always seems a little off. I worked like a dog six days a week and barely broke even for a couple of years, but I was my own boss. Which is what everyone thinks until they go into business and realize they just landed themselves a hard job with long hours, low pay, and no benefits. The American dream, baby. Anyway, one day the oven quit on me and I didn't have the cash to fix it, so the repo man came and took my cart away. Karen's husband at the time was loaded, so she told me to forget the loan and I limped away and slept for two weeks straight. The bank did have a venture capital division, and they did acquire the cart, so I felt good about leaving that part in.

I scrolled up and the smile left my face.

Consolidated Foodservice, Inc. – Sales Associate, Lead Sales Associate, Assistant Director of Sales. Consistent high performer for billion-dollar, national food servicer. Successfully worked cross-platform in a fast-paced, competitive environment. Met high expectations and often exceeded challenging sales quotas. Promoted twice based on merit to lead sales teams. Reported directly to the Director of Regional Sales with a dotted line to the Associate Vice-President of Regional Sales.

That part of my resume actually got me the job I've got now. I used it when my pal Tom Jacobs called and asked if I wanted to jump ship and join him at United. And I did. United Food is no small company but Consolidated is the big gorilla that pushes everybody else in our industry around. They have the whole supply chain wrapped around their little finger. They have better product. They set the prices. They have more trucks, more salespeople, more marketing dollars, and more assholes running the show. They're like McDonald's and we're Burger King. But that's okay with me because I love Whoppers and hate Big Macs. Well, I don't hate them. I'll eat them in a pinch, and that special sauce is pretty darn good.

Anyway, I was happy to get out of Consolidated and excited to join the United team. Until I met Jack Girard that is. And then Tom left less than six months after I got here because his wife Jane got a job in Washington D.C. and I ran out of excitement altogether. But right now I wished I was back at Consolidated where I could hide in the middle of the pack and run easy with the dozen other regional reps.

I think I hit quota maybe three times in five years, and I *was* promoted twice, but only because turnover there was so bad I was just the last guy standing. I did report to the regional sales director, who was almost as much of a jerk as Girard. I saw the associate VP exactly once and he blew me off. And I don't even know what "cross-platform" means. But my resume makes it sound like I was a superstar salesman, a team player and a leader.

I chuckled and wondered if maybe they'd take me back. They were plenty sore when I turned rat and went to United though, so probably not. Maybe somebody else will want me. Somebody who doesn't know my resume's a bunch of hot air. I shrugged and closed my laptop. It was getting late and I figured I could bang out the blurb for United at the office.

My resume gave me some laughs, and took my mind off Darlene for a few minutes, but by the end of it I was back to feeling down in the dumps. And when I glanced at the clock it was later than I thought.

"Dammit," I hissed, glaring at Mr. Coffee like he was to blame.

I'd been hoping to catch Darlene on her break, but it was almost ten and no way I'd make it now. I had it figured some fast talking could make up for last night, but I was also planning on dropping my two-week notice on Girard's desk and that made me a quitter for real. Open and shut case. I guess me and Darlene Camper were all washed up before we even got a chance to get dirty.

That thought took me in a totally different direction and glued me to my stool for another minute, but then I knew it was time to move. I gulped down the last of my coffee, shouldered the United bag, tucked my jacket under my arm because I didn't have time for the zipper right now, and headed out the door.

Darlene made it crystal clear last night what she thinks of quitters, so even if I did catch her she probably wasn't going to give me the time of day.

I couldn't help but try.

15

It was twenty after when I careened into the United parking lot on two wheels. As usual, I was a good hundred feet from the office by the time I found a spot, but I made double time through the lot hoping I might still catch Darlene in the break room. Despite being in near peak physical condition, I was a little out of breath when I reached the glass doors of the office, and when I saw my own face in the reflection it stopped me cold. I looked like twenty miles of rough road. Ten at least. Shaking my head, I made my way into the lobby and impatiently waited for an elevator. One finally came and by the time the door opened to the third floor I found myself standing face to face with Scott Sorenstam.

"Morning, E.C. You look kind of rough, brother." He sounded concerned. "You sick or something?"

I still wanted to look for Darlene and considered brushing past him without saying a word, but I was done playing the fool so I let him have it with both barrels.

"Sick? Yeah, *brother*, I'm sick alright." I had a hard time keeping my voice level. "Sick of this place and sick of everyone here." Scott's eyes narrowed and he took a step back. I was inches away from choking the bastard and he could probably tell.

"I thought I had friends here, and I thought they had my back. Turns out there's a bullseye on it. Vic's got Westerling feeding her the good accounts. Dan and his pal Scarpetti are making deals with mine. I'm trying to stop this crazy reorg, and all along you're giving Girard the lowdown."

Sorenstam was staring at me like I just stole his lunch. But he's a Big Mac guy so I probably wouldn't do that. Anyway, Scott was staring at me and looked like I caught him with his gloves down and landed a hard right cross. And that's my best punch. He just shook his head in disgust.

"You *are* sick."

Sorenstam's not that strong but he strong-armed me out of his way and got into the elevator. I guess he was mad. He had that look of disgust frozen on his face as the doors slowly shut, and I lingered for a few seconds as the elevator dinged its way back down. That was a rotten thing for me to say, and I wasn't sure whether it felt good or bad. I couldn't shake the feeling something was wrong with the play. That thought was eating at me as I walked briskly down the hall to the break room. Which was empty. No Darlene. That settled it, I felt bad.

Nice work, Chucky. He took the bullet alright but maybe you shot the wrong guy.

It felt like I'd dropped a hundred feet by the time I finally hit the chair in my office, and nothing seemed right as I went through the motions pulling stuff out of my bag and opening my laptop. Just as I clicked on the resignation letter I'd written, my desk phone rang and gave me the jumps. I slowly lifted the receiver to my ear.

"Hey, send me a truckload of frozen corn dogs willya? ASAP. I'm hungry."

A smile broke out in spite of my funk. It was Tom.

"What's the matter? No corn dogs in D.C.? Or do you just miss our restaurant-quality brand?"

"I'll tell you what's the matter. I miss *you* brother."

This time the word *brother* felt like it fit.

"Me too. Me too. I was just thinking about you this morning. You must've got the message."

153

The line was breaking up so he had to be on his cell.

"Where the hell are you? Inside the Washington Monument?"

There was a long pause on the other end before he started up again. Of course he was on his cell. He doesn't have a land line anymore. Who *does* except me?

"Can you hear me now?"

"Yeah."

"Sorry, I'm on the Metro and we were under the Potomac. There're so many damn tunnels in this town it's a wonder there's cell service at all. So talk to me. How the hell are you? How's work? How's your crappy condo? How's your golf game? Married with children yet?"

I took a deep breath.

"Well, let's see. Not very good. I'm quitting. Crappy. Even crappier. What dame would even kiss me let alone marry me? And I hate children. How are yours?"

"Don't know. They disappeared a month ago. They're on billboards and milk cartons but so far no luck."

Tom was kidding of course but his tone of voice had changed and I braced for what I knew was coming.

"What's going on, Chuck? You really quitting?"

By the time I finished laying out the whole story it was almost noon. I've known Tom since high school and he's my best friend. Facebook friends come and go with a click, but this is the real deal. We have the same sarcastic sense of humor, sometimes sick, sometimes silly. We both like sports, and both like watching sports. We like games too. Back at Lincoln High we were short and shy so we never got any dates. Not that we ever asked. We played games instead. Been in the same fantasy football league since college, and we're the only ones in the league for chrissakes.

Even though Tom moved to D.C., we still see each other over the holidays and we still play a big family game of Risk. And we play for keeps.

Anyway, Tom and I know each other better than we know ourselves and he knew something really was wrong. He's my biggest fan, and sometimes plays the cheerleader to a fault, but this time he wasn't giving me a shoulder to cry on. In fact, when I'd run out of gas telling him my sob story he got after me and was starting to sound an awful lot like Darlene.

"Okay, this reorg does sound like a bad idea and quitting United wouldn't be the end of the world. You're a talented guy and there are other places to hang your hat. I mean, look at me. You too could be selling ladies shoes at Nordstrom." He stopped while we shared a laugh. "Thing is, Chuck, I've never seen you scared of your own shadow. If I didn't know better I'd say you weren't just quitting on United, you're quitting on yourself. Maybe I need to hop on a plane, come out there, and kick your butt."

"Maybe you do," I sighed in agreement. "I sure would love to have a beer and see your face. It'd do me a world of good."

"I gotta run, Chuck. This is my stop. You say this big meeting is tomorrow afternoon?"

"Yeah."

"If you're taking my advice, which I've never known you to do, I'd stick that letter in your desk drawer and go to the meeting. And give 'em hell. I love you and I'm going to call you tomorrow and check on you. And the day after that, and the day after that."

"I love you too, T. Give Jane a big kiss for me. And hug those kids if they ever show up."

Tom had one more thing to say, but he was cutting out and the line went dead so I didn't catch what it was. I didn't have to.

I hung up and stared out the window. The sun was poking holes in the cloud cover and spotlighting a few crossover SUVs in the parking lot. A Kia Sorento here, a Nissan Murano there. After talking to my pal those rays looked a little bit like hope. But hope can be a real bastard.

Was my life really so empty I was just going to cut and run? I wanted to wipe this mess out of my life and quitting was the quickest way to do that, but I've been down that long road before and it goes nowhere. I mean, I think I could learn to like selling ladies shoes but that's not where I want to go. Or maybe it is. Slipping high-heeled shoes over the heels of well-heeled ladies doesn't sound half bad. And that led me back to Darlene.

When I drifted back to my laptop, the resignation letter was still on the screen so I tried it on one more time to see if it still fit. I'm one of those guys who can buy a suit right off the rack and it always fits, but now this one felt awfully tight through the shoulders, and the sleeves were a little too long. Plus, I prefer a more European cut that shows off my V-shaped back. Anyway, the letter sounded good last night but just didn't fit anymore.

I closed the laptop and stood up. Stretching felt good and made me realize I was hungry. I didn't finish my sausage biscuit this morning, and after talking to Tom I couldn't quit the idea a corn dog would taste pretty good. The halls were almost deserted as I made my way to the break room, which was definitely odd for this hour, but being alone right now was just fine by me. The run-in with Sorenstam earlier still had me shaky. There was something about the look on his face I couldn't read. Scott and I aren't tight but we get along just fine. He really doesn't seem the type to sing like a canary, but I learned long ago you can't read a book by its cover. And why else would he be talking to Girard?

The Jerk doesn't talk to anybody below him on the org chart unless he wants something. Like information.

Stepping into the United break room immediately took the edge off my appetite. The smell of day-old donuts, half-eaten sandwiches, and Pine-Sol filled my nose, and a little wave of nausea rippled through my gut. I briefly considered backing out and grabbing a bite on the road later, but I'm a big boy and needed to shovel some coal into the furnace, so I shook it off and opened the refrigerator.

Bad idea. A tsunami of nausea hit me this time when I found myself staring down the barrel of a rancid breakfast burrito. It looked almost black, and I don't think it was the beans. I knew I had a ham and cheese croissant in there somewhere but figured I had no more than five seconds to find it before the lights went out. One of the things that's kept me alive all these years is knowing when I'm outgunned and need to turn tail and run. And that burrito had me outgunned, so I closed the fridge and slowly backed away.

I needed a plan B and eyed the bank of vending machines against the back wall. As I fumbled in my pocket for a couple of bills, I spied something out of the corner of my eye. Something that wasn't right. The break room has had the same lovely decor for as long as I've been at United. Round tables with fake wood tops. Cheap plastic chairs in every color of the rainbow. A rolling cart with dishes and glassware, some clean, some not so much. And the walls cluttered with the same sorry collection of mandatory employee postings, inspirational sayings, and a couple of paintings of Mt. Hood that somebody in accounting did. That bean counter is no Rembrandt, I can tell you that.

Anyway, something was out of place and I couldn't put my

finger on it, but when I grabbed the PowerBar out of the slot and turned to my right I suddenly knew exactly what it was. Some gravedigger had disturbed this ancient tomb and hung a big yellow sign on the wall next to the OSHA poster.

Winners never quit, and quitters never win.

I froze, staring at the words. I might as well have disappeared into one of those worm holes they talk about and come out the other end in a separate universe. If there are any. It seems like ours is big enough but I guess there could be other ones too. I used to watch *Cosmos* a lot. Carl Sagan was always talking about things I couldn't understand but I liked the show anyway. It made me feel like there was something out there bigger than us. Probably better too. And worm holes seemed like the fastest way to get there.

Anyway, I've never been in a separate universe but suddenly it felt like I was. For the first time in a week I knew exactly who I was and where I stood. Chucky was standing in the break room of course, but seeing the world in a whole new light. And it was still that harsh florescent light that makes everything look radioactive, but I think you get my meaning. Tom was right, I won't need that letter of resignation because I'm not resigning. And that's what those letters are for. I thought to myself I'm no quitter, so I broke it down. There's no "me" in quitter, but there's an "i" in winner, and that's me. A winner.

If you want to get technical, the only things I've ever won were a trophy for the Sunset Little League championship when I was ten, and a Big Bertha driver in a raffle after the United Food Scramble a couple years back. But trophies and golf clubs aren't what make you a winner. I'm not exactly sure what makes you one, but Carl Sagan could probably explain it. Except he's dead.

Anyway, I suddenly knew what to do. It was time to take the bull by the horns. The halls were busy now like they usually are but I didn't pay attention to faces. I tore into my PowerBar and strode down the hall with only one thing on my mind. Well, two things actually because I wished I'd gotten Chocolate Peanut Butter instead of Chocolate Mint Cookie, but the big thing on my mind was the Jerk. His office was dead ahead now and through the frosted glass window I could just make out the soft silhouette of Darlene sitting at her desk. I thought about saving the last bite of my PowerBar for her, because she does prefer Chocolate Mint Cookie, but I knew she was probably still sore at me so I popped it in my mouth, swallowed hard, and burst into Girard's office foyer.

"Morning, doll face."

She looked up from her monitor and I thought I caught a smile in her eyes before her face dissolved into a scowl.

"It's after noon. What do you want?" She grunted her displeasure and returned to the screen.

"I want to see Girard. I know he's in there." The Jerk almost always eats lunch in his office about this time and I figured it was a good bet he'd be there.

The foyer is small but posh and Darlene's desk sits just outside the door that leads to Jack Girard's corner office. I'm not sure why the foyer feels posh. Foyer is a fancy word that you have to pronounce different than it looks so maybe that's why. Maybe it's because Darlene makes any room look posh. I don't really know, but I do know that posh is a fun word to say.

Anyway, I was staring a hole through the door of the corner office. You know it's Girard's office because there's a big sign on the door that says Jonathan J. Girard, Regional Sales Director. Everybody else has a small, standard-issue sign that slips into those holders beside their doors, but Girard's wasn't big enough to match his ego so he had one made special. Put it right on the door too.

"He's eating lunch."

I was right on the money. Darlene didn't bother to look up from her computer and kept tapping out something at a furious pace. We fell silent for a moment and I got lost watching her fingernails clattering on the keys.

"You know he hates to be bothered when he's eating," she said finally.

"Yeah, I know. That'll make it even better."

Darlene's eyes jumped up and locked on mine for a couple of sweet seconds before she could think of something to say.

"Make what better?" she asked with more than a little curiosity.

"Something I should've done a long time ago."

She swiveled around to face me. Which was nice because she was wearing another one of those surplice tops. There was still a frown on her face but I could tell she was dying to know what was on my mind. And maybe, just maybe, she was rethinking what she said last night. I flashed her a smile and opened the door to Girard's office.

"E.C., don't."

She started to say something else but her voice trailed off as I shut the door behind me.

Girard was sitting in his oversized chair at his oversized desk eating an oversized kale salad. He loves kale. Which is one more reason I hate him. He glared at me while he finished chewing the big bite he was working on. Girard chews with his mouth open, so there were little bits of kale fleeing the scene of the crime and some kind of white dressing trickling down his chin. Not a pretty sight. I shuddered and added that one to the list too. He made a half-hearted effort to wipe his face with a paper napkin and put down his little plastic fork.

"Come right in, Poole," he snarled. "I assume there's a good reason for this."

Girard looked past me and I turned back to see Darlene's face peeking through a sliver in the doorway.

"Sorry, I tried to..." she stammered, but Girard waved his hand dismissively so she aborted her apology and quickly disappeared.

I raised my chin up and dove in. "I thought it was time we had a meeting, Jack."

"Meeting's tomorrow, Poole," he said through tight lips.

"Yeah, well I decided to move it up."

Girard's pretty slow on the uptake, but he could tell I meant business so he shoved aside his salad and motioned me to one of the chairs facing his desk.

"Thanks, but I'd rather stand."

"Suit yourself."

Girard leaned back in his chair, folded his hands across his belt, and started twiddling his thumbs. That's standard procedure for him and together with the smirk it usually meant the answer was no before you even asked the question. Too bad for him I didn't come to ask questions.

"This reorg is a bad idea, Jack. We don't like it. Customers won't like it. Sales are going to suffer."

Girard snapped forward in his chair and cut me off.

"I told you to get on board with this, Poole, or get out of my way. Maybe it's time you find another shop. Or another line of work."

"I'm not quitting. No way. You can fire me if you want, but when the numbers go south and they're looking for a fall guy it's going to be you not me."

Girard glared at me for a few seconds and looked like he wanted to spit something out. Kale probably. Finally he just eased back in his chair and slapped the smirk back on.

"Well, Gloria's got a master's degree that says it's going to work," he said smugly as he resumed twiddling. "If you're so smart tell me why it won't."

"All that BS about sales sclerosis and competitive dynamics is just a fancy way to say you don't trust your people to do their jobs, and you can't think of a better way to motivate them. And you want to reduce *head count*," I said making exaggerated air quotes with my fingers and punching up the last word. "You may cut costs in the short run but you're going to lose accounts and revenue in the long haul. When was the last time you were out in the field, Jack? Customers are going to think we're nuts shuffling accounts like this."

Girard stopped twiddling and leaned forward again. I could tell he was steamed but something was making him think twice. I'm good at making people think twice. Sometimes I can make them think three times. Which I guess would be thrice, if that's even a word. Anyway, I caught him off guard so he was scrambling to find a flaw in my argument.

"If we lose accounts and revenue then people are going to lose their jobs," he said very slowly like he was trying to squeeze it out of his slow brain.

It obviously took a lot of mental effort, but after a few seconds he grinned and acted like he just got the Final Jeopardy answer. Although it's a question not an answer on that show, which I think is stupid. But it's a really popular show so what do I know? Anyway, he looked pretty pleased with himself.

"Exactly," I said sharply.

The word exploded out of me as I slapped both hands down on the edge of his desk. Girard reflexively leaned back. This time there was no twiddling.

"Summerhill just wants to churn and burn. Set the bar too high, have everyone at each other's throats, and then get rid of the poor saps who can't keep up."

"What's wrong with that, Poole?" he asked. For the first time I could tell he really didn't know the answer.

"What's wrong is you're creating a jungle where only one or two salespeople can survive. They'll be stretched thin and won't perform as well, you'll fire the others, hire some new ones, and then you'll end up with a bunch of wet-behind-the-ears punks who don't know what they're selling and probably can't find their own ass with both hands and a map."

Girard stared blankly at me for a few long seconds before reaching for his salad and picking up the little plastic fork. I was still leaning on his desk and it was another few seconds before he broke the silence.

"Sounds to me like you don't think *you'll* survive," he said while stuffing another large mound of leaves in his kale hole. His beady, black eyes were focused on mine but I could tell he was rattled and didn't have the stomach for more fight. More kale obviously, but no more fight.

"Don't worry about me, Jack, I'll survive alright," I crowed, nodding my head and poking myself in the chest with my forefinger.

Suddenly I felt good. Really good. Better than in a long time.

My chest was clean now, except for a little mint chocolate I'd just smeared on it, and I toyed with the idea of rubbing Girard's nose in it. Not the mint chocolate, the reorg. But I didn't want to watch him spit kale bits on his desk any longer so I walked to the door and yanked it open like I meant it. I turned around one last time and delivered a hard stare that would make any street tough run. And said it one more time.

"I *will* survive."

I slammed Girard's door shut and didn't leave any goodbyes behind me. Darlene was sitting sideways at her desk staring at me with those hazel eyes asking all kinds of questions, but the answers would have to wait. I winked, shot her a grin that had winner written all over it, and headed down the hall to my office without looking back. And with Gloria Gaynor ringing in my ears.

I will survive.

16

For the first time in a week I felt like I knew where I was headed. Maybe even for the first time in my life. Gloria Gaynor was still stuck in my head so I stuck my hands in my pockets and started to hum a few bars while I walked.

Do you think I'd crumble? Did you think I'd lay down and die? Oh no, not I. I will survive. I will survive.

The rain clouds had finally lifted and sun streamed through the high windows in the corridor by the break room, painting the vinyl floor yellow. The look I saw on Darlene's face made me crack a smile. Maybe I *could* get her back. I know I never had her, but I think I could have if I hadn't been such a chump. Anyway, I felt like a million bucks and when I looked down at my feet it was like I was walking on sunshine. Then, sadly, Katrina and the Waves started to drown out Gloria Gaynor just as I swung into my office.

I'm walking on sunshine, woooo. I'm walking on sunshine, woooo. I'm walking on sunshine, woooo. And don't it feel good?

Yeah it feels good, it just doesn't sound good. I hate that song.

I plopped down in my chair and took a few minutes to savor the set-to I had with Girard. I was pleased with the way I handled it. I had him on his heels from the opening bell and didn't let up. And that was real fear I saw in his eyes when I told him he was going to take the fall if this stupid reorg crashed and burned. That one caught him flush on the chin. I nodded at the wisdom of that and started thinking about tomorrow's meeting. Today I was just getting warmed up. Maybe I can't stop the reorg, but I can stop acting like a chump. And I can let the Jerk and everyone else know I'm going down swinging. Katrina was still woooo-wooing when it suddenly dawned on me I forgot the vendor audit for PRC.

I swore softly and shrugged while I opened my laptop. I'd done most of the work yesterday afternoon, but that was when I was ready to throw in the towel so I hadn't bothered to sharpen my pencil on the pricing. I knew I had to go through the whole thing again and that got me back to walking on solid ground. And suddenly it didn't feel so good. I guess that's why nobody's ever written a song about walking on linoleum.

Before I waded back into the audit, I made a cursory check of my orders, which didn't look all that bad today, and then checked my email. One from Chef Weatherspoon at Cosa Nostra caught my eye and I clicked on it. Obviously David Eastman had talked to him about my visit, which made me shake my head. I wasn't exactly on top of my game when I met Eastman, so I was surprised the chef followed up. And brother did he follow up.

"Jesus," I muttered as I scrolled down through what had to be the longest email I'd ever seen. I realized when I got to the bottom that most of it was a bio he must use as a default setting. Who puts a bio in their email? With a photo gallery? Chef Chastain Bowers Weatherspoon, that's who. And that's some moniker. He must be a real high hat. Reading through it I figured he was probably an army brat. Born in Berlin, lived for a while in South Korea, went to grade school in Norfolk, Virginia, and then prep school in Adelaide, Australia. He graduated from the Culinary Institute of America at Greystone in Napa, and rattled the pots and pans at Le Bernardin and Babbo in New York, and Gary Danko in San Francisco. Big time stuff. Really big. The bio also said he had an epiphany visiting a meatpacking plant a couple years back and became a vegetarian. Sounded almost religious about it. So I guess it makes perfect sense he's now the chef at a Stumptown steakhouse.

Anyway, the actual email was short, just asking for more information about United's farm-to-table program. Like where exactly we source our meat and produce.

Animals, Chef. And plants.

I made a mental note to get back to that one and clicked on another email, this one from Manning's Lakeside Grill. Manning's is Sorenstam's account, at least for another couple of days, so that seemed odd. But when I opened it there was a personal note from Tui. Somewhere in the middle of a scattered herd of emojis he managed to ask how I was doing and attach a digital coupon for a free appetizer with the purchase of two drinks. Sounded like a good idea to me.

There was also one from Tom. The subject line read "Watch This!" Tom and I exchange emails a lot and we like to share links and YouTube videos. Once in a while they're about things that make us mad, like politics, but most of the time they're just plain funny. He didn't sound funny earlier when he hung up though, so I was ready to take one on the chin when I clicked on the link. Knowing Tom, I thought it might be something inspirational from one of the Rocky movies, which wouldn't be inspiring. Or maybe that scene from *Raging Bull* when Jake LaMotta loses the fight and sticks his bloody face in Sugar Ray Robinson's and says, "You never got me down, Ray. You never got me down." Tom loves that movie, and so do I. But instead it was a five-minute clip of Jerry Lewis and Dean Martin from *Sailor Beware.* It's a boxing video of sorts, and it got me laughing alright, but I'm not sure it helped get me in the mood to fight.

The rest of the emails were the usual Google alerts for things I couldn't care less about, invitations on LinkedIn from people I don't know, and time-limited offers to buy things I don't need or want. I know Google's got smart algorithms, and I get it when somebody tries to sell me gym clothes after I buy an exercise bike online, or that five-star resort ads pop up because I spend my spare time looking at vacation spots I can't afford, but please tell me why I'm getting pitched on plus-sized dresses and swimwear. Sure I could lose a couple of pounds but I'm no plus-size. And I ain't no dame. I think their models are sexy though so I don't mind getting those.

Anyway, when I was done deleting, I closed email and pulled up the vendor audit for Chef Mercedes and the new PRC kingpin. There wasn't as much work left as I feared, but it still took half an hour to track down the last numbers and tighten up a few I knew would matter. What really fried my bacon was that they already have this dope and were just making me jump through the hoop so they could say they did it.

Also, it was after one and I was hungry. That PowerBar didn't do the job and for some reason fried bacon sounded really good right now. I could sure go for a BLT, or better yet some of those bacon-wrapped dates they have at Manning's. They stick an almond inside the date, wrap them in bacon like the name implies, and roast them. They're delicious. Halfway between the BLT and bacon-wrapped dates, I made the decision to head to Manning's when I finished the audit, have a couple of drinks and some fried bacon, and call it a day.

What is it about bacon? It might even be more popular than ranch dressing. We put bacon in a lot of things, on a lot of things, and wrap it around everything else. A chef I used to work with asked me why we use bacon in so many dishes. He was a smart guy. A walking encyclopedia of food. I wanted to impress him so I guessed it was for texture contrast, smokiness and the salt. He just stared at me like I was an idiot and said no, it's because bacon tastes good. As I fumbled in my coat pocket for my flip phone, I realized I was even *more* hungry now.

"What's up, E.C.?"

Chef Mercedes sounded tired as usual when she answered my call.

"Just finishing up the audit and needed to confirm you don't want the farm-to-table program pricing. You're top tier already obviously, but the organics are going to be cheaper if you're in the program."

"Fuck the organics," she barked into my ear. "What does that even mean anymore? Just because you don't dust your crops with DDT doesn't make it organic."

This time her f-bomb dropped like a dud. I'd heard this rant before and knew I had to give her lots of line before I could reel her in. But she must've been too busy because I dodged the full lecture about "organics" and "free-range" and "cage-free" and all the other buzz words in our business that don't mean what people think they mean. She's right, they don't. Big Food has a lot of money and a lot of clout with the swamp critters in Washington. They've had their pals water down the regulations so much there's not much difference anymore between a chicken that never sees the light of day and one that gets a little time in the prison yard. And the truth is you probably won't even taste any difference. Still, if it makes you feel better to eat organic, or free-range, or cage-free, or whatever, I guess it can't hurt.

"Just wanted to check, Chef. This is coming at you right now.

Let me know if you have any trouble with the document or if you got any questions. And I'll see you Monday morning."

I hit send and was just about to hang up when she brushed me back with a hard slider.

"Will I? Mr. Scarpetti was here yesterday and he said there was going to be a shakeup at United. That maybe you weren't going to be our rep anymore. That true?"

"Gee, I wonder where he heard that."

After the flap with Sorenstam I was feeling bad about busting his chops and had thought about going easier on Dan and Vic, but now my blood was starting to boil again.

"It was probably Conner, E.C., but it could've been your boss. What's going on?"

It was Conner alright.

"Oh, some suit back east cooked up a corporate reorg and wants to put the sales team in a blender. Looks like they may shift some accounts around."

I was trying to play it cool and sound casual, but my chest was in a vice and the voice coming out of my mouth sounded pretty thin to me so it must've tipped her off I was on edge. And it didn't help I used another couple of lame cooking references.

"Why didn't you tell me?"

She didn't sound angry, just disappointed, and that felt worse.

"Been a lot going on, Mercedes, and I didn't want to bother you with it. You know these big wheels like to blow smoke but five will get you one it turns out to be nothing new. Besides, we won't know for sure until the sales meeting tomorrow afternoon."

"Uh huh." She knew full well I was the one blowing smoke. "Well, good luck. And call me if we're breaking up. I don't want to get dumped by text."

"Not my style, doll. If it happens it'll be face to face with a fist full of flowers."

I don't think Chef Mercedes likes being called doll, so it was no surprise she didn't respond and just hung up.

I slowly closed the laptop and leaned back in my chair. I let Conner get my goat again, and I don't have many more goats to get. But Chucky isn't on the case anymore. I get around alright but I can't keep private eyes on everyone, and the thing is I just don't care about Dan and Scarpetti, or Vic and Westerling, or Scott and the Jerk. I've been on the wrong side of the street this week, but I'm working my own side now. It's a lonely place to be and that's where I belong.

Somehow I missed the turn to the business park where Manning's is and ended up on the wrong side of the street. The urban planning whizzes who lay out these suburban jungles should have to spend eternity trying to make a left turn across traffic to a Target parking lot. Or maybe just spend eternity shopping at Target. That ought to be punishment enough. Anyway, I was even more hungry and thirsty by the time I parked the Subaru and pushed open the double doors to Manning's.

"Oh, my god!"

I braced myself for the bear hug as Tui rushed around the corner of the desk to greet me, and he didn't disappoint. Only a small squeak came out when I tried to talk, so he went ahead and filled the dead air.

"I sent you an email today. Did you open it? I can't believe you're here so soon."

He seemed to be having a fine conversation with himself, so when he released me from the death grip I just stepped back and smiled. Tui kept right on talking as he grabbed me by the arm and hauled me into the bar.

"How are you? I've been worried about you," he said forcing me gently onto an open barstool. "You didn't look very happy at dinner the other night. Who were those people? The guy with the mustache looked like a creep. Is he your boss?"

I turned to face the big Tongan.

"Tui could you take a breath? And maybe put all those questions in writing?"

Clearly satisfied he'd stuck his nose far enough into my business, he simply beamed and motioned for the bartender. Before I could order a beer, which is really what I wanted, Tui ordered me a scotch and soda and slipped a menu under my elbow on the bar.

"I'll be back. Do *not* leave."

Tui danced out of the bar just as my drink arrived and I could only shake my head in amazement. It finally registered that Taylor Swift was telling everyone to *Shake It Off* and Tui really *was* dancing his way out of the bar. What a guy. I just wished his memory wasn't so damn good because I really didn't want a scotch and soda. I briefly considered dumping out the drink and ordering a beer but I was afraid if Tui caught me he might crush me. Or start crying. Or both.

When I swiveled back around, the slender young man tending bar was watching me with a grin that told me he's seen the dance act before. More than a few times.

"He *loves* this song," he said with a mixture of disgust and affection just as Taylor was wrapping up. "And a million others. Tui could be on the patio and completely out of earshot but if *Happy* started playing he'd be here in a heartbeat."

"I believe it."

And I do, but I needed some food PDQ and just caught the bartender to take my order before he turned to grab a ticket out of the printer. There was no way those bacon-wrapped dates were going to escape their fate today, and I teed up a grilled chicken burger with bacon and fries to follow. And a side of ranch dressing of course. And a Coors since I'd slammed the scotch and soda after Tui danced around the corner. Feeling satisfied I had all the major food groups covered, and a little buzzed from the rushed drink, I stretched my shoulders, settled down on my elbows, and started tipping the frosty bottle that just appeared.

It was hard to believe this was the same day that started with writing a resignation letter and polishing my resume. It was also hard to believe that a stupid quote on a cheap poster in a stinking break room turned everything around. I needed a slap in the face and Vince Lombardi was the man for the job. Darlene and Tom roughed me up too, so they get credit for finding my backbone. I still wasn't exactly sure how all the pieces fit but whatever the hell was going on, Chucky's back, and I'm not giving an inch to Girard, or Westerling, or anybody tomorrow. It's going to be a sporty meeting.

I was feeling good about myself and things were looking up. Hell, even Darlene was coming back around when I left Girard's office. Or so it seemed. I started to daydream when a pretty thing snuck up behind me and slipped the bacon-wrapped dates under my nose. She disappeared before I could say thanks, so I turned my attention to the appetizer and popped one of those bundles of joy in my mouth. They had to be right out of the oven because suddenly the roof of my mouth was on fire, and I must've made a scene sucking air in and out and waving my hand in front of my face because the dame at the end of the bar was laughing at me.

She was a buxom redhead wearing a blue dress and sporting a set of big bedroom eyes. I guess it was a dress. Spray paint would've done just about the same thing.

I swallowed the little fireball whole then tossed her a quick smile and shoulder shrug. My dentist tells me I've got unusually soft tissue in my palette, so this could be a serious burn, but I wasn't going to let anything bother me right now. Besides, it was nothing a little cold beer couldn't fix. I took another swig.

Just then the sound system found its way through my ears and into my brain and Tom Petty was talking to me.

Well I know what's right, I got just one life. In a world that keeps pushing me around. But I'll stand my ground. And I won't back down.

I love Tom Petty, and I love that song. I saw him at an Oregon Zoo concert and he opened with it. Don't ask me why they have concerts at the zoo, it's a Portland thing. I'm sure the animals hate it. Anyway, he didn't sing as much as he snarled the song, like he was sending a message. I never met the guy but to my knowledge he always stood his ground and never backed down. Tom's dead of course so he did once, but it's still a great song.

My mouth was still sore but I polished off the last date with no trouble just as Tui reappeared with my chicken burger. Tom Petty must not rate with him because he was moving through the bar propelled by something that looked more or less like walking. I tapped my empty beer bottle for the bartender's benefit and turned to face Tui.

"Bacon chicken burger with fries and a side of ranch," he announced loud enough to make the redhead perk up and shoot me a look. "And I brought you extra ranch."

Miss Blue Dress didn't let go of the look and I started thinking about offering to share my lunch with her. She looked pretty enough when I walked in, and after a couple of quick drinks she was even prettier, but I was still hungry and there was no way I was giving up even a bite. And though this gal could probably play AAA baseball she wasn't in Darlene's league.

"Thanks, Tui."

I took a big bite of sandwich but all I tasted was cologne because Tui had dropped down on the stool beside me. Even a couple of fries slathered with ranch dressing were no match for the overpowering musk. I don't get musk. I'm not sure, but I'd guess it's what sex-crazed bucks smell like when they're chasing does around the forest. Maybe it's sexy to does, and dames, but not to me. Especially when I can't taste my lunch.

"What's happening at United, E.C.? Are you getting fired?" Tui asked earnestly without showing the least bit of concern he was overstepping his bounds.

"Why do you ask?" I casually mumbled through a mouth full of French fries.

"Scotty said there was going to be a big shakeup. He said he might not be my rep anymore, and maybe he was going to get canned. He said you might too."

"He did, huh?" I said turning to face Tui, eyeing him with suspicion that probably wasn't warranted. I guess it's okay for Girard *and* Tui to call him Scotty but not me.

"Yes he did. Is it true, E.C.?"

I carefully put my bacon chicken burger down and slowly wiped the ranch dressing off my lips. Tui cocked his head waiting for my response but I wasn't sure yet how I wanted to play this. If he *was* Girard's mole it doesn't seem likely Sorenstam would get the chop, but it was pretty interesting he told Tui he might.

Maybe I was off base about Scott but there didn't seem to be any harm in telling Tui what's what.

"Don't know, Tui," I said truthfully. "There's a shakeup alright, but we won't know how the chips are going to fall until tomorrow afternoon."

Tui straightened his back, which pushed his big chest out over his big belly and stretched his already tight Manning's polo shirt to the limits of the fabric. I hadn't noticed when the ever-present smile disappeared and his eyes started to glow, but it made him look like the Incredible Hulk. If the Incredible Hulk were a South Pacific Islander. And wore cologne. It occurred to me there might be another side to the big guy, a dark side, and that made me shudder.

"They better not fire you and Scotty or I'll call my brothers and we'll go visit Mr. Mustache," he said flatly like he'd never meant anything more in his life.

"How many brothers do you have?" I asked.

"Seven."

"Seven? Wow. That must be a ton of Tongans," I said with a grin, trying to turn the temperature down.

With that, The Hulk disappeared and Tui returned. He stood up and gave me a quick sideways bear hug that I think tore my rotator cuff. I don't even know what a rotator cuff is, but baseball pitchers tear them sometimes and they say it hurts like hell.

"You and Scotty stand up to those bastards, you hear? They can't push you around like that," he said with that big smile beaming in my face. Somebody was yelling his name from the kitchen, which had him on his feet and moving towards the door, but he turned around and wagged a finger at me. "And I want a full report tomorrow at happy hour."

I settled back on the stool shaking my head and was returning my attention to the beer when I caught the blue dress staring at me again. She'd settled her bill and was standing up to leave. Maybe Tui scared her off, or maybe I just wasn't her type. I guess I did look like a fool with those dates but they really were hot. Anyway, she gave me a little wave like I was a parade that passed her by and flashed one last smile as she walked out.

Thankfully, my sense of smell returned as I finished the chicken burger and fries, and it was a good thing Tui brought me extra ranch because I was scraping the bottom of the second barrel with my last fry. I motioned for my check and drained the beer. I started daydreaming about Darlene again while I was paying my tab and almost left a two hundred percent tip. The credit card receipt was a mess but the bartender got his twenty percent and I hauled off the barstool and headed for the door.

Tui was nowhere to be found when I walked by the front desk, and I gave some thought to trying to track him down, but I figured I'd see him tomorrow after the meeting one way or another. Besides, my mind was on other things now. Namely Darlene. I stepped out into the pale sun and the music being piped outside stopped me in my tracks. It was Rickie Lee Jones singing her big hit from way back when. Her only hit really. And it wasn't that big, but it did get a lot of radio play for a few weeks.

He sure has acquired this kinda cool and inspired sorta jazz when he walks. Where's his jacket and his old blue jeans? Well, this ain't healthy, it's some kinda clean. That means Chuck E.'s in love. Yeah, yeah. Chuck E.'s in love.

There *was* a little jazz in my step as I walked to my car and I broke into a smile. I have no idea what Rickie Lee's talking about, but Chucky's definitely in love.

17

I must've jumped the gun at Manning's yesterday and kept it rolling last night because my tongue was stuck to the roof of my mouth and the daylight streaming in the bedroom window felt like a switchblade stuck in my one open eye. I winced and rolled over. Another half hour of sleep sounded good, but my brain needed a few words with me and I knew I was going to have to wake up and listen. My brain's like that. So I leaned back on the pillows, clasped my hands behind my head, and drew a deep breath. It took me a good fifteen minutes to reconstruct yesterday's tumble of events, but by the time I got it sorted into neat little piles I was starting to feel pretty darn good. Even the hangover felt good.

Today's the day.

"Let's do this," I said with gusto as I swung my legs out and fumbled with my feet for the slippers under the bed. As usual, I managed to kick one backwards and had to lie down on my stomach and stretch to retrieve it. How does that happen? You'd think once in a while you'd either kick the slipper only a little ways back, or sideways, or maybe even all the way to the other side. But no, it's always the middle of the bed. I hate that. Especially today because by the time I scrambled to my feet and got the damn slipper on, the hangover didn't feel so good anymore.

Mr. Coffee could tell I'd tied one on last night but said nothing. Mr. Coffee doesn't judge. He must've sensed my mood and wanted to congratulate me though, because the first cup of joe tasted especially good. Slow-roasted, strong and hot, just like a good dame. Not the slow-roasted part, that would be weird. But strong and hot is how I like 'em and that's just how Darlene rates.

Checking email felt strange, but something in the back of my head told me to just keep doing my job. Maybe it was a coincidence, or maybe it was business as usual, but all my customers were placing big orders this morning. That made me grin and nod my head.

Go ahead and fire me, you moron. I'll take these orders with me when I go, and it'll be the last you see of me.

I clicked on an email from Chef Mercedes expecting the biggest one, but it wasn't an order at all. It was just a short, sweet note thanking me for the audit and wishing me luck in today's meeting. I'm not one for getting sappy but there was a lump in my throat when I fired off a reply thanking her. It could've been a piece of sausage biscuit but I don't think so. Jimmy Dean doesn't usually make me cry.

I took a long shower to wash the hangover away and savored the steam. Maybe it was too long because the mirror was so fogged up when I was shaving I had to keep wiping little circles so I could see. It was really annoying, but I kept doing it anyway because I wanted to be extra careful today. Being a bleeder, I couldn't afford any nicks or cuts. Sure, I've tried styptic pencils and powders but I bleed right through that stuff. Little pieces of toilet paper work for a while, but they stick to your face and when you rip them off it hurts, and then you start to bleed again. Band-aids are the only thing that do the trick but you look stupid wearing one on your face. Anyway, it took too long but I managed to get the job done.

On most days I don't give much thought to what I'm wearing. I'm one of those guys who looks good in anything I throw on. Besides, khakis with a polo shirt is my work uniform and I don't like to mess with success. Today was a big day though, and my gut told me a new outfit was right for the occasion. And it was Casual Friday after all. I put on a pair of faded blue jeans, my favorite plaid Pendleton shirt, some Doc Marten boots, checked myself in the mirror and nodded with approval.

It's go time, Chucky.

Traffic was heavy like it always is on Friday mornings. The five miles on I-5 from the 217 interchange to Wilsonville was bumper to bumper and took twenty minutes, but today I didn't care. Just before the exit I noticed I had a Chevy Equinox in front of me and a Chevy Traverse on my tail. I don't like being the meat in a Chevy sandwich but the comparison was interesting. Neither one measured up to the Volvo XC60 on my right though, and the Lincoln MKT on my left put them all to shame. I made a mental note to test drive that one as I started to crawl up the off-ramp. When the Acura RDX in front of me peeled off, I made my way across the overpass and followed a blue-hair in a Jeep Grand Cherokee all the way to the United parking lot. I don't like the new Jeeps much. I liked them better when they looked like jeeps.

After squeezing my Outback into a tight spot, I trudged across the lot to the office doors but pulled up short when I saw Dan Conner coming through the lobby. I hadn't planned on talking to anyone before the meeting. All the hard feelings for Dan and Scott and Vic got flushed out of my system last night but seeing Dan's face, and thinking about him and Scarface cooking up their plan to steal my best account, made my feelings feel hard again.

"Hey, E.C.," Conner said sporting a sly grin and glancing at his watch. "Welcome to work. Did you forget to set the alarm last night?"

It was a quarter to ten and I felt a twinge of guilt for sleeping so late. And for sporting a hangover. But a twinge was all it was, and I'm used to twinges so I recovered real quick. I called his sly grin and raised him a full smirk.

"Had a couple of stops this morning, asshole. You know? Doing my job. Plus traffic was a bitch." Unlike David Eastman, Conner didn't flinch.

"Uh, huh."

Maybe I overplayed that one because Conner didn't look like he was buying it. Or maybe I still smelled like booze. Either way, that's when I decided to give him something else to think about.

"You and Carpelli seem pretty tight. You think you might get the PRC account?" I asked with practiced cool I don't really need to practice.

Conner rocked back on his heels and gave me his best surprised look, complete with raised eyebrows. Maybe raised too high, which has to be hard to do with *that* face. He must've had me figured for a fool, but nobody's playing Chucky today so I just smiled and waited for his next move. Dan could tell he didn't have any wiggle room, so the eyebrows dropped back down where they belong and he squinted.

"It's Scarpetti. Johnny Scarpetti." Even though his eyes were squinty now I could see the wheels turning. "Yeah, he and I go back a few years, but so what? I got no idea who's getting what accounts, E.C. Girard isn't showing his cards, and I couldn't get anything out of the lovely Miss Camper either."

The thought occurred to me that maybe I should see what *I* could get out of the lovely Miss Camper, but that investigation is for when we're off duty.

"Well, I guess we'll just have to wait and see, won't we?" I said with a shrug, still wearing a frozen smile I was getting tired of wearing. "But not much longer."

Conner cocked his head and gave me a quizzical look, but I was in no mood for quizzes so I kept my trap shut. I left him there to think that over and pulled open the glass door to the lobby. I could feel Dan's eyes on my back as I punched the button for the elevator.

Was that genuine surprise I saw on his face? Could be I suppose, but he sure didn't deny he and Scarface are tight. There was a lot to think about and my head started to spin. But that could be because I always get motion sickness in elevators and the ones at United are pretty wobbly. Relieved to be back on solid ground, I stepped out of the elevator on the third floor and told myself it doesn't matter and I don't care. And I don't.

I was grateful the halls were quiet as I made my way to the salt mine. But just when I thought I was home free, I turned the last corner and crashed into Sue Ann Pennington who was practically running to some four-alarm fire in her head. I caught her by both arms and muttered an apology as she held her hand to her chest and gasped for breath. Sue Ann doesn't weigh a hundred dripping wet, and I'm a pretty big guy, so she probably saw her life flash before her eyes. When she finally stopped gasping and started giggling, I let go and hoped to God she didn't collapse. She didn't, but she *did* take a couple of exaggerated steps backwards.

"My god, E.C.!" she panted. "I can't believe it!"

"Sorry, Sue Ann," I sputtered. I was wondering can't believe what? How rock solid I am? How catlike my reflexes are? Her statement was confusing but that's no surprise since Sue Ann specializes in confusion. She probably majored in confusion. With a minor in perkiness. Maybe it's just a gift, I don't know. Sue Ann's harmless enough but she's a real dizzy dame.

"Look at you!" she said wide-eyed, looking me up and down.

"Plaid shirt! Blue jeans! Boots!" Full sentence structure was apparently out of the question and her head was moving back and forth violently like she was trying to shake the words out. "You. You're *casual*," she finally shrieked and broke into a big toothy smile.

I'd completely forgotten about Casual Friday, but when I looked down at myself I realized she was right. I *was* pretty darn casual. And I don't like to toot my own horn but pretty darn outdoorsy. I guess I should've warned the girls in the office I was coming in hot like this. Anyway, I looked back up at Sue Ann and gave her a rugged grin.

"Hey, it's Friday babe. Gotta run."

With that, I gave her a quick wink and squeeze on the arm and strode down the hall the last few yards to my cubbyhole. I could've sworn I felt her pulse racing when I touched her arm and that had me worried that my outfit today might not be exactly heart-healthy for the fairer sex here at United. But what do you want me to do? Try to be less handsome?

I started to input orders but the hangover was still hanging around and reminded me I wasn't done paying the piper for last night. I figured another cup of joe couldn't hurt, so I got out of my chair with no small amount of difficulty and made my way toward the break room. After the encounter with Sue Ann I was a little more cautious and took the corners pretty slow, which was good because around the last one and headed my way was the Jerk. Some lucky star needs thanking because he was on his phone and I didn't have to act happy to see him. He looked up and nodded, but even his nods are condescending so I just gave him a quick chin up and kept on walking.

Buckle up, Jack. Yesterday was just a little taste.

Girard did a double take when my outfit registered. I could tell Sue Ann liked it alright but the Jerk no doubt didn't approve. His idea of going casual on Fridays is leaving the silk tie on the rack and loosening the top button of his monogrammed shirt. And wearing a pair of Sperry Top Siders instead of Manolo Blahniks. Who even wears Top Siders anymore? I guess they're still required for New England prep schools, and maybe rich people with sailboats. And Jack Girard on Casual Friday.

Anyway, what was he going to do, fire me? That thought made me chuckle to myself while I poured a big cup of United's finest and dumped in some non-dairy creamer. I chuckled out loud when I remembered this afternoon I was going to pour the Jerk a big cup of shut-the-fuck-up. That won't taste so good either.

I'm not sure who wrote the script for today but maybe I need a stuntman. I had another near miss leaving the break room and almost sideswiped Scott Sorenstam, and that got my heart racing. And my brain wondering why we call it a near miss? It's really a near hit isn't it? I mean a near miss would be Darlene sitting near me on the sofa, but that's the only thing I could think of. Still, we all say near miss so I guess that's what it is. Anyway, I almost hit Scott and that caused me to splash some of my coffee on the floor. Like Girard, he was on his phone. He said something I couldn't quite make out, then ended the call with a quick swipe of his finger.

"Excuse me," he said still staring at the little screen.

He seemed stiff so I figured he must still be sore.

"My bad, Scott," I said and ducked back into the break room to grab a couple of paper towels. When I emerged a few seconds later he was already halfway down the hall and back on his phone.

I was going to apologize for roughing him up yesterday but that could wait until after the meeting. It also occurred to me that Sorenstam might be who Girard was talking to, so maybe he should be the one doing the apologizing.

I quickly cleaned up the mess before the Portland Roast ate through to the sub-floor, topped off the cup, and headed back to my desk. When my head stopped pounding from the unexpected exercise, I opened my laptop and started scrolling through orders and email. It's a well-worn routine, and it's not like I ever relish the job, but today it felt more mechanical. Almost robotic. Which reminded me I've got to watch *RoboCop* again.

I dug back into the orders, and halfway through suddenly became aware of a shadow crossing the desk. My body coiled into a steel spring ready to strike. Or at least uncoil really fast. I instinctively reached under my left arm but I wasn't packing heat today. Because, as you already know, I don't own a gun. And it's against company policy anyway. My eyes feverishly scanned the surface of the desk for something lethal I could use to disable the intruder. I settled on the cup of Portland Roast and gripped it firmly in my right hand. Then, ever so slowly, looked up.

"There's nothing wrong with this, Poole."

It was Mark Westerling waving my old laptop at me. I put down the coffee and gave him a thin smile.

"Maybe there's something wrong with me, Mark," I chirped.

"Maybe it was that you didn't have your report ready, or didn't want to give it," he snarled.

Westerling and I locked eyes. I wasn't going to back down, not to Westerling that's for sure. On the other hand, he obviously meant business and kept glaring at me. There didn't seem any way out of this. We were in a Mexican standoff. I was still seated, but it was a standoff alright, and why do they call them Mexican? Don't other nationalities have disagreements that they can't seem to get out of? Anyway, there we were staring at each other waiting to see who blinked first.

"Think what you want, Mark. Maybe it was a 24-hour virus or something. I'm not an IT guy."

Westerling continued to glare at me. I didn't want to give back my new laptop, so I decided to zig when he zagged and changed the subject. I'm not sure how much zigging and zagging goes on in Mexican standoffs, and technically he didn't zag, but I zigged anyway.

"So, have you and Vic got it all ironed out for this afternoon?" I said, closing my laptop and firmly laying a hand on it to say it wasn't going anywhere.

"What do you mean?"

I could tell he didn't know what I meant so I let him stew for a few seconds.

"Well, you two have been spending a lot of time together recently. I thought maybe you'd worked out who's getting what accounts."

Westerling still looked confused and didn't respond. The cat must've got his tongue so I plowed ahead.

"You know, so sales stop stagnating and we become more dynamic?"

Westerling doesn't usually react well to sarcasm and this time was no different.

"I don't get you, Poole. You do a pretty good job, and your numbers aren't all that bad. If you put your back into it maybe you could even beat Vicky. At least once in a while."

I'd never heard Westerling say anything nice to me so this

time the cat got *my* tongue. Which is really weird if you think about it. Cats grabbing people's tongues I mean. Has that ever actually happened? If so, what did they use? Their claws? Their teeth? And why would they want to do that in the first place? Are human tongues considered a cat delicacy? Anyway, I didn't know what to say so Westerling kept at it.

"But you're just not a company man, are you? You've got to be the square peg in the round hole, don't you? I really don't get it. You don't have to like United, or Girard. You're not the only one who thinks he's a jerk but why not keep that to yourself? Why do you always have to be a smart ass and sabotage your own success?"

Okay, those were a lot of questions. Good ones too. Or maybe it was really one question. Either way, I didn't have any answers right now so I just nodded in silent agreement and shrugged. Maybe Westerling's part Mexican because it felt like he won the standoff. Although he sure doesn't look Mexican. Most Mexicans I know don't have pasty-white skin and a Roman nose. Anyway, at least he forgot about taking back my new laptop because he was walking out the door shaking his head with the old one in hand.

Even after Westerling was out of sight I kept staring a hole in the door. My door is always open so the hole wasn't necessary, but all those questions were a jumble in my brain and it wasn't firing on all cylinders yet. I don't like Westerling. We've never seen eye to eye. I'm a lot taller of course so that's no surprise, but we just don't seem to agree on anything. The guy's a company man if I ever saw one, but what if he's right? Summerhill's a snake in a designer dress, and Girard's a jerk alright, but what if they're not really the enemy? What if it's somebody else? Hell, what if it's me?

I was afraid I wouldn't get a chance to eat before the meeting unless I grabbed lunch right away, so I stowed all the hard questions for later and grabbed my coat and keys. I figured a couple of Costco hot dogs should do the trick, and I was just about at the elevators when I felt a presence behind me and caught a whiff of a dame. It wasn't perfume, just that clean, freshly-scrubbed scent guys don't have. I started to turn around but didn't get the chance because I suddenly found myself walking in lockstep with Vicky Mannheim right beside me.

"This is a new look for you, isn't it?" she asked giving my outfit the once-over. She was smiling and had a twinkle in her eyes so I assumed she liked it.

"I like it," she said.

I gave her a shrug and a little attitude.

"Yep, heading out to Estacada after the meeting to do some four-wheeling."

What does that even mean? Don't all cars have four wheels? On the road or off? I've never really been off road but my Outback has all-wheel drive so I suppose I could. That's like four-wheel drive, right? And what's the difference? Maybe I should try four-wheeling, or all-wheeling, or whatever it is. I've got a big appetite for adventure and can handle whatever's out there, and my phone doesn't have GPS but I can trust my nose to keep me pointed in the right direction. Still, all that bumping around would make me nauseous so I think I'll stick to blacktop.

"Where you *really* headed, E.C.?"

"Costco for a dog. Wanna come?"

I had decided I wanted one last cross-examination of Miss Mannheim before the meeting so it seemed like a perfect opportunity.

"Sounds delish, but I've got a fire to put out at the Spaghetti Factory and I don't want to be late for the meeting."

"Okay, but you're missing some fine cuisine. Good luck."

I wasn't ready to let Vic off the witness stand but something was eating me. Do you really need a factory to make spaghetti? And if you do, why not fettuccine too? I mean, it must be a big investment to build a spaghetti factory, and I would think you could retool the assembly line to make just about any pasta. Maybe not ziti or orzo, but the vast majority of pasta for sure. Anyway, I wanted to noodle some answers out of Vic so I used the elevator ride to grill her.

"You and Westerling have been chumming around a lot lately. Have he and Girard figured out how to use their star player?"

Vic's eyes had been glued to her phone, but that question got her attention and she snapped her head sideways with a stern look on her face. I could tell she was working hard on an answer, which would explain the long pause, but when she finally spoke her comeback stopped me in my tracks.

"This is a team sport, E.C.," she said pivoting to face me. "We are an *all star team*."

She carefully separated and punched up each of the last three words for emphasis. Vic stopped and turned just out of the elevator. She grabbed both my arms, forcing me to face her, and gave me a piercing look that felt like it was going right through my poor hungover brain.

"I don't like this reorg any more than you do, mister, but I'd rather do something positive than just feel sorry for myself."

My mom used to call me mister when I was in hot water, and Vic has never called me mister, so I figured I must be in hot water now. I opened my mouth to protest but she beat me to the punch.

"Scott and Dan both said you've been a jerk this week. That's Girard's job not yours, and it's not like you. You seem to think we're all against you, which I don't understand. We're friends, right?"

She seemed to want an answer but I couldn't find one.

"Mostly though you just seem to want to throw in the towel and quit before we've even started to fight. That's not like you either," she said in disgust.

I wished I could tell her I *was* ready to fight, but I still wasn't sure who to take a swing at. I had bumped into just about everybody this morning, literally, but I still couldn't sort anything out. Nobody admitted playing dirty pool, but nobody denied it either. I needed some room to think so I decided it was time to get away from Vic and head for Costco. They have plenty of room there. And cheap hot dogs.

"Sorry, Vic. I reckon I better saddle up and mosey along," I said in a guttural drawl hoping to lighten the mood. I thought my outdoorsy outfit might help pull it off, but Vic's eyes were still shooting daggers so I guessed not.

"God help you, E.C.," were the last words I heard as she headed out the door.

18

Two Costco hot dogs and a large Coke seemed like a good idea fifteen minutes ago but my stomach was now suggesting it wasn't. Taking stock of what I'd put in my gullet today, I counted three cups of strong coffee and a sausage biscuit at home, a big cup of weak coffee at the office, and now a couple of tube steaks with too much soda pop. Way too much. No wonder I still felt like hell. I slapped my forehead when it registered I hadn't had even a drop of water today. Forgetting to hydrate is a rookie hangover mistake and this wasn't the day for rookie mistakes so I staggered out into the Costco desert in search of an oasis.

After two passes through health and beauty aids, and one wrong turn that dead ended in the garden center, I finally arrived at the grocery section and ran into a display of bottled water that stretched to the ceiling like a sacred temple of plastic. Even though I don't always sort properly, I'm pretty good about recycling and the sad story is most of these bottles will wind up floating around the Pacific Ocean. The ones from Costco alone are probably enough to create a new continent. I just wanted one regular-size bottle of Smartwater but this is Costco so my only choice was a twelve-pack of half-liters. I was pretty dehydrated but not that much. Anyway, when I was finally able to tear open the surprisingly strong plastic wrapping I took a big swig from one of the bottles and headed for the front-end checkout.

By the time I arrived at the registers I'd drained half the bottle. The surly checker obviously didn't approve of opening products before you pay, especially since I evidently ripped apart the UPC code and she had to look it up. I gave her a wink and a smile by way of apology and wrestled the heavy load out the door. When I climbed behind the wheel of my car, I was working on my second bottle and starting to feel a little better with water in my system. But the smart part wasn't working since my brain still couldn't make heads or tails of all the close encounters I'd had this morning.

After playing bumper cars in the Costco parking lot, I finally escaped and wound my way back to United Food. I crawled up to my office, and when I sat down at my desk and opened my laptop the time jumped right off the screen. One forty. There were only twenty minutes to the meeting, and that sent a jolt through my wiring. Obviously I was lost in Costco longer than I realized because I'd hoped to have an hour or so to try and add things up.

"Damn it." I slapped the laptop shut and closed my eyes hard to focus. I could tell my brain still wasn't happy with me but I made it thumb through the card catalog of clues all the same.

Sorenstam's plenty mad and I don't blame him. Maybe he's been playing tipster for the Jerk, but there's something else I can't put a finger on. Conner didn't deny being cozy with Scarface. How could he? But I can read people like a People magazine and his face didn't read guilty when I popped him with the question about City Bar & Grill. Maybe Vic's stacking the deck, but maybe not. Maybe she doesn't have to. Maybe she's gearing up to kick ass with whatever accounts she gets. Which she will. Maybe I should too. And what the hell is up with Westerling? Our little chat really threw me for a loop. Whose side is he on? Or is he on anyone's side? He's a bean counter, but there must be a human being in there somewhere or he wouldn't have said what he did.

I still had more questions than answers, so I started over with Sorenstam and spun the wheel again trying to make sense of it.

It's been a full week since the announcement and it dawned on me I don't know any more now than I knew then. Maybe less.

"You coming, ace? We're going to be late."

My eyes popped open and I was startled to find Mikey Willard standing right in front of me. His usual playful mug was a study in serious.

"Uh, yeah. Right," I stammered as I pulled myself out of the chair. I felt like I was coming out of a deep sleep so I had to use the edge of the desk to steady myself. I guess deep thought is like deep sleep, but I don't think deep that much so I wouldn't know.

Mikey broke into a half grin watching me struggle. He could tell I was in a bad way and the hard slap on the back he gave me as we were walking out the door was just what I needed. Maybe a little more than I needed because it knocked the wind out of me. But it worked. After a few steps I started to find my stride.

"You have a couple of beers at lunch, E.C.?"

"I wish. No, just a couple of Costco dogs and a Coke."

Mikey eyed me carefully. I don't get a case of nerves very often, but he's the kind of guy who can do that to you. He obviously wanted an explanation, and I know from experience you can't put much over on Mikey so I gave it to him straight.

"Been doing a lot of thinking, Mikey. This reorg has had me screwed up tight and I'm not sure which end is up anymore. Not sure who to trust."

We were walking toward the conference room at a pretty good clip but Mikey hadn't taken his eyes off me once. I prayed Sue Ann wasn't around the next corner and kept talking.

"I don't know what it is, Mikey. Maybe I'm scared of losing my job. Maybe I'm scared of keeping it. Hell, maybe I'm scared of myself."

What came out of my mouth surprised me but sounded suspiciously like the truth, so for the first time since we left my office I risked looking Mikey straight in the eyes.

"Yeah, well there's a small group of people who feel like that. It's called everybody. And we all paddle around in the same boat," he said with a hard stare but soft eyes.

I wasn't aware of how we got there but suddenly realized we were at the door to the conference room. He turned to face me and this time I got the full Mikey Willard grin. And a much more pleasant slap on the shoulder.

"Everything's going to be fine, E.C. Just fine."

For the first time in a week I felt like it would, and with that he ambled in ahead of me. I tailed Mikey in and scoped the room to see if I was the last one. Really I was looking for Darlene. I figured my Casual Friday outfit would be a sight for those beautiful eyes, and my heart sank when I discovered everyone was there but her and the Jerk.

As usual, only the crappy chairs were left so I settled into a vintage black model with a bad gash in the seat and no padding on one armrest. This one tilted back too far but I could at least adjust the height of the seat. And it still swiveled alright, but complained bitterly every time it did. I was on the far side of the table where I could keep an eye on the door and near to the end where Girard always sits, which would put me in close proximity to Darlene. Just where I like to be. Sue Ann was on my right and the only thing standing between me and those two empty seats. Except she was sitting.

"Hi, E.C." she said giving my outfit another gander. I could tell she had more to say but she just shook her head in disbelief and smiled.

I smiled back and nodded, rubbing my eyes to adjust to the fluorescent light. Straight across from me was Westerling with Vicky on his left. I let out a soft snort at the now familiar sight of those two huddled over his laptop. Vic was pointedly pointing at something and he was nodding slowly but with a whole lot of conviction. Obviously they were in total agreement about that something. It struck me as odd they'd still be rigging the game just before kickoff but they seemed pleased with the finishing touch whatever it was. Westerling looked up at her and they shared a quick laugh.

Mikey was on Westerling's right and already on his phone playing Candy Crush. He loves that game. I'm pretty sure the world has moved on from that craze but Mikey's a lifer. Girard never calls on Mikey to talk in these meetings so he's just killing time, and I suppose Candy Crush is as good a way as any.

I scanned back to the head of the table and Scott was there across from where Darlene will be. He was on his phone too but locked eyes with me when I looked his way. His cold stare and blank expression told me he hadn't found any of the love we'd lost. He probably hadn't even looked. I gave him a half-hearted, two-finger salute and pivoted to my left where Conner was parked. He was staring at me too. I guess it was just my day.

"You feeling okay?"

He seemed to mean it.

"Not really."

"You still worried about losing City?"

"No, lunch," I said with a smirk trying to throw him off.

Conner cracked a slight smile, but before he could get anything out his eyes darted to the front of the conference room. Mine didn't dart but they followed right behind. It was ten after and Girard was late. Of course. He marched in with his awkward arrogant strut but I didn't pay attention. My eyes were on the gorgeous dame to his left. Darlene loves Casual Friday and today she was in a pair of tight red jeans with white Chuck Taylor high-tops and a loose-fitting, white cable-knit sweater. The contrast of baggy top with tight pants sure is sexy, but I don't like tight tops with baggy pants so maybe it's not the contrast. Anyway, my heart tried to pound its way out of my chest when she shot me a glance and a quick wink.

"Sorry I'm late," Girard boomed.

Girard always says that. He's always late, and I think by now you know he's not at all sorry. He'd like us to think he was on the horn with a big customer, or the CEO, or Jay-Z, or somebody, but he was probably just picking kale out of his teeth. Nobody said anything in response because we're all used to the drill, and even if somebody *had* said something I wouldn't have noticed because I was watching Darlene shuffling papers, straightening the edges with sharp raps on the conference table. Just then she reminded me of Ava Gardner in *Night of the Iguana.* I don't recall any paper shuffling in that one but for some reason that's what came to mind. I love that movie. Richard Burton was great too, wrestling with a guilty conscience. But for God's sake, why be a priest when you can hang out at that Mexican beach hotel with Ava? Seriously.

Girard put his phone on the table and opened his laptop. He stared at the little screen for a moment, then shifted his beady eyes to the bigger one, and back again. This went on for a minute and the room was so quiet you could hear a pin drop. Not that anyone's ever heard a pin drop. Especially on carpet. I know it's just a figure of speech, but let's face it, that would be hard to hear.

Anyway, it was quiet in the room.

"I'm expecting a call but let's get started," Girard said finally without looking away from the two screens. "Darlene?"

At this, Darlene stood up and made her way around the room handing out a handout. When she got to me, I looked up hoping for a little eye contact but hers were checking my jeans and boots. Her eyebrows were arched and I thought she was going to comment positively on my attire, but she just dropped the spiral-bound booklet in front of me and moved on without a word, leaving behind a trace of tropical fragrance. I'm no tropical fruit expert but it smelled like mango or papaya. Or maybe it was some other exotic fruit I'm unaware of. They're called exotic for a reason, right? Whatever it was, I wanted a taste and was picturing Darlene in a sarong when Girard interrupted my reverie.

"In front of you is the United Food Distributors Reorganization Plan to Stimulate Competition and Increase Sales."

It was in large bold type on the cover page so we had figured that out already, but he still looked around the room with his bushy eyebrows raised in case there were any questions. Or in case we couldn't read. Mikey and I were already thumbing through the plan and I could tell Girard was getting worked up.

"Let's go through this together, shall we? So we're all on the same page," he said looking directly at me.

I closed my handout and smiled. He glanced at his phone again and looked like he was ready to pass more gas, but before he could speak I stood up. The chair complained loudly when I did and everyone's head snapped around to look at me. This was the first time Darlene felt the full impact of my Casual Friday look and I could tell she was impressed with its ruggedness. That made me feel even *more* ready for what was about to happen.

"Before you start, Jack, I want something off my chest."

I had everyone's attention when I stood up, but my announcement turned expressions of curiosity and idle interest to something else altogether, and I couldn't make out what it was. They were still curious alright, and interested too, but what was written on their faces wasn't idle. I paused just long enough to make Girard uncomfortable and stop looking at his phone, and he turned to face me as well.

"I've been a real horse's ass this past week."

That line brushed aside the cobwebs in the back of my brain and rushed out of my mouth. I guess the group hadn't seen it coming because more than one head cocked to the side. Truth is I hadn't seen it coming either, but I kept my head screwed on straight with little or no cocking.

"I've given some of you a bum steer."

Setting aside confusion over horses and cattle, I started with Sorenstam and let my eyes land briefly on everyone as I worked my around the table.

"People who didn't deserve it. People I've known for a long time. Friends of mine."

I stopped short of giving Girard eye contact and instead lingered for a moment on Darlene's. They were open wide now and locked on mine. Not the cold hard eyes I saw in the car Wednesday night but soft and warm. I skipped eyeballing Girard because honestly there's no steer that's too bum for him.

"And believe it or not, I've been an even bigger ass to myself."

I realized for the first time that's the real truth and paused before continuing.

"I've sweated bullets for the past week trying to figure this thing out. Who's playing what game, and with who. The truth is

I've got no idea where *you all* stand on this reorg and it doesn't really matter." I said letting my eyes tour the table again.

"Now I know where *I* stand. This reorg is bad news. Not just for me. Not for any one person in this room. For *all* of us," I said swinging both arms out. "For the company."

For the first time since I started speaking my eyes landed on Girard. Hard.

"And especially for *you.*"

Girard was staring at me and I couldn't tell if he was ready to explode or crawl under the table. I had a lot more to add and plenty of good reasons to back me up, but before I could say anything, Girard's phone started to play *Live and Let Die.* Of course that's his ringtone. He squinted at it and held up one finger giving the universal signal for *I gotta take this one.* As he was walking out of the room, he hunched over in a bow of obedience and clearly said "Yes, sir," so we all knew it must be Stoddard.

Everyone watched Girard leave and then started exchanging nervous glances. I wanted to catch Darlene's eye but she was whispering something to Sue Ann. Westerling was nodding knowingly at Vic, Scott was checking his phone, and Dan mumbled, "Well, well, well" under his breath. And when I finally looked at Mikey, he arched one interested eyebrow at me before going back to crushing candy. When the chatter died, I noticed everyone staring at me again and realized I was still standing. With a sheepish grin I sat down. This time, whatever weak life force had been holding up my chair seat flickered out, and with a soft whoosh I dropped slowly to the lowest possible height. My grin got a lot more sheepish.

I looked back Darlene's way and she had those deep pools of hazel trained on me with a sweet smile on her face. I smiled back and nodded. She could've been smiling because my head and shoulders now barely reached the tabletop, but I figured she must've been pretty impressed with my speech and couldn't wait to hear the rest of the story over a couple of drinks.

"What do you think that's all about?" came a voice from behind me.

When I swiveled around Conner was staring at his phone.

"What's *what* all about?" I snapped back, annoyed I had lost eye contact with Darlene.

Dan swiped his phone off and looked down at me.

"Girard? The phone call?"

He was clearly annoyed too, but with me for playing dumb. I tried to focus on the issue at hand and when the gears finally meshed I realized he may be on to something.

"Well, he'd probably take a call from Stoddard during a meeting anyway, but obviously he knew that one was coming," I said without really knowing what that meant.

Girard goes ape if anyone takes a call during a meeting but he does it all the time. Another one of his little power trips. Conner now had his left elbow on the table with his cheek on his fist and was staring at me looking for answers.

"If that's true, the timing is a little weird don't you think?"

I knew he was right but it still didn't add up.

"Yeah," I said flatly. "If it was a scheduled call you'd think they'd work it around the meeting."

Dan was nodding like I was still a couple steps behind him when suddenly my spine started to tingle. Nothing was running up or down. It just tingled.

"Maybe I'm imagining things, but it seemed like Westerling knew the call was coming too. Also knew what it was about."

I was talking more to myself than Dan, and the picture was still blurry but felt like it was coming into focus. "And Vic acted like she was in on the deal."

Before Conner could respond, Girard walked back in and stopped at the head of the table. All eyes turned to him. With his knuckles resting on the tabletop and furrows in his brow, he took a deep breath and we all assumed was going to talk about the elephant in the room. But it wasn't an elephant on his mind. It was me.

"Poole, why don't you get another chair?"

Everyone turned toward me and I could hear the soft chuckling of voices high and low. I've played the fool before, and I don't mind doing it if it serves my purpose, but being neck high to a conference table in an important meeting didn't serve any purpose except to make me look short. And stupid. I didn't say anything to Girard and quickly traded my recently deceased black chair for a faded blue one stashed against the wall. One that I discovered didn't rock, swivel, or go up and down. I wanted to pay another visit to the used chair lot but Girard was clearly impatient and ready to start his address.

"That was Ray Stoddard on the phone," he said to no one's surprise. "Looks like you and Vicky were right, Mark."

Girard was looking straight at Westerling now, and so was everyone else.

"Consolidated tried it four years ago. Their revenue dipped a few points, they lost a bunch of good people, and their stock took a hit. They scrapped it after only ten months. I guess a dozen other Fortune 500s tried it too and then walked it back."

Girard returned his attention to the rest of us, but my mind was racing to catch up to the news flash.

Consolidated? Tried what? The same reorg? Must've been just after I left.

"Mr. Stoddard has officially pulled the plug on Gloria's plan," he continued, somehow sounding relieved and disappointed at the same time. "In fact he's pulled the plug on Gloria as well. Apparently she plagiarized most of her thesis, and that whole theory had been debunked anyway. Ray's pretty hot about it. Now he's looking for a new sales and marketing veep."

You could see a twinkle in Girard's eyes. He's always wanted to get the call from corporate, and can see his name on the door of that VP office. Probably already picking out the over-sized furniture. My mind was reeling and I just stared blankly at Girard to give it time to recover. Or unreel. Or whatever it needed to do.

"Mark, Vicky, that was good work crunching those numbers and shooting holes in the plan. I'm just glad I was able to sell it to Ray."

Typical Girard. Nowhere to be found when there's somebody to blame, but always first in line to take credit even when somebody else deserves it. Vic had a smile frozen on her face and I could tell she was proud, but pissed off too. To my great surprise, Westerling looked right at me and rolled his eyes.

Thinking back on all those times I spied Mark and Vic huddled up made sense now. Especially the meeting with Girard in Westerling's office. The Jerk was too stupid to understand what they were trying to tell him, and too scared to take it to Stoddard. I'll bet they made an end run around him and pitched headquarters themselves. Maybe Stoddard, but more likely the CFO. Westerling and him are real chummy.

I figured it would all come out in the wash but it didn't matter anyway. The reorg was dead. It seemed like my speech was a waste of breath but I was glad I did it anyway. I turned to face Dan and he gave me a thumbs up under the table.

"I guess it goes without saying, but the reorg is off," Girard announced pompously. "You all will keep your current accounts, and I expect great things this quarter because you know your customers so well." His upper lip curled into a sneer and he raised both eyebrows, daring us to defy his great expectations.

Don't get your hopes up you jerk. You're going to get what you get every quarter.

"Darlene, why don't you collect those handouts?" he said as if that would've never occurred to her. "I've got to jump on a conference call with Ray and the other directors. We'll go over sales reports next Friday. Meeting over folks."

With that, he straightened his collar, puffed his puny chest up best he could, and strutted out of the room. Everyone was silent for a moment and we all exchanged glances again. This time for a really good reason.

"You guys rock!"

It was Dan who broke the ice. And quite nearly my left ear drum. He stood up, slapped me on the back, and marched around to the other side of the table. Without thinking, I stood up and followed him. He shook hands with Westerling, who was still seated, and when Vic stood up to greet him he gave her a great big hug. I squeezed Mikey's shoulder on my way past and made a beeline for Vicky.

"You're my hero, girl scout," I whispered in Vic's ear as I took my turn hugging her. I mouthed "I'm sorry" to Mark and he shrugged and gave me a wide smile. I don't remember ever seeing him smile and it actually looked pretty good on him. I could see he's got good teeth.

Scott had been waiting his turn with Vicky and I impulsively grabbed him and hugged him too. Luckily he hugged me back.

"Sorry I was such an ass, Scott," I said stepping back and holding him at arm's length.

"You already said that, E.C." He had broken into a broad grin. "You were. But I appreciate the apology. Let's forget it."

"Right. Okay. Thanks."

When Dan had finished thanking Mark, he and I locked eyes and both started laughing before falling into a bear hug. More of a bro hug actually. Still it was a pretty serious hug.

"Dan, I'm sorry," I started to sputter but he raised his hand.

"Shut up, dawg," he said in mock anger.

We laughed, and I realized any remaining hard feelings for Vic and Scott and Dan had evaporated. Things started to change when I finally found my spine, and killing the reorg flushed them right out of my system. I still wasn't sure what was going on with Dan and Scarpetti, or Scott and Girard for that matter, but it didn't matter now anyway. Whatever it was shouldn't have stuck in my craw like it did. And I don't think I even have a craw.

"That was pretty impressive, big guy."

I spun on my heels and found myself face to face with Darlene. Before I could say anything she gave me a warm hug and a long kiss on the cheek. I may never wash that cheek again. The strange thing is I don't recall ever washing my cheeks. Not the ones on my face at any rate. I mean I'm sure I do, but it's just one of those things you do in the shower that doesn't really register. Not like washing your hair or your toes. Or the nether regions. Anyway, I'm not washing that particular cheek any time soon.

"I just decided to stop acting like a baby is all," I said. "And I owe you one for making me realize I was."

"I like it better when you act like a man."

The smile she wore looked suspiciously like an invitation, but before I could put any words together Mikey boomed out an invitation of his own.

"Ladies and germs, I think this calls for a couple rounds at Manning's. Whaddya say?"

"Let's go," Darlene cooed.

Let's do.

19

To say that Tui was happy to see us is an understatement. Any restaurant manager is happy seeing eight thirsty people walk into their bar, but not many of them start clapping and jumping up and down. He gave every one of us a crushing hug, and they weren't bro hugs either. I went last hoping he'd be tired after seven of them, but when I whispered that the reorg was off he gave me the longest and hardest hug of all. We all filed into the Manning's bar wearing his cologne, and I realized Tui was dancing again, this time to Bruno Mars.

Stylin', wilin', livin' it up in the city. Got Chucks on with Saint Laurent. Gotta kiss myself I'm so pretty.

I exchanged nods with the same bartender from yesterday. He gave me a loose smile and shook his head as Tui danced by.

It was a sunny fall afternoon but chilly and windy. Still, there were a few hardy souls out on the patio. Hardy fools if you ask me. Mikey and Dan looked like they were headed outside but the ladies didn't call for a vote and deposited themselves on a banquette in the far corner of the warm bar. Tui stopped dancing long enough to pick up a heavy marble-top table like it was an empty cardboard box and nestled it together with the one that was already there. Dan shot one last wistful look at the patio before he and Mikey admitted defeat and joined us. Tui blew us all a kiss and danced out to the last refrain from *Uptown Funk.*

Saturday night and we in the spot. Don't believe me just watch. Come on. Don't believe me just watch.

It sounded like Bruno knew just where we were. It was Friday night, and it wasn't even night yet, but still. It was quarter to four, the bar was almost full, the music was loud, and the reorg was just a bad dream. We *were* in the spot. A tall, black cocktail waitress with high cheekbones and the grace of a ballet dancer came by to get our drink order. She was all legs and drop-dead gorgeous, so Mikey had to pick his jaw up off the floor before he could stammer out he wanted a shot of tequila and a Corona. Mikey always drinks Cuervo Gold but when she asked for his preference in tequila he ordered Patron. She gave him a smile and nod of approval, then turned her attention to me.

"Macallan Fifteen. One cube."

She arched an eyebrow and said, "Nice."

When I turned back to the table, Darlene was staring a hole through my head. She was directly across from me and wore that little smile with a corner of her mouth up and lips puffed out. My mind drifted ahead to Saturday night and it wondered if she had plans. I know I should've asked her out before but something's been eating me for a long time. Something I couldn't figure. Whatever it was, it was dead and gone now, and I couldn't wait to be out on the town with that beautiful dame on my arm. I was going to ask her tonight for sure.

Don't believe me just watch.

That would have to wait until later, so I just gave her a wink and punched Mikey playfully in the arm. Like I've said, I don't really know my own strength, and it must not have been playful enough because he hit me back. Hard. I winced and groaned in spite of myself. Mikey actually *was* a Golden Glove champion.

"Back to business as usual, brother," I said casually, wondering if Mikey's punch would leave a mark. I don't know if I told you but I bruise easily too. "With any luck the Jerk will get Summerhill's job and we'll be rid of him for good."

I shot a self-conscious look at Darlene. I'm pretty sure she feels the same way I do about Girard, but she's been his secretary for over a year and probably doesn't appreciate all the nasty remarks directed his way. Or at least doesn't feel like she can join the party. Fortunately, she was leaning across Scott and laughing about something with Sue Ann so I didn't need to worry about any bruised feelings. I was more worried about my arm. I could see Scott was the one who was really worried though. Darlene was brushing up against him as she talked to Sue Ann and he was trying his best to disappear into the banquette. Knowing Scott, he'll probably tell Angela he had an office fling.

Suddenly I felt a presence behind me and caught a subtle whiff of fragrance that definitely wasn't Tui's Eau de Sledgehammer cologne. The black beauty had returned with our drinks and mine appeared in front of me before I had the chance to look up. Three fingers of Macallan and a single large ice cube. Today I wasn't interested in beer. I wanted the big boy drink.

The first sip of silky, smoky scotch slipped down my throat. It burned a little and made my eyes water. I liked it. I glanced up and caught Darlene smiling at me again as she was bringing a pink Cosmo up to her lips. The color of the drink and her lipstick were a perfect match and I got lost somewhere in between. Her eyes stayed glued to mine as I joined her in taking another sip.

"I'd like to propose a toast!"

The familiar loud voice snapped me back. Dan Conner was holding up a pint in his hand.

"To our saviors, Vicky and Mark," he said grandly with a broad smile, nodding in their direction. "The only ones smart enough to know what was wrong with the reorg, and strong enough to do something about it. Cheers mates!"

"Yeah, cheers," I echoed without much enthusiasm.

Yeah, and I was too dumb and too weak.

Hiding the hurt inside, I forced a smile during the tangled round of toasting. Everyone took a drink and this time my sip turned into a swig. When the hubbub died down, I turned to my left and slapped Mark on the back. And gave Vic a chin up and a *you go, girl.* When I turned back, Mikey had the full attention of our waitress and was ordering happy hour food. All of it as far as I could tell. Mikey likes to eat. When he finally finished and the dancer sashayed away, he turned to his right and continued a conversation with Dan they must've started before the toast.

"That's a big crew to take to Mexico, amigo. All those niños?"

It sounded like a playful warning, and Dan's smile confirmed that it was.

"It's a big crowd every year, Mikey. That's what alcohol is for. We just decided this year we might as well soak up some sun while you and everyone else are slogging through slush and shivering around the fire. I'll think about you when I'm sweating by the pool and drinking one of those giant margaritas."

"Thanks for *that* image, Slim," Mikey said redirecting his attention back to the Patron.

I got a funny feeling I was better off not knowing the answers but started asking questions anyway.

"Sounds good to me. I'm in. Where we going?"

Dan wiped foam off his upper lip and peered around Mikey.

"Cabo, baby. And you ain't coming. Unless you want to be my cabana boy."

"Sure. I can sling towels and carry drinks, but your giant margarita will be half gone by the time it arrives. Who all's going on this surfing safari?"

"Me and Sue and the kids, and Johnny and Sophie and their brood. A baker's dozen my friend."

My blood had already started to run cold, but now it turned to ice.

"Johnny? Do I know him?"

"Johnny Scarpetti?" Dan leaned all the way around Mikey and locked a look on me. "The new Portland veep for PRC? You do know that, right? We went to high school together in Bellevue. Been best friends ever since."

He kept talking but the words were bouncing off the walls of my brain like racquetballs. I was wondering if people even play racquetball anymore when Dan served up an ace.

"We get together every year at Christmas for a few days. Trade off who's house gets trashed. This year we decided to take the wrecking crew to Cabo. Johnny and I've been planning it for a couple of weeks now. It's a surprise and we're going to spring it on Sue and Sophie and the kids at Thanksgiving."

He and I must've come to the same realization at the same time because his puzzled look turned into a big, fat grin that stretched ear to ear.

"You think I was gunning for your account, E.C.? Is that it?"

Mikey turned to look at me too, sporting his signature grin. Now I was staring down both barrels of a shotgun grin. Guns don't scare me but grins do. I tried to join the grin party but I couldn't find anything to wear, so all I could do was rest my right elbow on the table and hold my forehead.

"Yeah," I muttered, trying to make it all go away.

I switched to my left hand and turned to face the music. Dan and Mikey were still grinning, even wider now which I wouldn't have thought possible. I finally managed a half grin of my own, but couldn't force any words so I just kept shaking my head.

"Hey, cabana boy. I need another drink," Dan said laughing.

"Bring me one too," Mikey chimed in snapping his fingers.

I realized my glass was empty and another scotch was just what the doctor ordered. "Si, señores," I said with a head bob and rose from my chair to search for our server. I didn't get far because another one was right behind me with a tray of drinks headed for another table that I damn near knocked off her arm. Thankfully, she was able to save it without spilling a drop.

"You break it you buy it, E.C."

I was surprised to hear that come out of Westerling's mouth but was grateful for the diversion and joined in the laughter around the table at my expense. I could see Darlene for the first time in a while and noticed she wasn't laughing. Instead she had one of those looks that dames give guys sometimes. The *aww, you're cute* look. Guys can't figure that one. Is it because we're acting like a little kid and we really *are* being cute? Is it because we're doing something off the wall and they think it's sexy? Or is it we're being stupid and they know it? It's probably all three but how the hell would we know? They'll never give up *that* secret.

I spent five long minutes hiding my face from Dan and keeping my eyes peeled for our waitress until she and Tui emerged from the kitchen with our food order. After all the plates managed to find a spot on the table, Mikey gave the whirling forefinger signaling for another round of drinks. Most people were already digging into the wings and dips and deep-fried whatever, but the Costco dogs weren't sitting well and I figured this was a good time to hit the john. Unless I missed my hunch, the food would be gone by the time I got back, but another Macallan would be waiting. That was fine by me.

It was almost five now and business had picked up, but the men's room was nearly empty. There was a guy using the urinals, so I took up position at the other end of the line. You don't take the one right next door unless you have to. Guys just don't do that. I hadn't seen him leave the table, but when I glanced over I saw it was Scott Sorenstam. I gave him a nod and grinned but he didn't return the gesture. I was thinking maybe he was still sore but when he cocked his head toward me I could see he was on his phone.

"That's great, Chef. I really appreciate it. Jack's tied up right now but I'll call him later and let him know. You're the best."

Scott's soft spoken but his words ricocheted off the tile walls like bullets and I clearly heard every single one. The call was over but he still had the phone pinched between his chin and shoulder while he zipped up. Why do people think it's okay to have a phone conversation while they're going to the bathroom? Don't they think people can tell? Don't they care? I hear it going on in stalls all the time too. I mean, chatting while you're doing number one is bad enough, but number two? Are you kidding me?

Anyway, Scott slipped the phone in his pocket and I finally got the return nod and grin as we both headed for the sinks.

"Who was that?" I asked.

I was starting to get the jumps again.

"Chef Bernard at the Excalibur in Eugene," he replied without looking up from some serious hand washing. "Girard's nephew wants to be a chef and Bernie's agreed to let him intern in the kitchen when the kid gets out of school next summer."

The bad feeling I got when Dan told me about his vacation with Scarpetti came flooding back. I was waving my hand in front of the towel dispenser, hoping to buy some time while drying, but nothing was coming out. I finally realized it wasn't one of the electronic kinds. I hate it when that happens. You look like a fool standing there waving at a towel dispenser like it's a loved one leaving on a long trip. This was the kind of dispenser you have to pull down gently so another one pops out. Nobody ever pulls down gently though, so you always have to work the little wheel to make a towel appear. And the wheels are always slimy so then you feel like you have to wash again. Anyway, I finally got a couple of towels out and started wiping my hands as I turned to face Scott. He was just finishing up.

"I guess it shouldn't surprise me but it sure bugs me," he said as we pushed our way out the men's room door.

"What's that?" I asked, immediately wishing I hadn't.

"Girard never talks to me. Never. I mean he talks to me at the meeting, although usually not unless he's making me feel bad because I missed quota, but never outside the meeting. Not even a hello in the hall."

"Me neither. I guess we should consider ourselves lucky," I offered weakly.

Scott stopped just as we reached the entrance to the bar.

"But three weeks ago he calls me out of the blue, on a Saturday. I'm at a soccer game and I tell him I'll call him back but he just keeps talking. Girard's sister lives in Eugene and she and her husband love the Excalibur. Go there all the time. Her boy Jerome wants to be a chef, so she tells Girard she wants him to work at Excalibur. And Girard tells me."

I was just staring dumbly at Scott. I had it all added up already but there was more to the story so I let him go.

"He figures Bernie owes United a favor. For what? Paying us a half million dollars a year? Anyway, that put me in a real bind.

Girard's been calling me twice a day every day. God bless Chef Bernie. He knew I was in trouble if I couldn't pull this off so he agreed to take little Jerry. How do you like that?"

I didn't. Now I was going to have to pick even more buckshot out of my hide. Maybe next week I'd come clean and tell him what I thought he was doing talking to Girard, but I was all out of sorry right now so I just shook my head and put a hand on Scott's shoulder to steer him back into the bar.

"What a jerk," he muttered under his breath. He was talking about Girard but the punch landed on *my* chin.

The scotch was a welcome sight when we got back to the table, but as I suspected little remained of the appetizers. I grabbed the last Buffalo wing, a few scrawny celery sticks, a handful of tortilla chips, and the last smear of guacamole. It didn't make for a pretty plate. The chips were colorful enough because they were the red and blue ones that nobody likes, but as I said, the celery sticks were scrawny and the last wing was the bony kind, not one of the little drumsticks. I love those things. But so does everybody else.

I took a good, long pull on the Macallan and forced a smile for Darlene, who was eying me with an inquisitive frown. Dames know when a guy's not right. Just seeing her made me feel better though, and I decided it was time to stand up and say something. Again. But the chair incident was still fresh in my mind, so I decided to remain seated and banged my glass with a fork.

"I said earlier I'd been a jerk," I started, again not knowing where I was headed. Conversation gradually died down and I waited for all eyes to find me.

"Seems I didn't know just how big a jerk I'd been. Not only did I throw in the towel before the fight even started, but I threw all my friends under the bus."

I realized immediately that was too much throwing for one sentence, but it felt like I was catching some wind so I plowed ahead anyway.

"You know, Girard's a pain in the ass but so what? United's like every other company on the planet and guys like the Jerk are a dime a dozen. The thing is, we're playing a team sport and I was playing for myself."

I could feel Darlene's eyes on me but couldn't risk meeting them, so I stayed focused on Vic and Mark and Scott and Dan. And the celery sticks.

"All of you tried to tell me this one way or another, but I gotta say it was that stupid poster about winners never quitting and quitters never winning that finally woke me up. I was being a quitter. And I sure wasn't winning. Not with any of you." My eyes finally fell on Darlene. "And most of all not with the man in the mirror."

By this time, half of the bar was watching and listening and I was starting to sweat, so I figured I'd better wrap things up. Besides, I wanted another drink.

"I really just want to say I'm sorry. And I want to say thanks. Thanks for putting up with me, for slapping me around when you got tired of putting up with me, and for propping me up when I needed it most. Thanks for being my friends."

With that I picked up my glass and saluted everyone at the table before draining the scotch. Nobody had said a word yet, so more out of embarrassment than thirst I held up my glass and rattled the ice cube while looking around the bar.

"Nurse!"

Our lovely waitress, who had caught my entire act, smirked and turned to go get more medicine.

When I looked back at Darlene I saw a vision of beauty with tears in her eyes. I'm no crybaby, but that choked me up so I grabbed a celery stick and chomped down trying to keep a handle on myself. Tears came to my eyes anyway, but mostly because I bit the side of my cheek so hard I could taste blood. I grabbed the blue cheese dressing from the empty wing platter and scooped some into my mouth with what little remained of the celery stick, but that didn't hide the taste or stop the bleeding. Despite the explosion of bloody blue cheese flavor I managed a smile and deep nod for Darlene. I wanted to mouth *I love you* but figured it was too early for that. I also figured blood and blue cheese dribbling out of my mouth wouldn't be sexy.

Suddenly I was aware of the world around me again and turned to Mikey on my right. He'd been watching the whole thing and was eyeballing me with that slightly wicked but kind and worldly-wise grin.

"Nice speech, E.C. You been practicing that one too?"

"Nope. Did it sound like it?"

"No. No, not at all. It sucked," he said through a chuckle. "But it sounded like it came from your heart. And that's better."

With that he patted me on the shoulder and finished the last of his Patron.

"Now shut up and forget it will you? Please?"

Even when it's in a million little pieces and you don't know where to start, leave it to Michael Willard to put the world back together for you.

"Thanks, Mikey," was all I could muster. I turned to Darlene, who was hanging on every word, and gave her a wink to let her know I was okay. I was more than okay. Chucky's back. And he's in love. I can mend the fence with Scott soon enough, but right now all I wanted to do was step outside with Darlene and make a date for tomorrow night. Or try to at any rate.

I looked around the crowded Manning's bar and saw lots of pretty girls getting plied with stiff drinks by cocky young guys in Joseph A. Bank suits who knew happy hour was winding down. A few people were reaching for their wallets and digging in their purses. I excused myself again to go to the men's room and check on the gash in my mouth that was still bleeding, but on the way I slipped Tui my American Express Rewards Gold Card and told him it was all on me. And it was. Tui had been keeping an eye on things, and I could tell he wanted to hug me again, but I hightailed it to the john before he had the chance.

Turns out the oral damage was worse than I thought, and there was no way I was going to stop the bleeding right now. I considered stuffing toilet paper in my cheek but figured that might queer my chances for a date with Darlene. Medical attention would just have to wait. When I got back to the table, there was a riot of protest going on and Tui was trying to put down the insurrection with a big smile on his face and his hands up like he was being robbed. When he saw me coming he turned and fingered me. The rat. He handed me the check folder and gave me the hug I was trying to avoid.

"E.C.! You are *not* doing this." Vicky wasn't the only one saying it, just the loudest.

"Sorry. Did it," I said writing in a big tip for the tall drink of water and scrawling my signature.

By this time, everybody was on their feet and I just waved my hand to quiet them and turned towards the door. There wouldn't be any arguments about who owes who and how much. Not today. As we slowly made our way out, everyone thanked me for paying the tab, and also for the ham-handed apology. Everyone except Darlene that is. After failing to escape one more hug from Tui, I was the last one out the door. I can't even say what was happening in my poor confused spine when I thought I'd missed Darlene, but when I got outside she was waiting for me. Amid the last few shouted goodbyes as people headed for their cars, she grabbed me by the collar with both hands.

"It takes a big man to admit he's wrong. Even bigger to do it in public like that."

She had tears in her eyes again. I was afraid I might blow a gasket too so I didn't wait for her to get the waterworks going.

"You got any plans for tomorrow night, doll?" I asked as casually as I could. Which wasn't very.

"Yeah. Should I break them?"

"That's up to you."

"What'd you have in mind, blue eyes?"

"You know. You. Me. Drinks. Dinner." I said with a shrug. She had a big smile but didn't answer. She just giggled.

"Is that a yes?" I'm usually pretty sure of myself around dames but this time I wasn't so sure.

"Yes it's a yes, stupid."

I guess I wasn't done acting stupid this week but still managed a shaggy grin.

"Pick you up at six?"

"I'll be ready," she said pulling me closer and giving me a quick kiss. This time on the lips.

Not as ready as me, doll. Not as ready as me.

The dream is the same of course but this time the ending is different. I now know why the bull is staring at me. I know what he's saying. His charges come in slow motion and I hear loud choruses of olés as I work smoothly and effortlessly with the cape. Each pass closer and closer to my body. Tired of the chase, the bull stops and turns to face me.

Suddenly I'm holding a huge sword and again invite the last charge. The crowd roars when he accepts and bears down on me at full speed. I know I must avoid the right horn and wait for the exact moment. After what seems like eternity, he is upon me and our eyes meet, but this time I stand my ground. I rise between the horns, directly over his head, and plunge the sword down between the shoulders and into his heart. His knees buckle and he crumples slowly to the ground. El Toro is dead. I feel sad but proud, and when I look up I see only white handkerchiefs waving in the bright sun. And Darlene's face with a smile as she offers me a rose.

Honor and love make life worth living.

20

When I woke the sheets were tangled, and my blanket was clutched in one hand and draped on the floor. Another big dream I guess, but it must've been a good one because I had a smile on my face. Even songbirds hanging on to summer were singing outside my window. I usually don't bother making the bed but today it seemed like a good idea for some reason and I enjoyed the work. The kitchen was sunny and warm, and Mr. Coffee and I had a good long talk about things, though what exactly I don't remember. And my pal Jimmy Dean took the edge off all the scotch I drank last night.

Most of Saturday went by without me really noticing.

I had called Chef Mercedes but she didn't pick up. I left her a message the reorg blew up in Summerhill's face, thanked her again for the email, and said I'd see her Monday for sure. I wished I'd gotten to talk to her but it felt good to tell somebody, especially my best customer. And I couldn't wait to see that Mediterranean smile Monday morning.

Around ten I went to the gym for a couple hours. I was in no mood for Zumba, so I just did a little lifting and core work while eyeing the dames on the Thigh Masters. Usually that's the best part of my workout but my heart wasn't in it today, it was somewhere else. I spent about twenty minutes on the elliptical, and as you know I hate the elliptical. I wondered what meathead PE major came up with that thing. Was the idea to make people look like drunk circus bears cross-country skiing for the first time? Anyway, I only did it because all the treadmills were in use and at least I didn't throw up this time.

When a treadmill did open up, I switched and jogged for forty minutes. It felt good to get a sweat going but it didn't end well. There was a hot tomato wearing yellow and black spandex on the one directly to my left, and I think she had eyes for me. There are bigger guys at 24-Hour Fitness but I'm nobody's weak sister so her attention didn't surprise me. I was really looking for a light jog but of course had to crank the speed up to eight because she was running at seven. Usually I like to cruise at five or six but I managed the eight okay without breathing too hard. Problem is, when I was done I didn't bother warming down or letting the conveyor belt stop and I forgot about the law of forward momentum, so when I stepped off to the side and put my left foot down, I pitched face first into the floor-to-ceiling mirrors in front of the treadmills. I quickly dropped to the mat and fired off about twenty push-ups to try and cover my mistake, but I'm pretty sure she didn't buy it because she was choking on a laugh.

Anyway, it wasn't a bad workout and at least I sweated out most of the Macallan. I would've showered at the gym but I had a one o'clock at the day spa in Lake Oswego and figured I'd need one after that too, so I just threw on my sweats and grabbed a bite to eat at Taco Bell on the way. I had time to spare and should've gone inside but it's a Taco Bell for chrissakes, and you sure don't want to run into anyone you know at Taco Bell. That's awkward. Even if it's fourth meal. Anyway, the food's okay there but I should've known better than to try and eat tacos in my car.

Luckily, there's one of those do-it-yourself car washes on Kerr Parkway, and after making change and shoving a hundred quarters into the machine, I was able to vacuum up most of the shredded cheese, lettuce, and taco shell bits. It didn't hurt to give the old Outback a fresh shine either. I even bought those little

ArmorAll wipes and tried to bring the fake leather back to life. Didn't bother to add up all the quarters but I probably could've made a down payment on a new car with the money. It was worth it though. Darlene deserves a proper chariot and I was satisfied with my work.

Sensuous Steam is a little day spa in a strip mall in downtown Lake Oswego. There really isn't much of a downtown Lake Oswego but the locals like to think so. I stopped in there by accident a couple years ago thinking it was an "adult store". I wasn't shopping for me, I was looking to find a gag gift for a bachelor party. Not that I'm a prude or anything. I mean, I think it's great they have stores for adults, I just don't think sex is a spectator sport is all. Chucky wants to be in the game. Anyway, the athletic-looking gal in a catsuit at the front desk talked me into a massage and a steam that day. She could've talked me into anything.

Today was special so I sprang for the *Me First* package, which includes a mud pack, exfoliation, steam, and a mani-pedi. Most guys wouldn't be comfortable doing that, but as you know I'm not most guys. It felt good and I was hoping Darlene would be close enough tonight to appreciate the manscaping. If I could get rid of the lingering hibiscus scent that is. Nice place the Sensuous Steam. *Make Some Me Time* is their tagline. Not a bad idea.

I gassed up the car and swung by the ATM at Umpqua Bank to gas up my wallet. The long shower I took when I got home took care of the hibiscus alright. I usually shower with Dove body wash because of my sensitive skin, but today I used a bar of Irish Spring. It's really harsh but that fresh Irish breeze will blow away any other scent within a mile radius. On the Internet they say it will even get rid of a rodent infestation. That's strong soap.

I put on a pair of black slacks, a silver shark-skin shirt, a black sport coat, and an old pair of black dress shoes, the same ones I wore to my wedding. When I had finished shining and lacing them up, I glanced at the clock and it read four forty-five. I don't remember much after that until I pulled up in front of Darlene's apartment building at six on the dot.

Saturday night traffic can be pretty bad, so I was proud of myself for allowing just the right amount of time. Darlene lives in the Rasmussen on NE 25th and Flanders. It's one of those old courtyard complexes from the twenties or thirties. They all have a U-shaped brick building, with tiny wrought-iron balconies you can't use, surrounding a carefully manicured lawn that only your grandmother could love. Sometimes they have benches so you can sit and admire the little shrubbery. Nobody does that of course because it would be weird, but you could. Anyway, they're all over Portland, most cities I guess, and they all look pretty much the same. Except the Rasmussen. Darlene lives there.

The buzzer was so loud it gave me a start when I pushed the button next to the carefully handwritten tag that read D. Camper. When her voice came on, it sounded rough and robotic through the old intercom but still wrapped around me like a velvet glove.

"Hi, E.C. The system's broken. I'll be right down to get you."

"Okay, doll."

I took a long time to carefully strike a casual pose leaning against the door jamb, and then I waited. When Darlene's legs came into view down the last flight of stairs I had the chance to drink it all in. She was wearing black leggings with a loose red sweater. But not that loose. She looked even better than I imagined driving over, and I had done a fair amount of imagining on the drive over.

"Hello, handsome," she said pulling me inside and giving me another quick kiss. "You clean up real good."

I stepped back and motioned with my hand from her head to her toes. From the brunette hair done up in a loose roll with a wisp hanging off to one side all the way down to the tips of her black high-heeled pumps.

"I'd better look good if I'm going to escort *this* around."

Darlene did a quick pirouette for my benefit, smiled and winked, then started up the steps motioning for me to follow.

"Sorry for the hike. It's only a couple of floors," she chirped without looking back.

I was sorry it was only a couple of floors because the view was nice from my current position. I could've gone another ten or twenty flights no problem. When she got to the top step, she wheeled around abruptly and I almost planted my face in that red sweater. Which would've been fine by me.

"That wasn't so bad," I said breathing heavily and beaming a broad smile.

She beckoned with a finger and I followed her down the hall. That musty smell old buildings have hung in the air, but inside her apartment it was carefully hidden by a faint feminine fragrance. The place was decorated just like you'd expect a dame to decorate a place. There were pretty paintings on the walls and fresh flowers in a vase on a stand inside the door. Across the room next to the leaded windows was a large, glass-topped formal dining table with high-backed white leather chairs, and a tall palm in a stone pot. In the middle of the room there was a big, overstuffed couch with jungle print fabric and matching overstuffed chair, and a low-slung glass-top coffee table over a bearskin rug. I was lost on that rug when Darlene's voice startled me.

"Do we have time for a drink, E.C.?"

"Sure."

I didn't make a reservation at the Fireside Steakhouse because I like to eat in the bar and there's always a seat to be had. Even if I'd booked a table and we were late I would've made time for a drink at Darlene's. She disappeared into the kitchen and I settled into the soft cushions of the couch. I pawed at the handful of magazines splayed out on the coffee table and picked up a *Cosmopolitan*. There's always a sex quiz in Cosmo, and I was tempted to take it, but chances are I'd ace the thing so I didn't bother. I thought maybe I should check out *Ten Things That'll Drive Him Crazy,* but that would drive me crazy, so I just rifled through the ads. There were plenty of pretty girls wearing next to nothing, pouting and posing with men who don't really look like men. The girls were too scrawny for my taste, and I wasn't interested tonight anyway, so I tossed the rag back on the pile just as Darlene returned with two tall glasses.

"Here you go, sweetie. I hope a scotch soda suits you."

She didn't wait for an answer and nestled up to me on the couch. She had a vodka tonic with lime and clinked my glass with a cute little flick of her wrist. I took a swig of mine and it tasted better than any drink I'd ever had.

"Suits me just fine, babe."

I swung my left leg up just a little and slid my arm across the back of the couch behind her neck. She moved a little closer. The stereo was whispering soft jazz and it felt like we'd been together on this couch, just like this, a thousand times. I almost kissed her out of habit. The look on her face said she wouldn't mind, but I figured there'd be time for that later.

"You smell fresh," she said leaning in a little closer.

I suddenly wished I'd skipped the Irish Spring but at least it was better than hibiscus.

"Thanks," I said cavalierly, "I shower at least once a week."

"Uh huh."

"How long you had these digs?" I asked idly to change the subject. The Irish breeze was still blowing pretty hard.

"Two and a half years."

"You like this neighborhood? It's kind of a long commute."

"Yeah, I like it just fine. It was a little sketchy when I moved in but it's all gentrified now. There are some cute shops and a few good restaurants up Glisan and over on Burnside. El Gato Loco is the best Mexican food in town, I think. You ever been there?"

"I'd love to try it," I said suggestively and took a big gulp of my drink that was a little too big.

She casually reached over and wiped away a couple drops that had found their way to my chin. She did it because it's second nature for dames but it sent a jolt through me, so I kept the small talk going while I tried to recover.

"You're Portland born and raised, right? What high school?" I asked, but I knew the answers already. It made me feel like a creep when I Googled her but I wanted to know who she was, where she was from, and what she'd been up to. I know a little bit about a lot of things but I didn't know enough about Darlene, and I wanted to know more. Hell, I wanted to know everything about her. Facebook probably would've been a better place to snoop but I'm not on Facebook. Never have been. Not even once. Social media has a lot of people hooked, some pretty bad. Off the deep end bad. That's not gonna happen to Chucky. If I want to know who likes who, or who likes what, or what somebody had for breakfast this morning at IHOP, I'll ask them.

"Hillsboro High," she said shaking a fist like it was a pom-pom. "Our family moved to the Sylvan area my senior year but I stuck it out at Hillhi. All my friends were there."

"And after that?"

"I went to Portland State for a year, then got married and my ex moved us to Vancouver." Darlene made a face like she just ate a bad clam. "The Couve. Vantucky."

The story of her life went on for fifteen minutes. I heard a few things I already knew, and found out a few things I didn't, but I was listening to her voice more than what she said. I wanted to keep that sultry voice talking but the clock in my head said it was time to hit the road, so I polished off the drink and placed it carefully on the glass table. I'd broken one of those before at a party and that wasn't going to happen tonight.

"Let's get something to eat, shall we?" I suggested with arched eyebrows.

"Sure," she purred. "Let me grab my coat."

She whisked the drinks away to the kitchen and rinsed the glasses out in the sink. I stood up when she returned.

"Give me a minute to freshen up?" she asked.

"Take your time."

I hunkered down on the arm of the couch to wait it out. Dames always want to freshen up. They spend hours on their hair and makeup but it's never good enough for them. She looked just fine to me but there must be details guys miss. My eyes toured the apartment for the second time and settled on the door to the bedroom where I could see Darlene's bed. It wore a silvery bedspread dropping to the floor and a pile of pillows a mile high. I got lost somewhere deep in those pillows and didn't hear doors opening and closing. When I snapped out of it, she was standing by the front door wearing a big smile and a long black overcoat. It looked like a million bucks and didn't try very hard to hide all the curves underneath.

"Let's go, maestro."

Nobody's ever called me maestro. I'm not even certain what that means, but it felt good when I tried it on for size so I just nodded and grinned and we stepped outside into the hallway.

Darlene locked the door behind us and slipped the keys into her black patent leather purse. With another wink and a smile we were down the stairs and out the door.

21

I opened the passenger door to the Outback and Darlene slid in gracefully. Buttoning my sport coat against the night chill, I swung around the back of the car, and when I got behind the wheel she gave me a sly smile.

"Last time I was in this seat it was a little different, wasn't it?"

I'll never forget *that* night, but I pretended I did and played it for a laugh.

"Yeah, it was raining."

"Jerk," she huffed, playfully cuffing the back of my head.

I shot her a grin, fired up the Outback, and we headed down Glisan street and onto East Burnside toward the city.

"The car smells nice. Did you clean this rattletrap for me?"

"I didn't want you passing out on the way to dinner."

She laughed with a snort and kissed my cheek.

"That's sweet," she cooed and settled back in her seat looking satisfied with the state of affairs.

Traffic was light at the moment and the rest of the drive went smoothly. Moonlight sparkled off the Willamette River as we crossed the Burnside Bridge and I turned my head to find Darlene staring out the side window. I caught a glimpse of her legs and decided I'd never get enough of them. And nearly drove up on the sidewalk. Luckily, my catlike reflexes and above-average driving skills saved us from plunging into the river and we safely made our way across the old bridge and up West Burnside.

It was quarter after seven when we pulled into the Fireside parking lot. I took the ticket from the valet and tugged Darlene's collar up around her neck as we made our way to the front door.

The Fireside Steakhouse is clubby and dark, just the way I like it. The whole restaurant is lit only by candles on the tables and the huge, crackling fireplace that dominates the dining room. Though it was dusky outside it took our eyes a moment to adjust. Which would explain why I smacked my elbow on the door jamb steering Darlene into the bar.

"Ow," she exclaimed loudly, wincing on my behalf.

I grinned at her bravely and flexed my arm a couple of times to process the pain. She tucked her arm in the crook of my injured elbow and rubbed it sympathetically with her other hand. Like most guys, I tensed my arm when she grabbed it to pump up my bicep. But not too much. I didn't want to scare her.

"Hey E.C., been a while."

My favorite Fireside bartender, Frank, was smiling at us while he stirred a drink. He motioned with his eyes toward a couple of open seats at the end of the bar. I smiled, shook my head no, and pointed to an empty booth in the corner. I've spent many nights sitting courtside with Frank, swapping lies and watching him work, but tonight Darlene deserved my undivided attention. He gave her a quick up and down and flashed me an approving grin as I pulled the table out to let her slide onto the leather.

The Fireside bar is a classic. The bar itself is a semi-circle with a sunken floor, so the bar stools aren't stools but leather swivel armchairs. And they actually swivel. I love those things. There's a long banquette with four tables, a couple of small two-tops along a brick wall, and a handful of small booths you can get lost in. There are grainy old photos of loggers standing beside big trees before they became logs, and it's all red leather and walnut wood and deep shag carpet. It's the kind of place where men used to drink strong drinks and smoke cigars and talk about business and sports and dames. You can't smoke in bars anymore, but if you could I would do it here. Except as you know, I don't smoke.

"I love this place. It's perfect," Darlene whispered, giving my elbow another rub as I settled in beside her. "This your account?"

"Used to be. The evil empire still has it, but I don't hold it against these guys for being loyal customers."

I've been to the big chain chop shops but the Fireside is my go-to place for steak. It's been around for sixty years and still owned by the same Portland family. That matters to me. And those other joints serve good red meat, but I feel like I'm eating in a hotel lobby instead of a steakhouse. Anyway, the Fireside fits me like a glove.

"Look who's back."

I didn't need to look up to know it was Annette, a longtime Fireside server and one of the best in the business. I tore myself away from Darlene's eyes and looked up anyway.

"Welcome in," she said bowing in Darlene's direction before turning her practiced gaze to me. "Makers Mark Manhattan?"

I'm more of a scotch guy but there's something about a steakhouse that makes me want a Manhattan. Big city. Big steak. Big drink. It all adds up. I nodded in the affirmative and Annette turned back to Darlene. She just held up two fingers and smiled and Annette wheeled toward the bar.

"And rings please," I shouted after her.

Annette waved the back of her hand acknowledging the order. The Fireside has the best onion rings in the world. Period. I don't know what the hell they use for batter but it's crisp and light and never falls apart. I'm told the recipe is a closely guarded family secret and people who've nosed around too much have ended up dead. That's what Frank says anyway.

When I turned back to face Darlene she was wearing the sweetest smile I've ever seen. The candlelight in her face showed her age and that made her all the more pretty.

"So, what's *your* story, blue eyes? Where you from? Who's your momma? How'd you get here? Where you going?"

She was asking in an airy voice like she didn't care, but I could tell she did. I was digging in my brain for answers and came up empty so I stalled for a little time.

"Not a very interesting story, doll."

"Bore me," she said plopping an elbow on the table and cupping her chin in one hand.

It was the first time tonight I noticed she had freshly manicured red nails. How'd I miss that? Those claws looked like they could be put to good use. The thought crossed my mind she maybe went to a day spa today too, and if she did, good thing it wasn't the Sensuous Steam. That would've been awkward. Anyway, I was still scrambling for the story when Annette saved me with a couple of Manhattans.

"Here's looking at you, kid," I growled, doing what I thought was a pretty good Bogart impression. The eye roll and smirk while we clinked and drinked told me Darlene didn't agree. I'm really much better doing Peter Lorre but that's just not date night material.

"So?" She resumed the inquisition.

No more stalling. My time was obviously up and I was just getting started with the whole Portland born and raised part when Annette placed a basket of hot, golden brown rings on the table between us. She lingered briefly and put both palms up.

"Do we know what's next or would you like to go slow?"

I did want to go slow. Real slow. But I figured it wouldn't hurt to get the rest of the order in, and Annette's a pro so I knew she wouldn't rush us. Without cracking the menu, I ordered a house salad to share, two New York strips medium rare, baked potatoes with the works, and a bottle of Caymus cabernet sauvignon. I glanced over at Darlene to see if I'd gone down the wrong track, but she was giving me that maestro look again so I figured I did okay. Annette collected the menus and wine list and I rewarded myself with another sip of Manhattan.

"*Yummm*," Darlene said holding onto the m for a long time.

She had gotten into the onion rings already and raced out to a two-zip lead. I'm a competitive guy with a healthy appetite and could've easily run her down, but this was no race. Besides, she looked like a pretty happy camper right now. I'm kind of indoorsy and not into camping, so I'm not really sure what a happy camper looks like, but Darlene's a Camper and she was obviously happy, so this must be it.

Anyway, we nibbled on the rings and sipped on the drinks and fell into easy conversation. Maybe the booze was starting to talk but I was getting more comfortable telling my story, and maybe it's not so boring after all because she was eating it up. Along with the last of the onion rings.

We called a brief time out when Annette returned to clear the basket and deliver the house salad and wine. The Fireside house salad is old school. It's a big bowl of chopped romaine hearts and mixed vegetables. Salads nowadays are all spring greens, or field greens, or gathered greens, or micro-greens, or whatever. They're green alright, but they're limp and flimsy and taste like you're eating out of a bag of lawn clippings. Anyway, the Firehouse salad is crisp and tastes like fresh lettuce and vegetables. The best part though is the house dressing. It's just good old-fashioned French with blue cheese chunks but it's genius in my book.

Annette popped the cork on the cabernet. I'm no wine expert but I know that Caymus makes some good grape juice. I'd had their cab here before and it goes with a New York strip like they were made for each other. Like Bogie and Bacall. Or Sonny and Cher. Or Starsky and Hutch. A perfect pair. Must be why they call it wine pairing.

I ignored the cork she placed on the table because they always smell like cork to me, and I didn't swirl the small taste of wine because I've had that go wrong before. When I downed the sip of Caymus it tasted delicious. I nodded my approval to Annette and she carefully poured the perfect amount in our glasses, wrapped the bottle in a napkin, placed it on the table, and took her leave.

I guess we were still hungry because there wasn't much chatter while the salad disappeared. For the first time, I became aware of the soft background music in the bar. I love the soundtrack at the Fireside. It's a mix of dinner music from crooners like Sinatra and Dino, torch singers like Dinah Washington and Billie Holiday and Peggy Lee, and some great old soul tunes from Ray Charles and Otis Redding and Solomon Burke. But the one that softly swayed into my consciousness just now was *You Send Me* by the incomparable Sam Cooke.

At first I thought it was infatuation, but whoa it's lasted so long. Now I find myself wanting to marry you and take you home. You, you, you, you send me. I know you send me. I know you send me. Honest you do. Honest you do. Honest you do.

Darlene had a curious look on her face when I snapped to.

"Who is this?"

I had let the music play in my head and got lost for a minute, so I took in a big breath of air and let out a soft sigh.

"Sam Cooke. One of the all-time greats."

"What's it called?"

"*You Send Me.*"

"Is this your favorite?" she asked arching her eyebrows.

"I like a lot of his stuff but it might be, yeah."

She must've sensed I was embarrassed because she smiled and looked away. Returning my attention to matters at hand, I noticed the song was gone. And so was the salad.

With the timing of a Swiss watch, Annette arrived with our steaks. I've always owned other nationalities of watch but people say Swiss are good. And so is Annette. The meat was seared black, smelled great, and still sizzling on the metal platter. And the baked potato was piled high with butter, sour cream, chives and bacon bits. I like potatoes as much as the next guy, but in this case they play second fiddle to all that other stuff. I gave Darlene a quick wink, took in the savory aroma, and grabbed my steak knife. This is as good as meat and potatoes get. The rings and salad had taken the edge off our appetites, so we settled into a slow delicious routine of eating, drinking and talking.

By the time Annette reappeared to clear our empty dinner plates we'd covered a lot of ground.

Darlene had told me her dad was in the merchant marine and not around much when she was growing up. He missed a lot of birthdays and graduations and other things that mattered, and that made it hard for her to trust men. I told her most men are jerks and that probably makes it even harder. Her mom got tired of waiting for him, and of the rain, and spends most of her time now in Mexico painting pictures of the desert. Darlene's got three sisters, and all four of them look alike, walk alike, and talk alike. I said that was hard to imagine but I'd try.

Darlene wanted to be a fashion designer and had a lot of drawings from her high school years, but the price tag for those snazzy schools is steep and her mom couldn't afford it. I said I'd like to see the drawings. Now she wants to be an artist, but not the starving kind, so that's on the back burner. She loves to dance. I told her I've got two left feet but was willing to learn. She loves cats, and lost hers a couple years back, but isn't ready to hire a replacement just yet. She worries about getting old and she worries about her health. But who doesn't?

I told her I like red meat and football. My ex was a vegetarian and hated sports, so I played along for five long years, but Chucky isn't playing that game anymore. Darlene looked pretty happy eating a New York steak and kept checking the Alabama-Auburn score on the TV in the corner of the bar, so I figured I was in good company. Maybe I told her I was a slick second baseman when I was young and wanted to be a baseball player, or maybe I didn't. I know I said I didn't really want to be a salesman but was pretty good at it. And that maybe down the road I'd be a writer or something. She liked that.

I said I was partial to stiff drinks, and dinners out, and dames who act like dames. She smiled. I told her I like to watch movies, and that I like to read when I'm tired of watching movies. She asked me what I like to read and who my favorite author is. I said I like the classics, especially Hemingway because he writes like he's throwing punches and makes no apologies. I told her I wanted to travel more and she asked where. I said I wanted to go to Africa and maybe climb Kilimanjaro before I have to ride a scooter in the grocery store. She thought that was funny. And that I wanted to go to Spain, especially Madrid, and maybe even watch a bullfight. She didn't bat an eye.

I told her that more than anything else I wanted to go to Paris. That I wanted to walk, no stroll, down the Champs Elysees with a gorgeous woman on my arm. To visit the book vendors strung along the Seine and buy an old book or two. To get hopelessly lost on the Left Bank and not care, and sit in a small sidewalk café on the Boulevard Saint Germain and sip wine all afternoon. Her eyes danced when I talked about Paris and she said she wanted to go there too. She'd talked to her sisters about going together someday and I said maybe it should be me. We had both laughed and let it drop. But those kinds of thoughts don't drop so easy.

Annette whisked away our plates and said she'd be right back.

"Dessert, or maybe a brandy?" I inquired with a cocked head. "Or maybe both?"

Darlene held her hand to her stomach and shook her head no.

"I'll explode. But I've got some Grand Marnier back at my place if you're interested."

I'm not into sweets, and especially not sweet liquor so Grand Marnier isn't my favorite. But I'm not stupid.

"I'm interested," I said, looking straight into her eyes.

When Annette came back I held up a hand to stop the dessert spiel she had teed up. I've heard it before, and even fell for it a time or two, but not tonight.

"No room, Annette. This is dessert tonight," I said pointing to the last of the wine in my glass. "L'addition s'il vous plaît." I made a quick checkmark in the air signaling for the bill and caught Darlene staring at me.

"You speak French?" she asked wide-eyed.

"Oui." I tried to play it straight but couldn't help the grin.

She gave me a withering look, then a smile, and I could feel another question coming. And I was right.

"Can I ask you a question?"

"Of course."

"I fell hard the second I saw you, E.C. What took *you* so long? I dropped a thousand hints. Was that not enough? Too subtle?"

"That's three questions."

"Do you want me to smack you?"

That was number four but who's counting?

"No." I swiveled on the bench to face her directly. "I don't know why, Darlene. You knocked me out when I first laid eyes on you too."

The right words were slow to come.

"I don't know what's been eating me. Seems like over a year now I feel like I've been stuck in first gear. Afraid of something."

"What are you afraid of?"

"Not sure. I don't scare easy but whatever it was turned my belly yellow."

I felt a presence and looked up to discover Annette holding out the check folder. She was discreetly looking away like she had other things to do but I wondered how long she might have been standing there.

"I guess you want me to pay for this, huh?" I said sheepishly reaching for my wallet.

"If you'd prefer to spend a couple of hours in the dish pit that can be arranged," she said cheerily like maybe she'd *prefer* that.

Doing dishes isn't my strong suit so I just held out my American Express Rewards Gold Card between two fingers.

"Suit yourself." Annette took my card, nodded, spun on her heels, and disappeared again.

I returned my attention to Darlene. She had her elbows on the table and face nestled between both palms.

"You were telling me about your yellow belly."

Something in her face or the tone of her voice made the block in my head break up and tumble out of my mouth.

"I haven't been afraid of you, doll. I'm not afraid of Girard. Or Vic, or Dan, or Scott, or anybody really. I'm not afraid of losing my job. I'm not afraid of failure, or success either, not that I'd know what that's like."

"So?"

"I've always taken the easy way out. Told myself it wasn't worth the fight. Thought it was the other guy's fault. I guess I've been afraid I'm not who I think I am. Not such a tough guy after all. Truth is I've been afraid I'm a coward."

I was wondering if you can actually be afraid of being afraid when Annette returned.

"Nice to see you, E.C. Don't wait so long for the next time. Pleasure to meet you, Darlene," she said extending her hand. "I hope we see you again." She put the folder down on the table and gave it a quick pat.

"Thanks for coming in."

With that, Annette was gone and I felt naked and alone with my thoughts. Darlene put her hand on my cheek and turned my face to hers.

"You don't seem afraid anymore, sweetie. What happened?"

"You happened, baby. That night in the car."

"I remember. It was raining, right?"

"Yeah," I said with a grin, feeling the sting of her counterpunch. She returned the grin and took her hand back.

"That look on your face tore me up," I continued. "When I went to bed that night I thought I'd lost you. And when I woke up I thought I'd lost myself. That was okay, but losing you wasn't.

Then when I got to the office and saw that stupid poster in the break room about winners and quitters, I realized the only way I could lose was by quitting. And that's what I was doing. So I decided right then and there to quit quitting."

"And start winning," she said with an approving nod of her head.

"So far, so good," I replied, confused as to whether it's even possible to quit quitting. I don't think that's a double negative but do they cancel each other out somehow? And if you quit quitting can you still quit doing other things like watching too much TV? Or eating poorly? Anyway, winning felt good so far.

"How about that Grand Marnier?"

Her question jarred me back from the then and there to the here and now.

"Let's go," I replied with relish, signing the bill and closing the folder.

I pushed the table out and stood up offering my hand. She handed me hers and slid out of the booth, standing to her full high-heeled height. Almost eye to eye but not quite.

"Thanks for dinner," she purred.

"My pleasure," I purred right back.

She turned around slowly and put both hands up and back asking for help with her coat. This wasn't exactly my first rodeo so I was ready. I guided her arms through the sleeves and pulled the coat up over her elegant shoulders, slipped my arm around her slender waist, and steered her through the crowded bar. I got a few glances that said I was a lucky guy with all that dame. Real lucky. And even though he had three drinks working, Frank didn't miss his cue.

"G'night, miss. G'night, E.C."

I gave Frank a quick salute and led Darlene out of the bar, and the front door of the restaurant.

It was raining lightly now but you could still see a gauzy moon through the mist. I can never tell if it's waxing or waning, but it was almost full and the effect was mesmerizing so we stopped to take it in. Despite the chill and the drizzle it felt like a perfect night. Darlene shivered so I wrapped her collar more tightly around her neck. I slipped the valet our ticket and a fiver and he jogged off into the mist to retrieve the Outback, leaving us alone under the awning.

Darlene stepped up real close and wrapped both arms around my neck. She looked up at me and I lost myself for the thousandth time in those big pools of hazel. Then she kissed me. Hard but soft. Hot but sweet. I don't know how long it lasted, but when she finally let go I licked my lips to make sure it was real. And to squeeze out every last drop of kiss. She stepped back into the moonlight and her eyes locked mine in a grip I couldn't escape. After what seemed like eternity, she threw me the toughest questions of the night.

"Why is a woman attracted to a man? Why is a man attracted to a woman? Why you? Why me? Why us?"

I gave her a knowing smile and pulled her back close.

"Some questions in life are better left unanswered, doll."

And then *I* kissed *her*.

ACKNOWLEDGMENTS

This being my first novel, I'd like to begin by acknowledging it may very well be my last. For that reason, it feels precocious to reel off a long list of people who were positive influences on the book, or my writing, or my life. Still, all authors of whatever station do it, and I owe debts of gratitude that should be paid. So here goes.

First of all, I need to thank Ernest Hemingway for allowing me to bastardize the title of one of his books. Technically, I didn't have his expressed permission, but I did reach out to him and received no response. I'm sure he wouldn't have minded. The truth is I had absolutely no idea what the title of this book should be, and it only came to me after I'd drafted the first three chapters. Why I don't know, but I thought it would be funny to twist the title of a classic piece of literature to suit my purpose, and having already written about an afternoon meeting, I decided *Death in the Afternoon Meeting* would be a suitably snarky title for a decidedly snarky book.

Only when I actually read *Death in the Afternoon* for the first time did I realize it was a brutal and bloody and entirely non-fictional description of bull fighting in Spain in the 1920s and 1930s. To borrow his legacy without incurring a huge karmic debt, I reasoned, I should honor Papa in some small way, so bull fighting became part of the fabric of the story as a dream sequence, and a rather obvious metaphor for cowardice and courage. The careful reader will note as well that I sprinkled a handful of phrases from his book in mine, which was another peculiar way of honoring him. There is a fair amount of what bulls produce from the non-horned end that fills the pages, so there's that too.

Next, I need to profusely thank all of those writers who churned out the great detective stories of the 1930s, '40s and '50s, most notably Dashiell Hammett, Raymond Chandler, and Mickey Spillane. To say that those three men were an inspiration and a huge influence for *Death in the Afternoon Meeting* probably goes without saying. But I just did. Their gritty crime novels, and many of the movies based on them, have always captivated me and sent my imagination prowling down the dark alleys of some sexy and stylized urban jungle. Many phrases in my book closely resemble theirs as a fond homage to a style of storytelling not seen or heard nearly enough these days. How and when it occurred to me that someone leading an unremarkable, prosaic life and imagining himself as a hard-boiled private dick would be a humorous device, I can't say. Surely it had nothing to do with my own unremarkable and prosaic life.

I also owe a huge debt to my dear friend, Ross Hawkins. Ross has been in the publishing business for the past 20 years, and in fact still is, although more as a hobby now than a vocation. Demonstrating his ability to learn from painful lessons and exhibiting more than a little horse sense, he declined to publish this book himself, but instead became an invaluable mentor and guidance counselor who urged me to self-publish *Death in the Afternoon Meeting,* then keep writing whatever popped into my head and just have fun with it. That is some of the best advice I've ever received.

The happiest part of all, though, was that it afforded Ross and me the welcome opportunity to reconnect after years apart and roll around in the mud of many fond and funny memories from our time together as waiters, bartenders, barflies, and business associates in the wild and crazy '80s.

There is also a small circle of friends who were kind, brave, and foolish enough to read the original manuscript when I asked. The first draft was awful, and their encouragement and generally constructive criticism did more than a little to help polish the book. To protect the innocent I will not name names, but my love and gratitude go out to my best friend Tom, my sister Karen, my sister-in-law Melanie, who did me the honor and favor of saying much more than a breezy "it was fun", and other dear friends Bill, Val, Jim and Steve, as well as new friends Mari and Emily.

Last, but certainly not least, I want to thank my wife of the past 31 years, Lori. She is smart, beautiful, funny, and the best dame a palooka like me could ever hope to be in the care of. In her own loving and gentle, and at other times not so gentle way, she has pleaded with and prodded me to write a book about my life experiences, including many stories from my years in the restaurant business. I have never been comfortable writing about myself but found that E.C. Poole somehow gave me a voice to tell some of those stories.

Really, though, I owe anyone who has gotten all the way to the end of this book and these acknowledgments the most heartfelt thanks of all. Chucky loves you.

Chucky might be back, in...

THE JADED JUNGLE

Life in the big city, it can kill you. I'm not talking about the toughs I have to dodge in my line of work. I'm talking about too many people in too little space with too few seats at the ballgame. Or the ballet if that's more your cup of chai. I'm talking about dirty air and dirty streets, and too many people living on them who can't afford a roof over their head. I'm talking about too many cars and not enough lanes. Jimi Hendrix wrote a song about crosstown traffic. He was high most of the time so it probably didn't seem so bad, but it can be a nightmare. Like that poor frog in the pot, most people don't notice until it's too late.

Life in the big city is toxic but I'm here to tell you the suburbs are worse. It's a jungle out there. I live in the suburbs. I work in the suburbs. I shop and eat and drink in the suburbs. Mostly I just sit in traffic though. Which is where I am now...

Made in the USA
Las Vegas, NV
09 November 2020

10660333R00144